"'MY CASTLE'S BURNING, EH? HA-HA!'"

DREAMERS OF DREAMS

"RUPERT WAS ALWAYS MERRY"

"SIEGFRIED VON PEPPERPOTZ GREW ILL OF IT"

MORE WILDSIDE CLASSICS

Dacobra, or The White Priests of Ahriman, by Harris Burland
The Nabob, by Alphonse Daudet
Out of the Wreck, by Captain A. E. Dingle
The Elm-Tree on the Mall, by Anatole France
The Lance of Kanana, by Harry W. French
Amazon Nights, by Arthur O. Friel
Caught in the Net, by Emile Gaboriau
The Gentle Grafter, by O. Henry
Raffles, by E. W. Hornung
Gates of Empire, by Robert E. Howard
Tom Brown's School Days, by Thomas Hughes
The Opium Ship, by H. Bedford Jones
The Miracles of Antichrist, by Selma Lagerlof
Arsène Lupin, by Maurice LeBlanc
A Phantom Lover, by Vernon Lee
The Iron Heel, by Jack London
The Witness for the Defence, by A.E.W. Mason
The Spider Strain and Other Tales, by Johnston McCulley
Tales of Thubway Tham, by Johnston McCulley
The Prince of Graustark, by George McCutcheon
Bull-Dog Drummond, by Cyril McNeile
The Moon Pool, by A. Merritt
The Red House Mystery, by A. A. Milne
Blix, by Frank Norris
Wings over Tomorrow, by Philip Francis Nowlan
The Devil's Paw, by E. Phillips Oppenheim
Satan's Daughter and Other Tales, by E. Hoffmann Price
The Insidious Dr. Fu Manchu, by Sax Rohmer
Mauprat, by George Sand
The Slayer and Other Tales, by H. de Vere Stacpoole
Penrod (Gordon Grant Illustrated Edition), by Booth Tarkington
The Gilded Age, by Mark Twain
The Blockade Runners, by Jules Verne
The Gadfly, by E.L. Voynich

Please see www.wildsidepress.com for a complete list!

DREAMERS OF DREAMS

An Anthology of Fantasy

Edited by

R. Reginald
and
Douglas Melville

WILDSIDE PRESS

To Jim Stinson —
fine photographer, good friend, fellow madman.

DREAMERS OF DREAMS

This edition published in 2006 by Wildside Press, LLC.
www.wildsidepress.com

ACKNOWLEDGMENTS

"The Blind God" by Laurence Housman from *Gods and Their Makers and Other Stories*, Copyright 1897, All rights reserved, published by George Allen & Unwin Ltd., London, 1920, was reprinted by permission of George Allen & Unwin Ltd.

"The Last Adventure of Don Quixote" by Kenneth Morris from *The Secret Mountain and Other Tales*, published by Faber & Gwyer, London, 1926, was reprinted by permission of Curtis Brown Ltd. on behalf of Kenneth Morris.

"Same Time, Same Place" by Mervyn Peake from *Science Fantasy*, Vol. 20, No. 60, August 1963, Copyright 1963 by Nova Publications Ltd., was reprinted by permission of Maurice Michael, Literary Agent for The Estate of Mervyn Peake.

"The Journey of the King" by Lord Dunsany from *Time and the Gods* published by William Heinemann, London, 1906, Copyright 1906, was reprinted by permission of Curtis Brown Ltd. on behalf of The Estate of Lord Dunsany.

CONTENTS

The Affliction of Baron Humpfelhimmel

The Affliction of Baron Humpfelhimmel

VERYBODY said it was an extraordinary affair altogether, and for once everybody was right. Baron Humpfelhimmel himself would say nothing about it for two reasons. The first reason was that nobody dared ask him what he thought about it, and the second was that he was too proud to speak to anybody concerning any subject whatsoever, unless questioned. That he always laughed, no matter what happened, was the melancholy fact, and had been a melancholy fact from his childhood's earliest hour. He was born laughing. He laughed in church, he laughed at home. When his father spanked him he roared with laughter, and when he suffered from the measles he could not begin to restrain his mirth.

The situation seemed all the more sin-

157

"REST, SINUHIT, SON OF AMENEMHAIT"

The Lady of the Island

To face page 68

gular when it was remembered that Rudolf von Pepperpotz, the previous Baron Humpfelhimmel, and father of the Laughing Baron, as he was called, was never known to smile from his childhood's earliest hour to his dying day, and, strangest of all, was a far more amiable person, despite his solemnity, than the present Baron for all his laughter.

"What does it mean, do you suppose?" Frau Ehrenbreitstein once asked of Hans Pumpernickel, her husband's private secretary, of whom you have already had some account.

"I cannot tell," Hans had answered, "and I have my reason for saying that I cannot tell," he added, significantly.

"What is that reason, Hans?" asked the good lady, her curiosity aroused by the boy's manner.

"It is this," said Hans, his voice sinking to a whisper. "I cannot tell, because—because I do not know!"

And this, let me say in passing, was why Hans Pumpernickel was thought by all to be so wise. He had a reason always for what he did, and was ever willing to give it.

Affliction of Baron Humpfelhimmel

"They say," the good Lady Ehrenbreitstein went on—"they do say that when last winter the Baron while hunting boars was thrown from his horse, breaking his leg and two of his ribs, they could not be set because of his convulsions of laughter, though for my part I cannot see wherein having one's leg and ribs broken is provocative of merriment."

"Nor I," quoth Hans. "I have an eye for jokes. In most things I can see the fun, but in the breaking of one's bones I see more cause for tears than smiles."

And it was true. As Frau Ehrenbreitstein had heard, the Baron Humpfelhimmel had broken one leg and two ribs—only it was while hunting wolves and not in a boar chase—and when the Emperor's physician, who was one of the party, came to where the suffering man lay he found him roaring with laughter.

"Good!" cried the physician, leaning over his prostrate form. "I am glad to see that you are not hurt. I feared you were injured."

"I am injured," the Baron replied, with a loud laugh. "My left leg — ha - ha - ha!—is nearly killing me—hee-hee!—with p-pain, and if I mistake not, either my heart —ha-ha-ha-ha!—or my ribs—hee-hee-hee! —are broken in nineteen places."

Then he went off into such an explosion of mirth as not only appeared unseemly, but also deprived him of the power of speech for five or six minutes.

"I fail to see the joke," said the physician, as the Baron's laughter echoed and reechoed throughout the forest.

"Th-there—hee-hee!—there isn't a-any joke," the Baron answered, smiling. "Confound you — ha-ha-ha-ha! — oho-ho-ho! — can't you see I'm suffering?"

"I see you are laughing," the physician replied—"laughing as if you were reading a comic paper full of real jokes. What are you laughing at?"

"Ha-ha! I—I d-dud-don't know," stammered the Baron, vainly endeavoring to suppress his mirth. "I—I don't feel like laughing—hee-hee!—but I can't help it." And off he went into another gale. Nor did he stop there. The physician tried vainly to quiet him down so that he could set the fractured bones, but in spite of all he could do for him the Baron either would not or could not stop laughing. When he was able to move about again it was only with a limp, and even that appeared to have its humorous side, for whenever the Baron appeared on the public streets he was always smiling, and when the Mayor ventured to express his sympathy with him over his misfortune the Baron laughed again, and mirthfully requested him to mind his own business.

Then it was recalled how that ten years before, when the famous Von Pepperpotz Castle was destroyed by fire, the Baron was found writing in his study by the messenger who brought the news.

"Baron," the messenger cried—"Baron, the château is burning. The flames have already destroyed the armory, and are now eating their way through the corridors to the state banquet-hall."

The Baron looked the messenger in the eye for an instant, and then his face wreathed with smiles.

"My castle's burning, eh? Ha-ha-ha!" was what he said; and then, rising hurriedly from his desk, he hastened, shouting with laughter, to the scene, where no one worked harder than he to stay the devastating course of the flames.

"You seem to be pleased," said one who noticed his merriment.

The Baron's answer was a blow which knocked the fellow down, and then, striking him across the shoulders with his staff, he walked away, muttering to himself:

"Pleased! Ha-ha-ha! Does ruin please anybody—tee-hee-hee! If the churls only —tee-hee!—only knew—ha-ha-ha-ha!"

That was it! If they only knew! And no one did know until after the Baron had died without children—for he had never married — and all his possessions and papers became the property of the state. Through these papers the secret of the Baron's laughter became known to the good people of Schnitzelhammerstein-on-the-Zugvitz, and through them it became known to me. Hans Pumpernickel himself told me the tale, and as he has risen to the exalted position of Mayor of Schnitzelhammerstein-on-the-Zugvitz, an honor conferred only on the truly good and worthy, I have no reason to doubt that the story is in every way truthful.

Affliction of Baron Humpfelhimmel

"When Baron Humpfelhimmel died," said Hans, as he and I walked together along the beautiful sylvan path that runs by the side of the Zugvitz River, "I am sorry to say there were few mourners. A man who laughs, as a rule, is popular, but the man who laughs always, without regard to circumstances, makes enemies. One learns to love a person who laughs at one's jests, but one who laughs at funerals, at conflagrations, at beggars, at the needy and the distressed, does not become universally beloved. Such was the habit of Fritz von Pepperpotz, last of the Barons Humpfelhimmel. If you were to go to him with a funny story, none would laugh more heartily than he; but equally loud would he laugh were you to say to him that you had a racking headache, and should it chance that you were to inform him you had been desperately ill, his mirth would know no bounds. Even in his greatest frenzies of rage he would smirk and laugh, and so it happened that the popularity which you would expect would go with a mirthful disposition was the last thing in the world he could hope for. I do

not exaggerate when I say that Baron
Humpfelhimmel could not have been elected
office-boy to the Mayor on a popular vote,
even if there were no opposing candidate.
Now that it is all over, however, and we
know the truth, we have changed our minds
about it, and already several hundred of our
citizens have raised a fund of twenty marks
to go towards putting up a monument to
the memory of the Laughing Baron.

"Fritz von Pepperpotz, my friend," said
Hans to me, in explanation of the situation,
"laughed because he could not help it, as a
statement found among his papers after he
died showed. The statement contained the
whole story, and in some of its details it is
a sad one. It was all the fault of the grandfather of the late Baron that he could do
nothing but laugh all his days, that he
died unmarried, and that the name of Von
Pepperpotz has died off the face of the earth
forever, unless some one else chooses to as-
sume that name, which, I imagine, no one
is crazy enough to do. The only thing
that could reconcile me to such a name
would be the estates that formerly went
with it, but now that they have become the

property of the government the house has lost all of its attractions, retaining, however, every bit of its homeliness. Pumpernickel is bad enough, but it is beautiful beside Von Pepperpotz."

Here Hans sighed, and to comfort him, rather than to say anything I really meant, I observed that I thought Pumpernickel was a good strong name.

"Yes," Hans said, with a pleased smile. "It certainly is strong. I have had mine twenty-five years now, and it doesn't show the slightest sign of wear. It's as good as the day it was made, But to return to the Von Pepperpotz family and its mysterious affliction.

"According to the Baron's statement, while he himself could not restrain his mirth, no matter how badly he felt, his father, Rupert von Pepperpotz, could never smile, although he was a man of most genial disposition. Just as Fritz was ushered into the world, grinning like a Cheshire cheese—"

"Cat," I suggested, noting Hans's error.

"Cat, is it?" he said. "Well, now, do

"Over the Plum-Pudding"

you know I am glad to hear that? I always supposed the term used was cheese, and positively I have lain awake night after night trying to comprehend how a cheese could grin, and finally I gave it up, setting it down as one of the peculiarities of the English language. If it's Cheshire cat, and not Cheshire cheese, why, it's all clear as a pikestaff. But, as I was saying, just as Fritz was born grinning like a Cheshire cat, his father Rupert was born frowning apparently with rage. He was the most ill-natured-looking baby you ever saw, according to the chronicles. Nothing seemed to please him. When you or I would have cooed, Rupert von Pepperpotz would wrinkle up his forehead until the furrows, if his nurse tells the truth, were deep enough to hide letters in.

"And yet he was rarely cross, and never disobedient. It was the strangest thing in the world. Here was a being who always frowned and never laughed, and yet who was as obliging in his actions as could be. As he grew older his active amiability increased, but his frown grew more terrible than ever. He became a great wit. As

Affliction of Baron Humpfelhimmel

he walked through the streets of Schnitz-elhammerstein-on-the-Zugvitz he was always merry, though none would have guessed it to look at him. He had a pleasant voice, and his neighbors all said it was a most startling thing to hear in the distance a jolly, roistering song, and then to walk along a little way and see that it was this forbidding-looking person who was doing the singing.

"How Rupert got Wilhelmina de Grootzenburg to become his wife, considering his seeming solemnity, which made him appear to be positively ugly, nobody ever knew. It is probable, however, that it was sympathy which moved her to like him, unless it was that his ugliness fascinated her. Rupert himself said that it was not sympathy for his inability to laugh or smile, because he did not want sympathy for that. He didn't feel badly about it himself. He never had smiled, and so did not know the pleasure of it. Consequently he didn't miss it. Smiling was an idiotic way of expressing pleasure anyhow, he said. Why just because a man thought of a funny idea he should stretch his mouth he couldn't

167

see. No more could he understand why it
was necessary to show one's appreciation
of a funny story by shaking one's stomach
and saying Ha-ha! On the whole, he said
that he was satisfied. He could talk and
could tell people he enjoyed their stories
without having to shake himself or disturb
the corners of his mouth. When little
Fritz was born, and did nothing but laugh
even when he had the colic, the solemn-
looking Rupert observed that the baby
simply proved the truth of what he said.

"'What a donkey the child is,' he cried,
'to spoil his pretty face by stretching his
mouth so that you almost fear his ears will
drop into it! And those wild whoops,
which you call laughter, what earthly use
are they? I can't see why, if he is glad
about something, he can't just say, "I'm
glad about so and so," mildly, instead of
making me deaf with his roars. Truly,
laughter is not what it is cracked up to be.'

"'Ah, my dear Rupert,' Wilhelmina,
his wife, had said, 'you do not really know
what you are talking about! If you could
enjoy the sensation of laughing once you
would never wish to be without it.'

WHEN THE LIGHT WENT OUT. LEAVING THE EARTH IN DARKNESS

Affliction of Baron Humpfelhimmel

"'Nonsense!' replied the Baron. 'My father never laughed, so why should I wish to?'

"'Now, then,' continued Hans, "according to Fritz von Pepperpotz's statement, there was where Rupert was wrong. Siegfried von Pepperpotz had known what it was to laugh, but he had not known when to laugh, which was why the family of Von Pepperpotz was afflicted with a curse, which only the final dying out of the family could remove, and there lay the solution of the mystery. It seems that Siegfried von Pepperpotz, grandfather of Fritz and father of Rupert, had been a wild sort of a youth, who smiled when he wished and frowned when he wished, no matter what the occasion may have been, and he smiled once too often. A miserable-looking figure of a man once passed through the village of Schnitzelhammerstein - on - the - Zugvitz, selling sugar dolls and other sweets. To Siegfried and his comrades it seemed good to play a prank on the old fellow. They sent him two miles off into the country, where, they said, was a rich countess, who would buy his whole stock, when in reality there was

HE DID HIS BEST TO MAKE HER CHEERFUL

no rich countess there at all, so that the old man had his trouble for his pains.

"That he was a magician they did not know, but so he was, and in those days magicians could do everything. Of course he was angry at the deception, and on his return to Schnitzelhammerstein-on-the-Zugvitz he sent for the young men, and got all of them to apologize and buy his wares except Siegfried. Siegfried not only refused to apologize and buy the old man's candies, but had the audacity to laugh in his face, and tell him about a wealthy old duke who lived two miles out on the other side of the village, which the magician immediately recognized as another attempt to play a practical joke upon him.

"'Enough, Siegfried von Pepperpotz!' he cried, in his rage. 'Laugh away while you can. After to-day may you never smile, and may your son never smile, and may your son's son, willing or unwilling, smile smiles that you two would have smiled, and so may it ever go! May every third generation get the laughter that the preceding two shall lose, according to my curse!'

"This made Siegfried laugh all the harder, for, not knowing, as I have said, that the old man was a magician, he had no fear of him. Next day, however, he changed his mind. He found that he could not laugh. He could not even smile. Try as he would, his lips refused to do his bidding.

"It ruined his disposition. Siegfried von Pepperpotz grew ill over it. The greatest doctors in the world were summoned to his aid, but to no avail. If the curse had ended with him he might not have minded it so much, but after the discovery that from the day of his birth his son Rupert was no more able to laugh than himself he began to brood over the affliction, and shortly died of it; and when Fritz found out from a paper he discovered in a secret drawer in the old chest in the château what the curse was—for Siegfried never told his son, and alone knew from what it was he suffered, and that it was perpetual—he resolved that there should be no further posterity to whom it should be handed down.

"That," said Hans, "is the story of Baron Humpfelhimmel's affliction."

"And a strange story it is," said I.

171

"Though I don't know that it has any particular moral."

"Oh yes, it has!" said Hans. "It has a good moral."

"And what is that?" I asked.

"Don't laugh at your own jokes," he replied.. "If Siegfried von Pepperpotz had not laughed when the magician came back, he never would have been cursed, and this story never would have been told."

THE BLIND GOD

Laurence Housman

THE BLIND GOD

THE Blind God sat paddling on the banks
of a stream; and as he did so he was
thinking, or at least he was trying to think.
Very slowly, very gradually, he had begun
to realize that this cool and liquid sensation
affecting him locally was not, as he had so
long believed, an accompaniment to the
processes within, but was truly something
outside of himself, different, apart and
independent. And the new thought interested him—gave him, in fact, for the first
time, a sense of himself.

Hitherto he had experienced no needs, no
motives, no desires; he had just let things
slide, without knowing that they did slide,
remaining himself all the while self-con-
tained and immovable. Now in his egg of
a brain something tapped, asking for investigation; something that seemed to require
either to be assimilated or controlled.

He reached down his hand to find out
what it was, and in doing so discovered, in
a vague, indefinite way, what he had not

known before—that he had a hand, something, that is to say, with which he could
reach and touch outwardness. He let down
the hollow of his palm till it came in contact with the stream; but when he raised
it, all the contents were spilled again: it
brought nothing back to him. This happened many times, and still he remained
interested; though his hand brought him
nothing, it was giving to things a new
relationship—inwardness and outwardness;
the falling drops made a sound new and
pleasant to his ears, and after a while he
perceived that it came in response to his
own action—something, not himself, making
for righteousness, applauding him for what
he was doing.

This called for further investigation.
Groping deeper, he grasped and drew up a
handful of mud, smooth and yielding to the
touch, less elusive than water, presenting
itself to his handling as something pliant
and adaptable, something which it was
possible to keep intact and to control. It
did not run away as he lifted it. With a
germinating sense of possession he clasped
it more tightly, and as he did so moisture
oozed out of it, trickling between his fingers
and separating itself with the same pleasant

sound of running water, a fresh offering of applause from the something which was not himself.

Gradually (for all his movements were deliberate) his small handful of mud co-agulated, hardened, and took form. This way and that he turned it, plying it into fresh shapes, then, as its stiffness increased, moulded it into a ball, and, setting it to roll from palm to palm, found in the even regularity of its motion a new and unexpected diversion.

Before long, from its continuous revolutions, the ball assumed a polished and uniform surface, while at the same time the constant manipulation and contact of the Blind God had begun to cause certain chemical changes and fermentations of a minute but profoundly important character. Here and there he dented it with finger-marks, personal impressions made for future reference and verification ; and having thus sealed it with his sign manual, he continued to let it roll.

And it rolled, and it rolled, and it rolled. To the god himself the whole interest of this process, so apparently monotonous, lay in his own gradual acquirement of the thing which we call skill. This little mud ball was giving him a new idea about himself; sleight of hand was communicating fresh life to his brain; he felt himself becoming an expert in rolling. It never entered into his head that the little mud ball which he had merely taken up for a plaything was also becoming an expert in being rolled. But though he knew little about it, it interested him. Enclosing it in the warmth of his palms, infecting it unconsciously with emanations from his own being, he had begun to evolve for himself a new idea, the idea of expansion by possession. Here he had got hold at last of something to think about that he would not willingly let go. He did not know what it was, and he had no use for it; but it was something for hand and brain to catch hold of, and so— find themselves. Slowly and precariously his mind worked toward a digestive adapta-tion of this new fact, till, tired with the unwonted exertion, he fell fast asleep.

A god sleeps and wakes without any idea of time; such a thing as " a forty winks sleep " forms no part of his composition, especially if in his winkless and waking state he happens to be blind. Time, in fact, has no concern for one who leads a life without motives, desires or interests. But by the time the Blind God woke up again it had had a good deal to do with the little ball of earth on which his interests were now beginning to be so blindly centred. As he sat holding it enlapped on the banks of the stream, sheltering its spinnings between curved palms, instilling into it by subtle expenditure the currents of his own divinely untroubled life, wonderful things had happened to it. It had begun to teem with minute forms of existence, very busy, very urgent about their own concerns, paying no attention to him whatsoever —no, none ; not conscious of him any more than he was conscious of them, and so wasting no time in asking, as we mortals do nowadays, " Where do we come from ? " or " How did we get here ? " or " Where are we going to next ? " None of those superfluous and parenthetic inquiries disturbed or deflected the quick courses of its blood from the immediate business in hand —not to begin with, at all events.

The Blind God had no such thoughts about himself, and in that matter these small emanating life-atoms which he held in the hollow of his hand took after him. But in other respects they were infinitely his inferiors they had lost all sense of repose.

THE DIRGE OF SHIMONO KANI.
(The Journey of the King.)

[Face page 142.

Gripping life in a feverish and fractious clutch, they had rendered it fragmentary. They were tremendously busy and worried about things which did no good to anybody else and only harm to themselves—they were, that is to say, extraordinarily intent on living at each other's expense ; and they did so by a continual process of killing and being killed, eating and being eaten, with long bad bouts of indigestion as the result.

The Blind God sat holding in his hands all those innumerable and continuously struggling issues of life and death ; and he knew no more of the one than of the other. And yet, all unintentionally, he had made them, fashioned them out of clay, infected and warmed them into life, setting them there in his own likeness to make other lives on their own account—lives which would succeed or fail without any direct help or sustenance from him. Here within the hollow of his hand they ran, up and down, to and fro, killing each other, eating each other, loving and hating each other, but caring nothing about him, and he caring nothing about them—though they were all made by him and without him was not anything made that was made.

Just in the same way, if you think of it,

does the sun, where once the creative process has been started, breed life upon our
own earth, and open sweetly within us those
light-given gifts of the five senses ; yet all
the while it knows nothing about us and
remains itself unconquerably blind, deaf,
mute and intractable, rejoicing at nothing,
sorrowing at nothing, caring nothing for all
the love and hatred and hunger and satiety
which have been bred in us out of its
own superabundant heats.   So it was with
this little ball of mud which a blind
god's hands had fashioned, and into which,
without knowing it, he had put so much
life.

And so time went on—time measured
monotonously by the revolutions of a little
ball of mud in a blind god's hands, and
the monotonous but responsive revolutions
of the god's brain.   The main thing was
that though everything appeared to stand
still around them, they two had set up
between them a new relationship—the relationship of motion.   It was so huge an
advance in comparison with the nothingness
that went before, that the Blind God, even
though it seemed to lead nowhere, could
not divest himself of the acquirement.
Waking or sleeping, he continued to let the

ball roll within the hollow of his hands. And it rolled and it rolled.

But after a time some of the life-atoms, taking after their maker, began to have an idea that this ball of mud upon which they lived was not everything, that there was something outside, not themselves, which they could not account for, but which could perhaps account for them. And presently one or two of them who happened to be very far-sighted detected the dim form of the divinity stretching immeasurably above and beyond them. At once they began pointing, directing the attention of those more short-sighted than themselves. " See, see ! " they cried, " up there, and out yonder ! There lies He—the object of our search, the key to all wisdom."

Immediately all the other life-atoms came running to look, and, not seeing so clearly, they built tall towers, and ran up to the top of them in order to look again ; and then taller towers, and taller, till every one of them either saw or said he saw—for having built a tower and climbed up to the top of it, no one was willing to admit that he was so blind or such a fool that he could not see anything. So the little ball of mud became full of towers with people standing on the top of them, gazing. "Look," they said, "He is watching us. We must be careful how we behave!"

But those life-atoms were so tiny and their towers so small that the Blind God's touch passed over them, discovering nothing; and their little voices were too thin and weak to raise question or answer to his ears. For him the mud ball remained as smooth as it had ever been, and though he continued to roll it this way and that, he never detected the swarms of life that were on it or knew that he had at his beck a clamorously worshipping community. Very faithfully he attached himself to that one aspect of life which he had discovered, the keeping in motion of a small mud ball which he had picked up for himself and dried and moulded. Dimly, behind that, other ideas of life were preparing to follow.

Meantime, though he remained thus unconscious of their existence, the little life-atoms had begun to study him more and more. And the whole root of their philosophy about him was that he, having made them, saw and knew all that they were doing, and that if they themselves could only see as they were seen and know as

PATTERING LEAVES DANCED.   [*Face page* 176.
(*The Journey of the King.*)

they were known, life would have for them no further mystery. At the top of their towers some of them had begun to fix magnifying glasses so as to get a better view of him, but others said that magnifying glasses were a wicked device impiously invented, and that to look at a god through any such artificial aids was a negation to faith, a danger to hope, and a hindrance to charity. So they came and broke the magnifying glasses and killed those who looked through them, and pulled down their towers, till at last those who looked through the magnifying glasses began to retaliate, killing them in turn and pulling down their towers, and building bigger and stronger ones of their own. And in the end the people with the magnifying glasses won.

And so, as their glasses got bigger and stronger, they began to find out more about the things outside of them, and about that great still form of divinity that lay beyond and seemed, without motion, to be watching them. And at last one of them, on the top of the biggest tower of all and with the biggest magnifying glass of all, made a great discovery. He discovered that the god was blind !

This discovery filled him, apparently, with

joy; it seemed to him to explain away everything in the most satisfactory manner possible; and he called out for all the other little life-atoms to come and hear what he had discovered and bow to the logic of his conclusions. And the plain unanswerable fact of the discovery so dazzled them that they did so. "This god of ours," he said, "is blind; he knows nothing about us, has no conception of us whatever. And if he has no conception, then he does not exist, and he is not really there. What you thought was a form is only space, and where you saw eyes is only emptiness."

When the other little life-atoms heard that what they had believed to be eyes was only emptiness, and that what they had conceived to be form and design were only side issues from space and chance, many of them were glad, but some were very sorry and out of heart. And they sat and moped at the foot of their ruined towers, and, cursing the eye-glasses which had told them so much more than they wished to know, declared that life was no longer worth living. "What is the use?" they cried. "If He is not watching how we behave, what reason have we for behaving at all?"

And all the while the Blind God sat rolling his little mud ball from palm to palm and loving it—loving it, and wishing that he could make more of it, and find in it the self-expression and the companionship which his heart had begun to crave. For the little mud ball had taught him to think and to feel and to wish, and to let his thoughts go outside of himself in directions he had never tried. And because of the little mud ball he now found that time hung heavy on his hands, and his feet were weary of the chill waters that flowed around them, and his body was weary of its rest. He wanted to have things outside of himself, like himself, with which he might exchange the ideas of life which were beginning to formulate within him—all the product of this little ball of mud which he had taken into his hands and fathered with blind warmth! But though he wanted all those things he had no way of getting them, for he was a blind god, and he did not know.

But down below him, on his little mud world, the life-atoms had found out all about *him*—so they thought. They had found out that he was blind, that he knew nothing about them, and therefore—knowing nothing about them—did not really exist.

But though they had discovered his in-
firmities and his limitations, they had not
got at his heart. About that they knew
nothing—nor did he; the little mud ball
could not teach him everything—not all at
once.

But after a long time it taught him to
feel very tired ; and all at once he sighed
a deep sigh that passed in a soft shudder
through his whole being. And as he so
sighed the little mud ball slipped through
his fingers and fell into the stream and was
drowned.

The Blind God did not sorrow for it
much ; he only felt a little vexed with himself. " I must be more careful next time,"
he thought. And, stooping down, he
gathered up a fresh handful of mud and
moulded it into form, and once more started
rolling it.

THE GRAY WOLF

George MacDonald

THE GRAY WOLF

ONE evening-twilight in spring, a young English student, who had wandered northwards as far as the outlying fragments of Scotland called the Orkney and Shetland Islands, found himself on a small island of the latter group, caught in a storm of wind and hail, which had come on suddenly. It was in vain to look about for any shelter; for not only did the storm entirely obscure the landscape, but there was nothing around him save a desert moss.

At length, however, as he walked on for mere walking's sake, he found himself on the verge of a cliff, and saw, over the brow of it, a few feet below him, a ledge of rock, where he might find some shelter from the blast, which blew from behind. Letting himself down by his hands, he alighted upon something that crunched beneath his tread, and found the bones of many small animals scattered about in front of a little cave in the rock, offering the refuge he sought. He went in, and sat upon a stone. The storm increased in violence, and as the darkness grew he became uneasy, for he did not relish the thought of spending the night in the cave. He had parted from his companions on the opposite side of the island, and it added to his uneasiness that they must be full of apprehension about him. At last there came a lull in the storm, and the same instant he heard a footfall, stealthy and light as that of a wild beast, upon the bones at the mouth of the cave. He started up in some fear, though the least thought might have satisfied him that there could be no very dangerous animals upon the island. Before he had time to think,

239

however, the face of a woman appeared in the opening. Eagerly the wanderer spoke. She started at the sound of his voice. He could not see her well, because she was turned towards the darkness of the cave.

"Will you tell me how to find my way across the moor to Shielness?" he asked.

"You cannot find it to-night," she answered, in a sweet tone, and with a smile that bewitched him, revealing the whitest of teeth.

"What am I to do, then?"

"My mother will give you shelter, but that is all she has to offer."

"And that is far more than I expected a minute ago," he replied. "I shall be most grateful."

She turned in silence and left the cave. The youth followed.

She was barefooted, and her pretty brown feet went catlike over the sharp stones, as she led the way down a rocky path to the shore. Her garments were scanty and torn, and her hair blew tangled in the wind. She seemed about five and twenty, lithe and small. Her long fingers kept clutching and pulling nervously at her skirts as she went. Her face was very gray in complexion, and very worn, but delicately formed, and smooth-skinned. Her thin nostrils were tremulous as eyelids, and her lips, whose curves were faultless, had no colour to give sign of indwelling blood. What her eyes were like he could not see, for she had never lifted the delicate films of her eyelids.

At the foot of the cliff they came upon a little hut leaning against it, and having for its inner apartment a natural hollow within. Smoke was spreading over the face of the rock, and the grateful odour of food gave hope to the hungry student. His guide opened the door of the cottage; he followed her in, and saw a woman bending over a fire in the middle of the floor. On the fire lay a large fish broiling. The daughter spoke a few words, and the mother turned and welcomed the stranger. She had an old and very wrinkled, but honest face, and looked troubled. She dusted the only chair in the cottage, and placed it for him by the side of the fire, opposite the one window, whence he saw a little patch of yellow sand over which the spent waves spread themselves out listlessly. Under this window there was a bench, upon which the daughter threw herself in an unusual posture, resting her chin upon her hand. A moment after, the youth caught the first glimpse of her blue eyes. They were fixed upon him with a strange look of greed, amounting to craving, but, as if aware that they belied or betrayed her, she dropped them instantly. The moment she veiled them, her face, notwithstanding its colourless complexion, was almost beautiful.

When the fish was ready, the old woman wiped the deal table, steadied it upon the uneven floor, and covered it with a piece of fine table-linen. She then laid the fish on a wooden platter, and invited the guest to help himself. Seeing no other provision, he pulled from his pocket a hunting knife, and divided a portion from the fish, offering it to the mother first.

"Come, my lamb," said the old woman; and the daughter approached the table. But her nostrils and mouth quivered with disgust.

The next moment she turned and hurried from the hut.

"She doesn't like fish," said the old woman, "and I haven't anything else to give her."

"She does not seem in good health," he rejoined.

The woman answered only with a sigh, and they ate their fish with the help of a little rye bread. As they finished their supper, the youth heard the sound as of the pattering of a dog's feet upon the sand close to the door; but ere he had time to look out of the window, the door opened, and the young woman entered. She looked better, perhaps from having just washed her face. She drew a stool to the corner of the fire opposite him. But as she sat down, to his bewilderment, and even horror, the student spied a single drop of blood on her white skin within her torn dress. The woman brought

16

out a jar of whisky, put a rusty old kettle on the fire,
and took her place in front of it.   As soon as the water
boiled, she proceeded to make some toddy in a wooden
bowl.

Meantime the youth could not take his eyes off
the young woman, so that at length he found himself
fascinated, or rather bewitched.   She kept her eyes for
the most part veiled with the loveliest eyelids fringed
with darkest lashes, and he gazed entranced; for the
red glow of the little oil-lamp covered all the strangeness
of her complexion.   But as soon as he met a stolen
glance out of those eyes unveiled, his soul shuddered
within him.   Lovely face and craving eyes alternated
fascination and repulsion.

The mother placed the bowl in his hands.   He drank
sparingly, and passed it to the girl.   She lifted it to her
lips, and as she tasted—only tasted it—looked at him.
He thought the drink must have been drugged and have
affected his brain.   Her hair smoothed itself back, and
drew her forehead backwards with it; while the lower
part of her face projected towards the bowl, revealing,
ere she sipped, her dazzling teeth in strange prominence.
But the same moment the vision vanished; she returned
the vessel to her mother, and rising, hurried out of the
cottage.

Then the old woman pointed to a bed of heather in
one corner with a murmured apology; and the student,
wearied both with the fatigues of the day and the
strangeness of the night, threw himself upon it, wrapped
in his cloak.   The moment he lay down, the storm began
afresh, and the wind blew so keenly through the crannies
of the hut, that it was only by drawing his cloak over
his head that he could protect himself from its currents.
Unable to sleep, he lay listening to the uproar which
grew in violence, till the spray was dashing against the
window.   At length the door opened, and the young
woman came in, made up the fire, drew the bench before
it, and lay down in the same strange posture, with her
chin propped on her hand and elbow, and her face turned

towards the youth. He moved a little; she dropped her head, and lay on her face, with her arms crossed beneath her forehead. The mother had disappeared.

Drowsiness crept over him. A movement of the bench roused him, and he fancied he saw some four-footed creature as tall as a large dog trot quietly out of the door. He was sure he felt a rush of cold wind. Gazing fixedly through the darkness, he thought he saw the eyes of the damsel encountering his, but a glow from the falling together of the remnants of the fire revealed clearly enough that the bench was vacant. Wondering what could have made her go out in such a storm, he fell fast asleep.

In the middle of the night he felt a pain in his shoulder, came broad awake, and saw the gleaming eyes and grinning teeth of some animal close to his face. Its claws were in his shoulder, and its mouth in the act of seeking his throat. Before it had fixed its fangs, however, he had its throat in one hand, and sought his knife with the other. A terrible struggle followed; but regardless of the tearing claws, he found and opened his knife. He had made one futile stab, and was drawing it for a surer, when, with a spring of the whole body, and one wildly contorted effort, the creature twisted its neck from his hold, and with something betwixt a scream and a howl, darted from him. Again he heard the door open; again the wind blew in upon him, and it continued blowing; a sheet of spray dashed across the floor, and over his face. He sprung from his couch and bounded to the door.

It was a wild night—dark, but for the flash of whiteness from the waves as they broke within a few yards of the cottage; the wind was raving, and the rain pouring down the air. A gruesome sound as of mingled weeping and howling came from somewhere in the dark. He turned again into the hut and closed the door, but could find no way of securing it.

The lamp was nearly out, and he could not be certain whether the form of the young woman was upon the bench or not. Overcoming a strong repugnance, he approached it, and put out his hands—there was nothing there. He sat down and waited for the daylight: he dared not sleep any more.

When the day dawned at length, he went out yet again, and looked around. The morning was dim and gusty and gray. The wind had fallen, but the waves were tossing wildly. He wandered up and down the little strand, longing for more light.

At length he heard a movement in the cottage. By and by the voice of the old woman called to him from the door.

"You're up early, sir. I doubt you didn't sleep well."

"Not very well," he answered. "But where is your daughter?"

"She's not awake yet," said the mother. "I'm afraid I have but a poor breakfast for you. But you'll take a dram and a bit of fish. It's all I've got."

Unwilling to hurt her, though hardly in good appetite, he sat down at the table. While they were eating, the daughter came in, but turned her face away and went to the farther end of the hut. When she came forward after a minute or two, the youth saw that her hair was drenched, and her face whiter than before. She looked ill and faint, and when she raised her eyes, all their fierceness had vanished, and sadness had taken its place. Her neck was now covered with a cotton handkerchief. She was modestly attentive to him, and no longer shunned his gaze. He was gradually yielding to the temptation of braving another night in the hut, and seeing what would follow, when the old woman spoke.

"The weather will be broken all day, sir," she said. "You had better be going, or your friends will leave without you."

Ere he could answer, he saw such a beseeching glance on the face of the girl, that he hesitated, confused. Glancing at the mother, he saw the flash of wrath in her face. She rose and approached her daughter, with her hand lifted to strike her. The young woman stooped her head with a cry. He darted round the table to interpose between them. But the mother had caught hold of her; the handkerchief had fallen from her neck; and the youth saw five blue bruises on her lovely throat —the marks of the four fingers and the thumb of a left hand. With a cry of horror he darted from the house, but as he reached the door he turned. His hostess was lying motionless on the floor, and a huge gray wolf came bounding after him.

There was no weapon at hand; and if there had been, his inborn chivalry would never have allowed him to harm a woman even under the guise of a wolf. Instinctively, he set himself firm, leaning a little forward, with half outstretched arms, and hands curved ready to clutch again at the throat upon which he had left those pitiful marks. But the creature as she sprung eluded his grasp, and just as he expected to feel her fangs, he found a woman weeping on his bosom, with her arms around his neck. The next instant, the gray wolf broke from him, and bounded howling up the cliff. Recovering himself as he best might, the youth followed, for it was the only way to the moor above, across which he must now make his way to find his companions.

All at once he heard the sound of a crunching of bones —not as if a creature was eating them, but as if they were ground by the teeth of rage and disappointment; looking up, he saw close above him the mouth of the little cavern in which he had taken refuge the day before. Summoning all his resolution, he passed it slowly and softly. From within came the sounds of a mingled moaning and growling.

Having reached the top, he ran at full speed for some distance across the moor before venturing to look behind him. When at length he did so, he saw, against the sky, the girl standing on the edge of the cliff, wringing her hands. One solitary wail crossed the space between. She made no attempt to follow him, and he reached the opposite shore in safety.

THE INVISIBLE GIANT

Bram Stoker

THE INVISIBLE GIANT.

IME goes on in the Country Under the Sunset much as it does here.

Many years passed away : and they wrought much change. And now we find a time when the people that lived in good King Mago's time would hardly have known their beautiful Land if they had seen it again.

It had sadly changed indeed. No longer was there the same love or the same reverence towards the king, —no longer was there perfect peace. People had become more selfish and more greedy, and had tried to grasp all they could for themselves. There were some very rich and there were many poor. Most of the beautiful gardens were laid waste. Houses had grown up close round the palace ; and in some of these dwelt many persons who could only afford to pay for part of a house.

All the beautiful Country was sadly changed, and changed was the life of the dwellers in it. The people had almost forgotten Prince Zaphir, who was dead many, many years ago; and no more roses were spread on the pathways. Those who lived now in the Country Under the Sunset laughed at the idea of more Giants, and they did not fear them because they did not see them. Some of them said,

"Tush! what can there be to fear? Even if there ever were giants there are none now."

And so the people sang and danced and feasted as before, and thought only of themselves. The Spirits that guarded the Land were very, very sad. Their great white shadowy wings drooped as they stood at their posts at the Portals of the Land. They hid their faces, and their eyes were dim with continuous weeping, so that they heeded not if any evil thing went by them. They tried to make the people think of their evil-doing; but they could not leave their posts, and the people heard their moaning in the night season, and said,

"Listen to the sighing of the breeze; how sweet it is!"

So is it ever with us also, that when we hear the wind sighing and moaning and sobbing round our houses in the lonely nights, we do not think that our Angels may be sorrowing for our misdeeds, but only that there is a storm coming. The Angels wept evermore, and they felt the sorrow of dumbness—for though they could speak, those they spoke to would not hear.

Whilst the people laughed at the idea of Giants, there was one old old man who shook his head, and made answer to them, when he heard them, and said :

" Death has many children, and there are Giants in the marshes still. You may not see them, perhaps— but they are there, and the only bulwark of safety is in a land of patient, faithful hearts."

The name of this good old man was Knoal, and he lived in a house built of great blocks of stone, in the middle of a wild place far from the city.

In the city there were many great old houses, storey upon storey high ; and in these houses lived much poor people. The higher you went up the great steep stairs the poorer were the people that lived there, so that in the garrets were some so poor, that when the morning came they did not know whether they should have anything to eat the whole long day. This was very, very sad, and gentle children would have wept if they had seen their pain.

In one of these garrets there lived all alone a little maiden called Zaya. She was an orphan, for her father had died many years before, and her poor mother, who had toiled long and wearily for her dear little daughter —her only child—had died also not long since.

Poor little Zaya had wept so bitterly when she saw her dear mother lying dead, and she had been so sad and sorry for a long time, that she quite forgot that she had no means of living. However, the poor people who lived in the house had given her part of their own food, so that she did not starve.

Then after a while she had tried to work for herself and earn her own living. Her mother had taught her to make flowers out of paper; so she made a lot of flowers, and when she had a full basket she took them into the street and sold them. She made flowers of many kinds, roses and lilies, and violets, and snowdrops, and primroses, and mignonette, and many beautiful sweet flowers that only grow in the Country Under the Sunset. Some of them she could make without any pattern, but others she could not, so when she wanted a pattern she took her basket of paper and scissors, and paste, and brushes, and all the things she used, and went into the garden which a kind lady owned, where there grew many beautiful flowers. There she sat down and worked away, looking at the flowers she wanted.

Sometimes she was very sad, and her tears fell thick and fast as she thought of her dear dead mother. Often she seemed to feel that her mother was looking down at her, and to see her tender smile in the sunshine on the water; then her heart was glad, and she sang so sweetly that the birds came around her and stopped their own singing to listen to her.

She and the birds grew great friends, and sometimes when she had sung a song they would all cry out

together, as they sat round her in a ring, in a few notes
that seemed to say quite plainly :

"Sing to us again.   Sing to us again."

So she would sing again.   Then she would ask them

to sing, and they would sing till there was quite a con-
cert.   After a while the birds knew her so well that
they would come into her room, and they even built
their nests there, and they followed her wherever she
went.   The people used to say :

"Look at the girl with the birds ; she must be half a

H

bird herself, for see how the birds know and love her."
From so many people coming to say things like this,
some silly people actually believed that she was partly a
bird, and they shook their heads when wise people
laughed at them, and said:

" Indeed she must be; listen to her singing; her voice
is sweeter even than the birds."

So a nickname was applied to her, and naughty boys
called it after her in the street, and the nickname was
" Big Bird." But Zaya did not mind the name; and
although often naughty boys said it to her, meaning
to cause her pain, she did not dislike it, but the contrary,
for she so gloried in the love and trust of her little sweet-
voiced pets that she wished to be thought like them.

Indeed it would be well for some naughty little boys
and girls if they were as good and harmless as the
little birds that work all day long for their helpless baby
birds, building nests and bringing food, and sitting so
patiently hatching their little speckled eggs.

One evening Zaya sat alone in her garret very sad and
lonely. It was a lovely summer's evening, and she sat in
the window looking out over the city. She could see
over the many streets towards the great cathedral whose
spire towered aloft into the sky higher by far even than
the great tower of the king's palace. There was hardly
a breath of wind, and the smoke went up straight from
the chimneys, getting fainter and fainter till it was lost
altogether.

Zaya was very sad. For the first time for many days her birds were all away from her at once, and she did not know where they had gone. It seemed to her as if they had deserted her, and she was so lonely, poor little maid, that she wept bitter tears. She was thinking of the story which long ago her dead mother had told her, how Prince Zaphir had slain the Giant, and she wondered what the prince was like, and thought how happy the people must have been when Zaphir and Bluebell were king and queen. Then she wondered if there were any hungry children in those good days, and if, indeed, as the people said, there were no more Giants. So she thought and thought, as she went on with her work before the open window.

Presently she looked up from her work and gazed across the city. There she saw a terrible thing—something so terrible that she gave a low cry of fear and wonder, and leaned out of the window, shading her eyes with her hand to see more clearly.

In the sky beyond the city she saw a vast shadowy Form with its arms raised. It was shrouded in a great misty robe that covered it, fading away into air so that she could only see the face and the grim, spectral hands.

The Form was so mighty that the city below it seemed like a child's toy. It was still far off the city.

The little maid's heart seemed to stand still with fear as she thought to herself, "The Giants, then, are not dead. This is another of them."

Quickly she ran down the high stairs and out into the street. There she saw some people, and cried to them,

"Look! look! the Giant, the Giant!" and pointed towards the Form which she still saw moving slowly onwards to the city.

The people looked up, but they could not see anything, and they laughed and said,

"The child is mad."

Then poor little Zaya was more than ever frightened, and ran down the street crying out still,

"Look! look! the Giant, the Giant!" But no one heeded her, and all said, "The child is mad," and they went on their own ways.

Then the naughty boys came around her and cried out,

"Big Bird has lost her mates. She sees a bigger bird in the sky, and she wants it." And they made rhymes about her, and sang them as they danced round.

Zaya ran away from them; and she hurried right through the city, and out into the country beyond it, for she still saw the great Form before her in the air.

As she went on, and got nearer and nearer to the Giant, it grew a little darker. She could see only the clouds; but still there was visible the form of a Giant hanging dimly in the air.

A cold mist closed around her as the Giant appeared to come onwards towards her. Then she thought of all the poor people in the city, and she hoped that the

Giant would spare them, and she knelt .down before him and lifted up her hands appealingly, and cried aloud :

"Oh, great Giant ! spare them, spare them ! "

But the Giant moved onwards still as though he never heard. She cried aloud all the more,

"Oh, great Giant! spare them, spare them !" And she bowed down her head and wept, and the Giant still, though very slowly, moved onward towards the city.

There was an old man not far off standing at the door of a small house built of great stones, but the little maid saw him not. His face wore a look of fear and wonder, and when he saw the child kneel and raise her hands, he drew nigh and listened to her voice. When he heard her say, "Oh, great Giant!" he murmured to himself,

"It is then even as I feared. There are more Giants, and truly this is another." He looked upwards, but he saw nothing, and he murmured again,

"I see not, yet this child can see; and yet I feared, for something told me that there was danger. Truly knowledge is blinder than innocence."

The little maid, still not knowing there was any human being near her, cried out again, with a great cry of anguish :

"Oh, do not, do not, great Giant, do them harm. If someone must suffer, let it be me. Take me. I am willing to die, but spare them. Spare them, great Giant;

and do with me even as thou wilt." But the giant heeded not.

And Knoal—for he was the old man—felt his eyes fill with tears, and he said to himself,

" Oh, noble child, how brave she is, she would sacrifice herself!" And, coming closer to her, he put his hand upon her head.

Zaya, who was again bowing her head, started and looked round when she felt the touch. However, when she saw that it was Knoal, she was comforted, for she knew how wise and good he was, and felt that if any person could help her, he could. So she clung to him, and hid her face in his breast; and he stroked her hair and comforted her. But still he could see nothing.

The cold mist swept by, and when Zaya looked up, she saw that the Giant had passed by, and was moving onward to the city.

" Come with me, my child," said the old man; and the two arose, and went into the dwelling built of great stones.

When Zaya entered, she started, for lo! the inside was as a tomb. The old man felt her shudder, for he still held her close to him, and he said:

" Weep not, little one, and fear not. This place reminds me and all who enter it, that to the tomb we must all come at the last. Fear it not, for it has grown to be a cheerful home to me."

Then the little maid was comforted, and began to

examine all around her more closely. She saw all sorts of curious instruments, and many strange and many common herbs and simples hung to dry in bunches on the walls. The old man watched her in silence till her fear was gone, and then he said:

"My child, saw you the features of the Giant as he passed?"

She answered, "Yes."

"Can you describe his face and form to me?" he asked again.

Whereupon she began to tell him all that she had seen. How the Giant was so great that all the sky seemed filled. How the great arms were outspread, veiled in his robe, till far away the shroud was lost in air. How the face was as that of a strong man, pitiless, yet without malice; and that the eyes were blind.

The old man shuddered as he heard, for he knew that the Giant was a very terrible one; and his heart wept for the doomed city where so many would perish in the midst of their sin.

They determined to go forth and warn again the doomed people; and making no delay, the old man and the little maid hurried towards the city.

As they left the small house, Zaya saw the Giant before them, moving still towards the city. They hurried on; and when they had passed through the cold mist, Zaya looked back, and saw the Giant behind them.

Presently they came to the city.

It was a strange sight to see that old man and that
little maid flying to tell the people of the terrible Plague
that was coming upon them. The old man's long white
beard and hair and the child's golden locks were swept
behind them in the wind, so quick they came. The
faces of both were white as death. Behind them,
seen only to the eyes of the pure-hearted little maid
when she looked back, came ever onward at slow pace
the spectral Giant that hung a dark shadow in the
evening air.

But those in the city never saw the Giant; and
when the old man and the little maid warned them,
still they heeded not, but scoffed and jeered at them,
and said,

" Tush! there are no Giants now;" and they went on
their way, laughing and jeering.

Then the old man came and stood on a raised place
amongst them, on the lowest step of the great fountain with the little maid by his side, and he spake
thus :

" Oh, people, dwellers in this Land, be warned in time.
This pure-hearted child, round whose sweet innocence
even the little birds that fear men and women gather in
peace, has this night seen in the sky the form of a Giant
that advances ever onward menacingly to our city. Believe, oh, believe; and be warned, whilst ye may.
To myself even as to you the sky is a blank; and yet see
that I believe. For listen to me: all unknowing that

another Giant had invaded our land, I sat pensive in my dwelling; and, without cause or motive, there came into my heart a sudden fear for the safety of our city. I arose and looked north and south and east and west, and on high and below, but never a sign of danger could I see. So I said to myself,

" ' Mine eyes are dim with a hundred years of watching and waiting, and so I cannot see.' And yet, oh people, dwellers in this land, though that century has dimmed mine outer eyes, still it has quickened mine inner eyes— the eyes of my soul. Again I went forth, and lo! this little maid knelt and implored a Giant, unseen by me, to spare the city; but he heard her not, or, if he heard, answered her not, and she fell prone. So hither we come to warn you. Yonder, says the maid, he passes on- ward to the city. Oh, be warned! be warned in time."

Still the people heeded not; but they scoffed and jeered the more, and said,

" Lo, the maid and the old man both are mad; " and they passed onwards to their homes—to dancing and feasting as before.

Then the naughty boys came and mocked them, and said that Zaya had lost her birds, and had gone mad; and they made songs, and sang them as they danced round.

Zaya was so sorely grieved for the poor people that she heeded not the cruel boys. Seeing that she did not heed them, some of them got still more rude and wicked;

they went a little way off, and threw things at them, and mocked them all the more.

Then, sad of heart, the old man arose, and took the little maid by the hand, and brought her away into the wilderness; and lodged her with him in the house built with great stones. That night Zaya slept with the sweet smell of the drying herbs all around her; and the old man held her hand that she might have no fear.

In the morning Zaya arose betimes, and awoke the old man, who had fallen asleep in his chair.

She went to the doorway and looked out, and then a thrill of gladness came upon her heart; for outside the door, as though waiting to see her, sat all her little birds, and many many more. When the birds saw the little maid they sang a few loud joyous notes, and flew about foolishly for very joy—some of them fluttering their wings and looking so funny that she could not help laughing a little.

When Knoal and Zaya had eaten their frugal breakfast and given to their little feathered friends, they set out with sorrowful hearts to visit the city, and to try once more to warn the people. The birds flew around them as they went, and to cheer them sang as joyously as they could, although their little hearts were heavy.

As they walked they saw before them the great shadowy Giant; and he had now advanced to the very confines of the city.

Once again they warned the people, and great crowds

came around them, but only mocked them more than
ever; and naughty boys threw stones and sticks at the
little birds and killed some of them.   Poor Zaya wept
bitterly, and Knoal's heart was very sad.   After a time,
when they had moved from the fountain, Zaya looked
up and started with joyous surprise, for the great shadowy
Giant was nowhere to be seen.   She cried out in joy,
and the people laughed, and said,

"Cunning child! she sees that we will not believe
her, and she pretends that the Giant has gone."

They surrounded her, jeering, and some of them
said,

"Let us put her under the fountain and duck her,
as a lesson to liars who would frighten us."   Then they
approached her with menaces. She clung close to Knoal,
who had looked terribly grave when she had said she
did not see the Giant any longer, and who was now as
if in a dream, thinking. But at her touch he seemed to
wake up; and he spoke sternly to the people, and re-
buked them.   But they cried out on him also, and said
that as he had aided Zaya in her lie he should be ducked
also, and they advanced closer to lay hands on them
both.

The hand of one who was a ringleader was already
outstretched, when he gave a low cry, and pressed his
hand to his side; and, whilst the others turned to
look at him in wonder, he cried out in great pain, and
screamed horribly. Even whilst the people looked, his

face grew blacker and blacker, and he fell down before them, and writhed a while in pain, and then died.

All the people screamed out in terror, and ran away, crying aloud,

"The Giant! the Giant! he is indeed amongst us!"

They feared all the more that they could not see him.

But before they could leave the market-place, in the centre of which was the fountain, many fell dead, and their corpses lay.

There in the centre knelt the old man and the little

maid, praying; and the birds sat perched around the fountain, mute and still, and there was no sound heard save the cries of the people far off. Then their wailing sounded louder and louder, for the Giant—Plague—was amongst and around them, and there was no escaping, for it was now too late to fly.

Alas! in the Country Under the Sunset there was much weeping that day; and when the night came there was little sleep, for there was fear in some hearts and pain in others. None were still except the dead, who lay stark about the city, so still and lifeless that even the cold light of the moon and the shadows of the drifting clouds moving over them could not make them seem as though they lived.

And for many a long day there was pain and grief and death in the Country Under the Sunset.

Knoal and Zaya did all they could to help the poor people, but it was hard indeed to aid them, for the unseen Giant was amongst them, wandering through the city to and fro, so that none could tell where next he would lay his ice-cold hand.

Some people fled away out of the city; but it was little use, for go how they would and fly never so fast they were still within the grasp of the unseen Giant. Ever and anon he turned their warm hearts to ice with his breath and his touch, and they fell dead.

Some, like those within the city, were spared, and of these some perished of hunger, and the rest crept

sadly back to the city and lived or died amongst their
friends. And it was all, oh! so sad, for there was
nothing but grief and fear and weeping from morn till
night.

Now, see how Zaya's little bird friends helped her
in her need.

They seemed to see the coming of the Giant when
no one—not even the little maid herself—could see
anything, and they managed to tell her when there was
danger just as well as though they could talk.

At first Knoal and she went home every evening to
the house built of great stones to sleep, and came again
to the city in the morning, and stayed with the poor
sick people, comforting them and feeding them, and
giving them medicine which Knoal, from his great wisdom, knew would do them good. Thus they saved
many precious human lives, and those who were rescued
were very thankful, and henceforth ever after lived
holier and more unselfish lives.

After a few days, however, they found that the poor
sick people needed help even more at night than in the
day, and so they came and lived in the city altogether,
helping the stricken folk day and night.

At the earliest dawn Zaya would go forth to breathe
the morning air; and there, just waked from sleep,
would be her feathered friends waiting for her. They
sang glad songs of joy, and came and perched on her
shoulders and her head, and kissed her. Then, if she

went to go towards any place where, during the night,
the Plague had laid his deadly hand, they would flutter
before her, and try to impede her, and scream out in
their own tongue,

"Go back! go back!"

They pecked of her bread and drank of her cup
before she touched them; and when there was danger—
for the cold hand of the Giant was placed everywhere
—they would cry,

"No, no!" and she would not touch the food, or let
anyone else do so. Often it happened that, even whilst
it pecked at the bread or drank of the cup, a poor little
bird would fall down and flutter its wings and die; but
all they that died, did so with a chirp of joy, looking
at their little mistress, for whom they had gladly perished.
Whenever the little birds found that the bread and
the cup were pure and free from danger, they would
look up at Zaya jauntily, and flap their wings and try
to crow, and seemed so saucy that the poor sad little
maiden would smile.

There was one old bird that always took a second,
and often a great many pecks at the bread when it was
good, so that he got quite a hearty meal; and sometimes
he would go on feeding till Zaya would shake her finger
at him and say,

"Greedy!" and he would hop away as if he had done
nothing.

There was one other dear little bird—a robin, with a

K

breast as red as the sunset—that loved Zaya more than one can think.   When he tried the food and found that it was safe to eat, he would take a little tiny piece in his bill, and fly up and put it in her mouth.

Every little bird that drank from Zaya's cup and

found it good raised its head to say grace; and ever since then the little birds do the same, and they never forget to say their grace—as some thankless children do.

Thus Knoal and Zaya lived, although many around them died, and the Giant still remained in the city. So many people died that one began to wonder that so many were left; for it was only when the town began to get thinned that people thought of the vast numbers that had lived in it.

Poor little Zaya had got so pale and thin that she looked like a shadow, and Knoal's form was bent more with the sufferings of a few weeks than it had been by his century of age. But although the two were weary and worn, they still kept on their good work of aiding the sick.

Many of the little birds were dead.

One morning the old man was very weak—so weak that he could hardly stand. Zaya got frightened about him, and said,

"Are you ill, father?" for she always called him father now.

He answered her in a voice alas! hoarse and low, but very, very tender:

"My child, I fear the end is coming: take me home, that there I may die."

At his words Zaya gave a low cry and fell on her knees beside him, and buried her head in his bosom and wept bitterly, whilst she hugged him close. But she had little time for weeping, for the old man struggled up to his feet, and, seeing that he wanted aid, she dried her tears and helped him.

The old man took his staff, and with Zaya helping to support him, got as far as the fountain in the midst of the market-place; and there, on the lowest step, he sank down as though exhausted. Zaya felt him grow cold as ice, and she knew that the chilly hand of the Giant had been laid upon him.

Then, without knowing why, she looked up to where she had last seen the Giant as Knoal and she had stood beside the fountain. And lo! as she looked, holding Knoal's hand, she saw the shadowy form of the terrible Giant who had been so long invisible growing more and more clearly out of the clouds.

His face was stern as ever, and his eyes were still blind.

Zaya cried to the Giant, still holding Knoal tightly by the hand:

"Not him, not him! Oh, mighty Giant! not him! not him!" and she bowed down her head and wept.

There was such anguish in her heart that to the blind eyes of the shadowy Giant came tears that fell like dew on the forehead of the old man. Knoal spake to Zaya:

"Grieve not, my child. I am glad that you see the Giant again, for I have hope that he will leave our city free from woe. I am the last victim, and I gladly die."

Then Zaya knelt to the Giant, and said:

"Spare him! oh! spare him and take me! but spare him! spare him!"

The old man raised himself upon his elbow as he lay, and spake to her:

"Grieve not, little one, and repine not. Sooth I know that you would gladly give your life for mine.

But we must give for the good of others that which is dearer to us than our lives. Bless you, my little one, and be good. Farewell! farewell!"

As he spake the last word he grew cold as death, and his spirit passed away.

Zaya knelt down and prayed; and when she looked up she saw the shadowy Giant moving away.

The Giant turned as he passed on, and Zaya saw that his blind eyes looked towards her as though he were trying to see. He raised the great shadowy arms, draped still in his shroud of mist, as though blessing her; and she thought that the wind that came by her moaning bore the echo of the words :

" Innocence and devotion save the land."

Presently she saw far off the great shadowy Giant Plague moving away to the border of the Land, and passing between the Guardian Spirits out through the Portal into the deserts beyond—for ever.

A PROFESSOR OF EGYPTOLOGY

Guy Boothby

A PROFESSOR OF EGYPTOLOGY

FROM seven o'clock in the evening until half past, that is to say for the half-hour preceding dinner, the Grand Hall of the Hôtel Occidental, throughout the season, is practically a lounge, and is crowded with the most fashionable folk wintering in Cairo. The evening I am anxious to describe was certainly no exception to the rule. At the foot of the fine marble staircase—the pride of its owner—a well-known member of the French Ministry was chatting with an English Duchess whose pretty, but somewhat delicate, daughter was flirting mildly with one of the Sirdar's Bimbashis, on leave from the Soudan. On the right-hand lounge of the Hall an Italian Countess, whose antecedents were as doubtful as her diamonds, was apparently listening to a story a handsome Greek *attaché* was telling her ; in reality, however, she was endeavouring to catch scraps of a conversation being carried on, a few

37

A Professor of Egyptology

feet away, between a witty Russian and an equally clever daughter of the United States. Almost every nationality was represented there, but, fortunately for our prestige, the majority were English. The scene was a brilliant one, and the sprinkling of military and diplomatic uniforms (there was a Reception at the Khedivial Palace later) lent an additional touch of colour to the picture. Taken altogether, and regarded from a political point of view, the gathering had a significance of its own.

At the end of the Hall, near the large glass doors, a handsome, elderly lady, with grey hair, was conversing with one of the leading English doctors of the place—a grey-haired, clever-looking man, who possessed the happy faculty of being able to impress everyone with whom he talked with the idea that he infinitely preferred his or her society to that of any other member of the world's population. They were discussing the question of the most suitable clothing for a Nile voyage, and as the lady's daughter, who was seated next her, had been conversant with her mother's ideas on the subject ever since their first visit to Egypt (as indeed had been the Doctor), she preferred to lie back on the divan and watch the people about her. She

A Professor of Egyptology

had large, dark, contemplative eyes. Like her
mother she took life seriously, but in a somewhat different fashion. One who has been
bracketed third in the Mathematical Tripos
can scarcely be expected to bestow very much
thought on the comparative merits of Jæger,
as opposed to dresses of the Common or
Garden flannel. From this, however, it must
not be inferred that she was in any way a
blue stocking, that is, of course, in the vulgar
acceptation of the word. She was thorough
in all she undertook, and for the reason that
mathematics interested her very much the
same way that Wagner, chess, and, shall we
say, croquet, interest other people, she made
it her hobby, and it must be confessed she
certainly succeeded in it. At other times she
rode, drove, played tennis and hockey, and
looked upon her world with calm, observant
eyes that were more disposed to find good
than evil in it. Contradictions that we are,
even to ourselves, it was only those who
knew her intimately, and they were few and
far between, who realised that, under that
apparently sober, matter-of-fact personality,
there existed a strong leaning towards the
mysterious, or, more properly speaking, the
occult. Possibly she herself would have
been the first to deny this—but that I am

A Professor of Egyptology

right in my surmise this story will surely be sufficient proof.

Mrs Westmoreland and her daughter had left their comfortable Yorkshire home in September, and, after a little dawdling on the Continent, had reached Cairo in November —the best month to arrive, in my opinion, for then the rush has not set in, the hotel servants have not had sufficient time to become weary of their duties, and what is better still, all the best rooms have not been bespoken. It was now the middle of December, and the fashionable caravanserai, upon which they had for many years bestowed their patronage, was crowded from roof to cellar. Every day people were being turned away, and the manager's continual lament was that he had not another hundred rooms wherein to place more guests. He was a Swiss, and for that reason regarded hotel-keeping in the light of a profession.

On this particular evening Mrs Westmoreland and her daughter Cecilia had arranged to dine with Dr Forsyth—that is to say, they were to eat their meal at his table in order that they might meet a man of whom they had heard much, but whose acquaintance they had not as yet made. The individual in question was a certain Professor Con-

A Professor of Egyptology

stanides—reputed one of the most advanced Egyptologists, and the author of several well-known works. Mrs Westmoreland was not of an exacting nature, and so long as she dined in agreeable company did not trouble herself very much whether it was with an English earl or a distinguished foreign *savant*.

"It really does not matter, my dear," she was wont to observe to her daughter. "So long as the cooking is good and the wine above reproach, there is absolutely nothing to choose between them. A Prime Minister and a country vicar are, after all, only men. Feed them well and they'll lie down and purr like tame cats. They don't want conversation." From this it will be seen that Mrs Westmoreland was well acquainted with her world. Whether Miss Cecilia shared her opinions is another matter. At any rate, she had been looking forward for nearly a fortnight to meeting Constanides, who was popularly supposed to possess an extraordinary intuitive knowledge—instinct, perhaps, it should be called—concerning the localities of tombs of the Pharaohs of the Eleventh, Twelfth and Thirteenth Dynasties.

"I am afraid Constanides is going to be late," said the Doctor, who had con-

A Professor of Egyptology

sulted his watch more than once. "I hope, in that case, as his friend and your host, you will permit me to offer you my apologies."

The Doctor at no time objected to the sound of his own voice, and on this occasion he was even less inclined to do so. Mrs Westmoreland was a widow with an ample income, and Cecilia, he felt sure, would marry ere long.

"He has still three minutes in which to put in an appearance," observed that young lady, quietly. And then she added in the same tone, "Perhaps we ought to be thankful if he comes at all."

Both Mrs Westmoreland and her friend the Doctor regarded her with mildly reproachful eyes. The former could not understand anyone refusing a dinner such as she felt sure the Doctor had arranged for them; while the latter found it impossible to imagine a man who would dare to disappoint the famous Dr Forsyth, who, having failed in Harley Street, was nevertheless coining a fortune in the Land of the Pharaohs.

"My good friend Constanides will not disappoint us, I feel sure," he said, consulting his watch for the fourth time. "Possibly I am a little fast, at anyrate I have never known him to be unpunctual. A remarkable

A Professor of Egyptology

—a very remarkable man is Constanides. I cannot remember ever to have met another like him. And such a scholar!"

Having thus bestowed his approval upon him the worthy Doctor pulled down his cuffs, straightened his tie, adjusted his *pince-nez* in his best professional manner, and looked round the hall as if searching for someone bold enough to contradict the assertion he had just made.

"You have, of course, read his *Mythological Egypt*," observed Miss Cecilia, demurely, speaking as if the matter were beyond doubt.

The Doctor looked a little confused.

"Ahem! Well, let me see," he stammered, trying to find a way out of the difficulty. "Well, to tell the truth, my dear young lady, I'm not quite sure that I have studied that particular work. As a matter of fact, you see, I have so little leisure at my disposal for any reading that is not intimately connected with my profession. That, of course, must necessarily come before everything else."

Miss Cecilia's mouth twitched as if she were endeavouring to keep back a smile. At the same moment the glass doors of the vestibule opened and a man entered. So remarkable was he that everyone turned to look at him—a fact which did not appear to disconcert him in the least.

He was tall, well shaped, and carried himself with the air of one accustomed to command. His face was oval, his eyes large and set somewhat wide apart. It was only when they were directed fairly at one that one became aware of the power they possessed. The cheek bones were a trifle high, and the forehead possibly retreated towards the jet-black hair more than is customary in Greeks. He wore neither beard nor moustache, thus enabling one to see the wide, firm mouth, the compression of the lips of which spoke for the determination of their possessor. Those who had an eye for such things noted the fact that he was faultlessly dressed, while Miss Cecilia, who had the precious gift of observation largely developed, noted that, with the exception of a single ring and a magnificent pearl stud, the latter strangely set, he wore no jewellery of any sort.

He looked about him for Dr Forsyth, and, when he had located him, hastened forward.

" My dear friend," he said in English, which he spoke with scarcely a trace of foreign accent, " I must crave your pardon a thousand times if I have kept you waiting."

"On the contrary," replied the Doctor, effusively, "you are punctuality itself. Permit me to have the pleasure—the very great pleasure—of introducing you to my friends, Mrs Westmoreland and her daughter, Miss Cecilia, of whom you have often heard me speak."

Professor Constanides bowed and expressed the pleasure he experienced in making their acquaintance. Though she could not have told you why, Miss Cecilia found herself undergoing very much the same sensation as she had done when she had passed up the Throne Room at her presentation. A moment later the gong sounded, and, with much rustling of skirts and fluttering of fans, a general movement was made towards the dining-room.

As host, Dr Forsyth gave his arm to Mrs Westmoreland, Constanides following with Miss Cecilia. The latter was concious of a vague feeling of irritation; she admired the man and his work, but she wished his name had been anything rather than what it was.

(It should be here remarked that the last Constanides she had encountered had swindled her abominably in the matter of a turquoise brooch, and in consequence the name had been an offence to her ever since.)

Dr Forsyth's table was situated at the further end, in the window, and from it a good view of the room could be obtained. The scene was an animated one, and one of the party, at least, I fancy, will never forget it—try how she may.

During the first two or three courses the conversation was practically limited to Cecilia and Constanides; the Doctor and Mrs Westmoreland being too busy to waste time on idle chatter. Later, they became more amenable to the discipline of the table—or, in other words, they found time to pay attention to their neighbours.

Since then I have often wondered with what feelings Cecilia looks back upon that evening. In order, perhaps, to punish me for my curiosity, she has admitted to me since that she had never known, up to that time, what it was to converse with a really clever man. I submitted to the humiliation for the reason that we are, if not lovers, at least old friends, and, after all, Mrs Westmoreland's cook is one in a thousand.

From that evening forward, scarcely a

A Professor of Egyptology

day passed in which Constanides did not
enjoy some portion of Miss Westmoreland's
society. They met at the polo ground,
drove in the Gezîreh, shopped in the Muski,
or listened to the band, over afternoon tea,
on the balcony of Shepheard's Hotel. Constanides was always unobtrusive, always
picturesque and invariably interesting.
What was more to the point, he never
failed to command attention whenever or
wherever he might appear. In the Native
Quarter he was apparently better known
than in the European. Cecilia noticed that
there he was treated with a deference such
as one would only expect to be shown to a
king. She marvelled, but said nothing.
Personally, I can only wonder that her
mother did not caution her before it was
too late. Surely she must have seen
how dangerous the intimacy was likely to
become. It was old Colonel Bettenham
who sounded the first note of warning.
In some fashion or another he was connected with the Westmorelands, and therefore had more or less right to speak his
mind.

"Who the man is, I am not in a position
to say," he remarked to the mother; "but
if I were in your place I should be very

A Professor of Egyptology

careful. Cairo at this time of the year is
full of adventurers."

"But, my dear Colonel," answered Mrs
Westmoreland, "you surely do not mean
to insinuate that the Professor is an ad-
venturer. He was introduced to us by
Dr Forsyth, and he has written so many
clever books."

"Books, my dear madam, are not everything," the other replied judicially, and with
that fine impartiality which marks a man who
does not read. "As a matter of fact I am
bound to confess that Phipps—one of my
captains—wrote a novel some years ago,
but only one. The mess pointed out to
him that it wasn't good form, don't you
know, so he never tried the experiment
again. But as for this man, Constanides,
as they call him, I should certainly be more
than careful."

I have been told since that this conversation worried poor Mrs Westmoreland more
than she cared to admit, even to herself.
To a very large extent she, like her daughter,
had fallen under the spell of the Professor's
fascination. Had she been asked, point
blank, she would doubtless have declared
that she preferred the Greek to the Englishman—though, of course, it would have

48

A Professor of Egyptology

seemed flat heresy to say so. And yet
—well, doubtless you can understand what
I mean without my explaining further.

I am inclined to believe that I was the
first to notice that there was serious trouble
brewing. I could see a strained look in the
girl's eyes for which I found it difficult to
account. Then the truth dawned upon me,
and I am ashamed to say that I began to
watch her systematically. We have few
secrets from each other now, and she has
told me a good deal of what happened during
that extraordinary time—for extraordinary
it certainly was. Perhaps none of us
realised what a unique drama we were
watching—one of the strangest, I am
tempted to believe, that this world of ours
has ever seen.

Christmas was just past and the New Year
was fairly under way when the beginning of
the end came. I think by that time even
Mrs Westmoreland had arrived at some sort
of knowledge of the case. But it was then
too late to interfere. I am as sure that
Cecilia was not in love with Constanides
as I am of anything. She was merely
fascinated by him, and to a degree that,
happily for the peace of the world, is as
rare as the reason for it is perplexing.

A Professor of Egyptology

To be precise, it was on Tuesday, January the 3rd, that the crisis came. On the evening of that day, accompanied by her daughter and escorted by Dr Forsyth, Mrs Westmoreland attended a reception at the palace of a certain Pasha, whose name I am obviously compelled to keep to myself. For the purposes of my story it is sufficient, however, that he is a man who prides himself on being up-to-date in most things, and for that and other reasons invitations to his receptions are eagerly sought after. In his drawing-room one may meet some of the most distinguished men in Europe, and on occasion it is even possible to obtain an insight into certain political intrigues that, to put it mildly, afford one an opportunity of reflecting on the instability of mundane affairs and of politics in particular.

The evening was well advanced before Constanides made his appearance. When he did, it was observed that he was more than usually quiet. Later, Cecilia permitted him to conduct her into the balcony, whence, since it was a perfect moonlight night, a fine view of the Nile could be obtained. Exactly what he said to her I have never been able to discover; I have, however, her mother's assurance that she was visibly

A Professor of Egyptology

agitated when she rejoined her. As a matter of fact, they returned to the hotel almost immediately, when Cecilia, pleading weariness, retired to her room.

And now this is the part of the story you will find as difficult to believe as I did. Yet I have indisputable evidence that it is true. It was nearly midnight and the large hotel was enjoying the only quiet it knows in the twenty-four hours. I have just said that Cecilia had retired, but in making that assertion I am not telling the exact truth, for though she had bade her mother "Good-night" and had gone to her room, it was not to rest. Regardless of the cold night air she had thrown open the window, and was standing looking out into the moonlit street. Of what she was thinking I do not know, nor can she remember. For my own part, however, I incline to the belief that she was in a semi-hypnotic condition and that . for the time being her mind was a blank.

From this point I will let Cecilia tell the story herself.

How long I stood at the window I cannot say; it may have been only five minutes, it might have been an hour. Then, suddenly, an extraordinary thing happened. I knew

51

A Professor of Egyptology

that it was imprudent, I was aware that it was even wrong, but an overwhelming craving to go out seized me. I felt as if the house were stifling me and that if I did not get out into the cool night air, and within a few minutes, I should die. Stranger still, I felt no desire to battle with the temptation, It was as if a will infinitely stronger than my own was dominating me and that I was powerless to resist. Scarcely conscious of what I was doing I changed my dress, and then, throwing on a cloak, switched off the electric light and stepped out into the corridor. The white-robed Arab servants were lying about on the floor as is their custom; they were all asleep. On the thick carpet of the great staircase my steps made no sound. The hall was in semi-darkness and the watchman must have been absent on his rounds, for there was no one there to spy upon me. Passing through the vestibule I turned the key of the front door. Still success attended me, for the lock shot back with scarcely a sound and I found myself in the street. Even then I had no thought of the folly of this escapade. I was merely conscious of the mysterious power that was dragging me on. Without hesitation I turned to the right and hastened along

52

A Professor of Egyptology

the pavement, faster I think than I had ever walked in my life. Under the trees it was comparatively dark, but out in the roadway it was well-nigh as bright as day. Once a carriage passed me and I could hear its occupants, who were French, conversing merrily—otherwise I seemed to have the city to myself. Later I heard a *muezzin* chanting his call to prayer from the minaret of some mosque in the neighbourhood, the cry being taken up and repeated from other mosques. Then at the corner of a street I stopped as if in obedience to a command. I can recall the fact that I was trembling, but for what reason I could not tell. I say this to show that while I was incapable of returning to the hotel, or of exercising my normal will power, I still possessed the faculty of observation.

I had scarcely reached the corner referred to, which, as a matter of fact, I believe I should recognise if I saw it again, when the door of a house opened and a man emerged. It was Professor Constanides, but his appearance at such a place and at such an hour, like everything else that happened that night, did not strike me as being in any way extraordinary.

"You have obeyed me," he said by way

53

of greeting. "That is well. Now let us be going—the hour is late."

As he said it there came the rattle of wheels and a carriage drove swiftly round the corner and pulled up before us. My companion helped me into it and took his place beside me. Even then, unheard-of as my action was, I had no thought of resisting.

"What does it mean?" I asked. "Oh, tell me what it means? Why am I here?"

"You will soon know," was his reply, and his voice took a tone I had never noticed in it before.

We had driven some considerable distance, in fact, I believe we had crossed the river, before either of us spoke again.

"Think," said my companion, "and tell me whether you can remember ever having driven with me before?"

"We have driven together many times lately," I replied. "Yesterday to the polo, and the day before to the Pyramids."

"Think again," he said, and as he did so he placed his hand on mine. It was as cold as ice. However, I only shook my head.

"I cannot remember," I answered, and yet I seemed to be dimly conscious of something that was too intangible to be a recol-

lection. He uttered a little sigh and once
more we were silent. The horses must have
been good ones for they whirled us along at
a fast pace. I did not take much interest in
the route we followed, but at last something
attracted my attention and I knew that we
were on the road to Gizeh. A few moments
later the famous Museum, once the palace of
the ex-Khedive Ismail, came into view.
Almost immediately the carriage pulled up
in the shadow of the *Lebbek* trees and my
companion begged me to alight. I did so,
whereupon he said something, in what I can
only suppose was Arabic, to his coachman,
who whipped up his horses and drove swiftly
away.

"Come," he said, in the same tone of
command as before, and then led the way
towards the gates of the old palace.
Dominated as my will was by his I could
still notice how beautiful the building looked
in the moonlight. In the daytime it presents
a faded and unsubstantial appearance, but
now, with its Oriental tracery, it was almost
fairylike. The Professor halted at the gates
and unlocked them. How he had obtained
the key, and by what right he admitted us,
I cannot say. It suffices that, almost before
I was aware of it, we had passed through

A Professor of Egyptology

the garden and were ascending the steps
to the main entrance. The doors behind
us, we entered the first room. It is only
another point in this extraordinary adventure
when I declare that even now I was not
afraid; and yet to find oneself in such a
place and at such an hour at any other time
would probably have driven me beside
myself with terror. The moonlight
streamed in upon us, revealing the ancient
monuments and the other indescribable
memorials of those long-dead ages. Once
more my conductor uttered his command
and we went on through the second room,
passed the Shekh-El-Beled and the Seated
Scribe. Room after room we traversed,
and to do so it seemed to me that we ascended stairs innumerable. At last we came
to one in which Constanides paused. It
contained numerous mummy cases and was
lighted by a skylight through which the rays
of the moon streamed in. We were standing before one which I remembered to have
remarked on the occasion of our last visit.
I could distinguish the paintings upon it distinctly. Professor Constanides, with a deft-
ness which showed his familiarity with the
work, removed the lid and revealed to me
the swathed-up figure within. The face

A Professor of Egyptology

was uncovered and was strangely well-preserved. I gazed down on it, and as I did so a sensation that I had never known before passed over me. My body seemed to be shrinking, my blood to be turning to ice. For the first time I endeavoured to exert myself, to tear myself from the bonds that were holding me. But it was in vain. I was sinking—sinking—sinking—into I knew not what. Then the voice of the man who had brought me to the place sounded in my ears as if he were speaking from a long way off. After that a great light burst upon me, and it was as if I were walking in a dream; yet I knew it was too real, too true to life to be a mere creation of my fancy.

It was night and the heavens were studded with stars. In the distance a great army was encamped and at intervals the calls of the sentries reached me. Somehow I seemed to feel no wonderment at my position. Even my dress caused me no surprise. To my left, as I looked towards the river, was a large tent, before which armed men paced continually. I looked about me as if I expected to see someone, but there was no one to greet me.

"It is for the last time," I told myself. "Come what may, it shall be the last time!"

A Professor of Egyptology

Still I waited, and as I did so I could hear the night wind sighing through the rushes on the river's bank. From the tent near me—for Usirtasen, son of Amenemhait—was then fighting against the Libyans and was commanding his army in person—came the sound of revelry. The air blew cold from the desert and I shivered, for I was but thinly clad. Then I hid myself in the shadow of a great rock that was near at hand. Presently I caught the sound of a footstep, and there came into view a tall man, walking carefully, as though he had no desire that the sentries on guard before the Royal tent should become aware of his presence in the neighbourhood. As I saw him I moved from where I was standing to meet him. He was none other that Sinûhît—younger son of Amenemhait and brother of Usirtasen—who was at that moment conferring with his generals in the tent.

I can see him now as he came towards me, tall, handsome, and defiant in his bearing as a man should be. He walked with the assured step of one who has been a soldier and trained to warlike exercises from his youth up. For a moment I regretted the news I had to tell him—but only for a moment. I could hear the voice of Usir-

A Professor of Egyptology

tasen in the tent, and after that I had no thought for anyone else.

"Is it thou, Nofrît?" he asked as soon as he saw me.

"It is I!" I replied. "You are late, Sinûhît. You tarry too long over the wine cups."

"You wrong me, Nofrît," he answered, with all the fierceness for which he was celebrated. "I have drunk no wine this night. Had I not been kept by the Captain of the Guard I should have been here sooner. Thou art not angry with me, Nofrît?"

"Nay, that were presumption on my part, my lord," I answered. "Art thou not the King's son, Sinûhît?"

"And by the Holy Ones I swear that it were better for me if I were not," he replied. "Usirtasen, my brother, takes all and I am but the jackal that gathers up the scraps wheresoever he may find them." He paused for a moment. "However, all goes well with our plot. Let me but have time and I will yet be ruler of this land and of all the Land of Khem beside." He drew himself up to his full height and looked towards the sleeping camp. It was well known that between the brothers there was but little love, and still less trust.

A Professor of Egyptology

"Peace, peace," I whispered, fearing lest his words might be overheard. "You must not talk so, my lord. Should you by chance be heard you know what the punishment would be!"

He laughed a short and bitter laugh. He was well aware that Usirtasen would show him no mercy. It was not the first time he had been suspected, and he was playing a desperate game. He came a step closer to me and took my hand in his. I would have withdrawn it—but he gave me no opportunity. Never was a man more in earnest than he was then.

"Nofrît," he said, and I could feel his breath upon my cheek, "what is my answer to be? The time for talking is past; now we must act. As thou knowest, I prefer deeds to words, and to-morrow my brother Usirtasen shall learn that I am as powerful as he."

Knowing what I knew I could have laughed him to scorn for this boastful speech. The time, however, was not yet ripe, so I held my peace. He was plotting against his brother, whom I loved, and it was his desire that I should help him. That, however, I would not do.

"Listen," he said, drawing even closer to

me, and speaking in a voice that showed me plainly how much in earnest he was, "thou knowest how much I love thee. Thou knowest that there is nought I would not do for thee or for thy sake. Be but faithful to me now and there is nothing thou shalt ask in vain of me hereafter. All is prepared, and ere the moon is gone I shall be Pharaoh and reign beside Amenemhait, my father."

"Are you so sure that your plans will not miscarry?" I asked, with what was almost a sneer at his recklessness—for recklessness it surely was to think that he could induce an army that had been admittedly successful to swerve in its allegiance to the general who had won its battles for it, and to desert in the face of the enemy. Moreover, I knew that he was wrong in believing that his father cared more for him than for Usirtasen, who had done so much for the kingdom, and who was beloved by high and low alike. But it was not in Sinûhît's nature to look upon the dark side of things. He had complete confidence in himself and in his power to bring his conspiracy against his father and brother to a successful issue. He revealed to me his plans, and, bold though they were, I could see that it was impossible that they could succeed. And in the event of his failing, what mercy could he hope to receive? I knew Usirtasen too well to think that he would show any. With all the eloquence I could command I implored him to abandon the attempt, or at least to delay it for a time. He seized my wrist and pulled me to him, peering fiercely into my face.

"Art playing me false?" he asked. "If it is so it were better that you should drown yourself in yonder river. Betray me and nothing shall save you—not even Pharaoh himself."

That he meant what he said I felt convinced. The man was desperate; he was staking all he had in the world upon the issue of his venture. I can say with truth that it was not my fault that we had been drawn together, and yet on this night of all others it seemed as if there were nothing left for me but to side with him or to bring about his downfall.

"Nofrît," he said, after a short pause, "is it nothing, thinkest thou, to be the wife of a Pharaoh? Is it not worth striving for, particularly when it can be so easily accomplished?"

I knew, however, that he was deluding himself with false hopes. What he had in his mind could never come to pass. I was

A Professor of Egyptology

like dry grass between two fires. All that was required was one small spark to bring about a conflagration in which I should be consumed.

"Harken to me, Nofrît," he continued. "You have means of learning Usirtasen's plans. Send me word to-morrow as to what is in his mind and the rest will be easy. Your reward shall be greater than you dream of."

Though I had no intention of doing what he asked, I knew that in his present humour it would be little short of madness to thwart him. I therefore temporised with him, and allowed him to suppose that I would do as he wished, and then, bidding him good-night, I sped away towards the hut where I was lodged. I had not been there many minutes when a messenger came to me from Usirtasen, summoning me to his presence. Though I could not understand what it meant I hastened to obey.

On arrival there I found him surrounded by the chief officers of his army. One glance at his face was sufficient to tell me that he was violently angry with someone, and I had the best of reasons for believing that that someone was myself. Alas! it was as I had expected. Sinûhît's plot had been

A Professor of Egyptology

discovered; he had been followed and watched, and my meeting with him that evening was known. I protested my innocence in vain. The evidence was too strong against me.

"Speak, girl, and tell what thou knowest," said Usirtasen, in a voice I had never heard him use before. "It is the only way by which thou canst save thyself. Look to it that thy story tallies with the tales of others!"

I trembled in every limb as I answered the questions he put to me. It was plain that he no longer trusted me, and that the favour I had once found in his eyes was gone, never to return.

"It is well," he said when I had finished my story. "And now we will see thy partner—the man who would have put me— the Pharaoh who is to be—to the sword had I not been warned in time."

He made a sign to one of the officers who stood by, whereupon the latter left the tent, to return a few moments later with Sinûhît.

"Hail, brother!" said Usirtasen, mockingly, as he leaned back in his chair and looked at him through half-shut eyes. "You tarried but a short time over the wine cup this night. I fear it pleased thee but little. Forgive me; on another occasion better shall be found for thee lest thou shouldst deem us lacking in our hospitality."

"There were matters that needed my attention and I could not stay," Sinûhît replied, looking his brother in the face. "Thou wouldst not have me neglect my duties."

"Nay! nay! Maybe they were matters that concerned our personal safety?" Usirtasen continued, still with the same gentleness. "Maybe you heard that there were those in our army who were not well disposed towards us? Give me their names, my brother, that due punishment may be meted out to them."

Before Sinûhît could reply, Usirtasen had sprung to his feet.

"Dog!" he cried, "darest thou prate to me of matters of importance when thou knowest thou hast been plotting against me and my father's throne. I have doubted thee these many months and now all is made clear. By the Gods, the Holy Ones, I swear that thou shalt die for this ere cock-crow."

It was at this moment that Sinûhît became aware of my presence. A little cry escaped him, and his face told me as plainly as any words could speak that he believed that I had betrayed him. He was about to speak, probably to denounce me, when the sound of voices reached us from outside. Usirtasen bade the guards ascertain what it meant, and presently a messenger entered the tent. He was travel-stained and weary. Advancing towards where Usirtasen was seated, he knelt before him.

"Hail, Pharaoh," he said. "I come to thee from the Palace of Titoui."

An anxious expression came over Usirtasen's face as he heard this. I also detected beads of perspiration on the brow of Sinûhît. A moment later it was known to us that Amenemhait was dead, and, therefore, Usirtasen reigned in his stead. The news was so sudden, and the consequences so vast, that it was impossible to realise quite what it meant. I looked across at Sinûhît and his eyes met mine. He seemed to be making up his mind about something. Then with lightning speed he sprang upon me; a dagger gleamed in the air; I felt as if a hot iron had been thrust into my breast, and after that I remember no more.

As I felt myself falling I seemed to wake from my dream—if dream it were—to find myself standing in the Museum by the mummy case, and with Professor Constanides by my side.

A Professor of Egyptology

"You have seen," he said. "You have
looked back across the centuries to that day
when, as Nofrît, I believed you had betrayed
me, and killed you. After that I escaped from
the camp and fled into Kaduma. There I
died ; but it was decreed that my soul should
never know peace till we had met again and
you had forgiven me. I have waited all these
years, and see—we meet at last."

Strange to say, even then the situation
did not strike me as being in any way im-
probable. Yet now, when I see it set down
in black and white, I find myself wondering
that I dare to ask anyone in their sober
senses to believe it to be true. Was I in
truth that same Nofrît who, four thousand
years before, had been killed by Sinûhît, son
of Amenemhait, because he believed that I
had betrayed him ? It seemed incredible,
and yet, if it were a creation of my imagina-
tion, what did the dream mean ? I fear it is
a riddle of which I shall probably never
know the answer.

My failure to reply to his question seemed
to cause him pain.

"Nofrît," he said, and his voice shook
with emotion, "think what your forgive-
ness means to me. Without it I am lost,
both here and hereafter."

A Professor of Egyptology

His voice was low and pleading and his face in the moonlight was like that of a man who knew the uttermost depths of despair.

"Forgive—forgive," he cried again, holding out his hands to me. "If you do not, I must go back to the sufferings which have been my portion since I did the deed which wrought my ruin."

I felt myself trembling like a leaf.

"If it is as you say, though I cannot believe it, I forgive you freely," I answered, in a voice that I scarcely recognised as my own.

For some moments he was silent, then he knelt before me and took my hand, which he raised to his lips. After that, rising, he laid his hand upon the breast of the mummy before which we were standing. Looking down at it he addressed it thus,—

"*Rest, Sinûhît, son of Amenemhait*—for that which was foretold for thee is now accomplished, and the punishment which was decreed is at an end. Henceforth thou mayest sleep in peace."

After that he replaced the lid of the coffin, and when this was done he turned to me.

"Let us be going," he said, and we went together through the rooms by the way we had come.

A Professor of Egyptology

Together we left the building and passed through the gardens out into the road beyond. There we found the carriage waiting for us, and we took our places in it. Once more the horses sped along the silent road, carrying us swiftly back to Cairo. During the drive not a word was spoken by either of us. The only desire I had left was to get back to the hotel and lay my aching head upon my pillow. We crossed the bridge and entered the city. What the time was I had no idea, but I was conscious that the wind blew chill as if in anticipation of the dawn. At the same corner whence we had started, the coachman stopped his horses and I alighted, after which he drove away as if he had received his orders beforehand.

"Will you permit me to walk with you as far as your hotel?" said Constanides, with his customary politeness.

I tried to say something in reply, but my voice failed me. I would much rather have been alone, but as he would not allow this we set off together. At the corner of the street in which the hotel is situated we stopped.

"Here we must part," he said. Then, after a pause, he added, "And for ever.

A Professor of Egyptology

From this moment I shall never see your face again."

"You are leaving Cairo?" was the only thing I could say.

"Yes, I am leaving Cairo," he replied with peculiar emphasis. "My errand here is accomplished. You need have no fear that I shall ever trouble you again."

"I have no fear," I answered, though I am afraid it was only a half truth.

He looked earnestly into my face.

"Nofrît," he said, "for, say what you will, you are the Nofrît I would have made my Queen and have loved beyond all other women, never again will it be permitted you to look into the past as you did to-night. Had things been ordained otherwise we might have done great things together, but the gods willed that it should not be. Let it rest therefore. And now—farewell! To-night I go to the rest for which I have so long been seeking."

Without another word he turned and left me. Then I went on to the hotel. How it came about I cannot say, but the door was open and I passed quickly in. Once more, to my joy, I found that the watchman was absent from the hall.

Trembling lest anyone might see me, I

A Professor of Egyptology

sped up the stairs and along the corridor, where the servants lay sleeping just as I had left them, and so to my room. Everything was exactly as I had left it, and there was nothing to show that my absence had been suspected. Again I went to the window, and, in a feeling of extraordinary agitation, looked out. Already there were signs of dawn in the sky. I sat down and tried to think over all that had happened to me that evening, endeavouring to convince myself, in the face of indisputable evidence, that it was not real and that I had only dreamt it. Yet it would not do! At last, worn out, I retired to rest. As a rule I sleep soundly; it is scarcely, however, a matter for wonderment that I did not do so on this occasion. Hour after hour I tumbled and tossed—thinking—thinking—thinking. When I rose and looked into the glass I scarcely recognised myself. Indeed, my mother commented on my fagged appearance when we met at the breakfast table.

"My dear child, you look as if you had been up all night," she said, and little did she guess, as she nibbled her toast, that there was a considerable amount of truth in her remark.

Later she went shopping with a lady

A Professor of Egyptology

staying in the hotel, while I went to my room to lie down. When we met again at lunch it was easy to see that she had some news of importance to communicate.

"My dear Cecilia," she said, "I have just seen Dr Forsyth, and he has given me a terrible shock. I don't want to frighten you, my girl, but have you heard that *Professor Constanides was found dead in bed this morning?* It is a most terrible affair! He must have died during the night!"

I am not going to pretend that I had any reply ready to offer her at that moment.

THE END OF PHÆACIA.

Andrew Lang

THE END OF PHÆACIA.

I.

INTRODUCTORY.*

THE Rev. Thomas Gowles, well known in
Colonial circles where the Truth is valued,
as "the Boanerges of the Pacific," departed
this life at Hackney Wick, on the 6th of
March, 1885. The Laodiceans in our midst
have ventured to affirm that the world at
large has been a more restful place since Mr.
Gowles was taken from his corner of the
vineyard. The Boanerges of the Pacific was,
indeed, one of those rarely-gifted souls, souls
like a Luther or a Knox, who can tolerate no
contradiction, and will palter with no com-
promise, where the Truth is concerned.

* From *Wandering Sheep*, the Bungletonian Missionary
Record.

Papists, Puseyites, Presbyterians, and Pagans
alike, found in Mr. Gowles an opponent whose
convictions were firm as a rock, and whose
method of proclaiming the Truth was as the
sound of a trumpet. Examples of his singular
courage and daring in the work of the ministry
abound in the following narrative. Born and
brought up in the Bungletonian communion,
himself collaterally connected, by a sister's
marriage, with Jedediah Bungleton, the revered
founder of the Very Particular People, Gowles
was inaccessible to the scepticism of the age.

His youth, it is true, had been stormy, like
that of many a brand afterwards promoted to
being a vessel. His worldly education was of
the most elementary and indeed eleemosynary
description, consequently he despised secular
learning, and science "falsely so called." It is
recorded of him that he had almost a distaste
for those difficult chapters of the Epistles in
which St. Paul mentions by name his Greek
friends and converts. In a controversy with
an Oxford scholar, conducted in the open air,
under the Martyrs' Memorial in that centre
of careless professors, Gowles had spoken of
" Nĭcŏdĕmus," " Eubŭlus," and " Stephānas."
His unmannerly antagonist jeering at these

slips of pronunciation, Gowles uttered his celebrated and crushing retort, "Did Paul know Greek?" The young man, his opponent, went away, silenced if not convinced.

Such a man was the Rev. Thomas Gowles in his home ministry. Circumstances called him to that wider field of usefulness, the Pacific, in which so many millions of our dusky brethren either worship owls, butterflies, sharks, and lizards, or are led away captive by the seductive pomps of the Scarlet Woman, or lapse languidly into the lap of a bloated and Erastian establishment, ignorant of the Truth as possessed by our community. Against all these forms of soul-destroying error the Rev. Thomas Gowles thundered nobly, "passing," as an admirer said, "like an evangelical cyclone, from the New Hebrides to the Aleutian Islands." It was during one of his missionary voyages, in a labour vessel, the *Blackbird*, that the following singular events occurred, events which Mr. Gowles faithfully recorded, as will be seen, in his missionary narrative. We omit, as of purely secular interest, the description of the storm which wrecked the *Blackbird*, the account of the destruction of the steamer with all hands (not, let us try to hope, with all souls) on board, and everything that transpired till Mr. Gowles found himself alone, the sole survivor, and bestriding the mast in the midst of a tempestuous sea. What follows is from the record kept on pieces of skin, shards of pottery, plates of metal, papyrus leaves, and other strange substitutes for paper, used by Mr. Gowles during his captivity.

II.

NARRATIVE OF MR. GOWLES.[*]

" I MUST now, though in sore straits for writing materials, and having entirely lost count of time, post up my diary, or rather commence my narrative. So far as I can learn from the jargon of the strange and lost people among whom Providence has cast me, this is, in their speech, the last of the month, *Thargeelyun*, as near as I can imitate the sound in English. Being in doubt as to the true time, I am resolved to regard to-morrow, and every seventh day in succession, as the

[*] 1884. Date unknown. Month probably June.

Sabbath. The very natives, I have observed with great interest, keep one day at fixed intervals sacred to the Sun-god, whom they call Apollon, perhaps the same word as Apollyon. On this day they do no manner of work, but *that* is hardly an exception to their usual habits. A less industrious people (slaves and all) I never met, even in the Pacific. As to being more than common idle on one day out of seven, whether they have been taught so much of what is *essential* by some earlier missionary, or whether they may be the corrupted descendants of the Lost Tribes (whom they do not, however, at all resemble outwardly, being, I must admit, of prepossessing appearance), I can only conjecture. This Apollon of theirs, in his graven images (of which there are many), carries a bow and arrows, *fiery darts of the wicked*, another point in common between him and Apollyon, in the *Pilgrim's Progress.* May I, like Christian, turn aside and quench his artillery!

To return to my narrative. When I recovered consciousness, after the sinking of the *Blackbird*, I found myself alone, clinging to the mast. Now was I tossed on the crest of the wave, now the waters opened beneath me, and I sank down in the valleys of the sea. Cold, numbed, and all but lifeless, I had given up hope of earthly existence, and was nearly insensible, when I began to revive beneath the rays of the sun.

The sea, though still moved by a swell, was now much smoother, and, but for a strange vision, I might have believed that I was recovering my strength. I must, however, have been delirious or dreaming, for it appeared to me that a foreign female, of prepossessing exterior, though somewhat indelicately dressed, arose out of the waters close by my side, as lightly as if she had been a sea-gull on the wing. About her head there was wreathed a kind of muslin scarf, which she unwound and offered to me, indicating that I was to tie it about my waist, and it would preserve me from harm. So weak and exhausted was I that, without thinking, I did her bidding, and then lost sight of the female. Presently, as it seemed (but I was so drowsy that the time may have been longer than I fancied), I caught sight of land from the crest of a wave. Steep blue cliffs arose far away out of a white cloud of surf, and, though a

strong swimmer, I had little hope of reaching
the shore in safety.

Fortunately, or rather, I should say, providentially, the current and tide-rip carried me
to the mouth of a river, and, with a great
effort, I got into the shoal-water, and finally
staggered out on shore. There was a wood
hard by, and thither I dragged myself. The
sun was in mid heavens and very warm, and
I managed to dry my clothes. I am always
most particular to wear the dress of my
calling, observing that it has a peculiar and
gratifying effect on the minds of the natives.
I soon dried my tall hat, which, during the
storm, I had attached to my button-hole by
a string, and, though it was a good deal
battered, I was not without hopes of partially
restoring its gloss and air of British respecta-
bility. As will be seen, this precaution was,
curiously enough, the human means of
preserving my life. My hat, my black
clothes, my white neck-tie, and the hymn-
book I carry would, I was convinced, secure
for me a favourable reception among the
natives (if of the gentle brown Polynesian
type), whom I expected to find on the island.

Exhausted by my sufferings, I now fell

asleep, but was soon wakened by loud cries of anguish uttered at no great distance. I started to my feet, and beheld an extraordinary spectacle, which at once assured me that I had fallen among natives of the worst and lowest type. The dark places of the earth are, indeed, full of horrid cruelty.

The first cries which had roused me must have been comparatively distant, though piercing, and even now they reached me confused in the notes of a melancholy chant or hymn. But the shrieks grew more shrill, and I thought I could distinguish the screams of a woman in pain or dread from the groans drawn with more difficulty from a man. I leaped up, and, climbing a high part of the river bank, I beheld, within a couple of hundred yards, an extraordinary procession coming from the inner country towards the mouth of the stream.

At first I had only a confused view of bright stuffs—white, blue, and red—and the shining of metal objects, in the midst of a crowd partly concealed by the dust they raised on their way. Very much to my surprise I found that they were advancing along a wide road, paved in a peculiar manner, for I had never seen anything of this kind among the heathen tribes of the Pacific. Their dresses, too, though for the most part mere wraps, as it were, of coloured stuff, thrown round them, pinned with brooches, and often clinging in a very improper way to the figure, did not remind me of the costume (what there is of it) of Samoans, Fijians, or other natives among whom I have been privileged to labour.

But these observations give a more minute impression of what I saw than, for the moment, I had time to take in. The foremost part of the procession consisted of boys, many of them almost naked. Their hands were full of branches, wreathed in a curious manner with strips of white or coloured wools. They were all singing, and were led by a woman carrying in her arms a mis-shapen wooden idol, not much unlike those which are too frequent spectacles all over the Pacific. Behind the boys I could now distinctly behold a man and woman of the Polynesian type, naked to the waist, and staggering with bent backs beneath showers of blows. The people behind them, who were almost as light in colour as ourselves, were

cruelly flogging them with cutting branches
of trees.   Round the necks of the unfortunate victims—criminals I presumed—were
hung chains of white and black figs, and
in their hands they held certain herbs, figs,
and cheese, for what purpose I was, and
remain, unable to conjecture.   Whenever
their cries were still for a moment, the woman
who carried the idol turned round, and lifted
it in her arms with words which I was unable
to understand, urging on the tormentors to
ply their switches with more severity.

Naturally I was alarmed by the strangeness
and ferocity of the natives, so I concealed
myself hastily in some brushwood behind a
large tree.   Much to my horror I found that
the screams, groans, and singing only drew
nearer and nearer.   The procession then
passed me so close that I could see blood
on the backs of the victims, and on their faces
an awful dread and apprehension.   Finally,
the crowd reached the mouth of the river, at
the very place where I had escaped from the
sea.   By aid of a small pocket-glass I could
make out that the men were piling great
faggots of green wood, which I had noticed
that some of them carried, on a spot beneath

the wash of high tide. When the pile had reached a considerable height, the two victims were placed in the middle. Then, by some means, which I was too far off to detect, fire was produced, and applied to the wild wood in which the unhappy man and woman were enveloped. Soon, fortunately, a thick turbid smoke, in which but little flame appeared, swept all over the beach. I endeavoured to stop my ears, and turned my head away that I might neither see nor hear more of this spectacle, which I now perceived to be a human sacrifice more cruel than is customary even among the Fijians.

When I next ventured to look up, the last trails of smoke were vanishing away across the sea; the sun gazed down on the bright, many-coloured throng, who were now singing another of their hymns, while some of the number were gathering up ashes (human ashes!) from a blackened spot on the sand, and were throwing them into the salt water. The wind tossed back a soft grey dust in their faces, mixed with the surf and spray. It was dark before the crowd swept by me again, now chanting in what appeared to be a mirthful manner, and with faces so smiling and happy that I could scarcely believe they had just taken part in such abominable cruelty. On the other hand, a weight seemed to have been removed from their consciences. So deceitful are the wiles of Satan, who deludes the heathen most in their very religion!

Tired and almost starved as I was, these reflections forced themselves upon me, even while I was pondering on the dreadful position in which I found myself. Way of escape from the island (obviously a very large one) there was none. But, if I remained all night in the wood, I must almost perish of cold and hunger. I had therefore no choice but to approach the barbarous people, though, from my acquaintance with natives, I knew well that they were likely either to kill and eat me, or to worship me as a god. Either event was too dreadful to bear reflection. I was certain, however, that, owing to the dress of my sacred calling, I could not be mistaken for a mere beach-comber or labour-hunter, and I considered that I might easily destroy the impression (natural among savages on first seeing a European) that I was a god. I therefore followed the throng from a distance, taking advantage for concealment of turns in the way, and of trees and underwood beside the road. Some four miles' walking, for which I was very unfit, brought us across a neck of land, and from high ground in the middle I again beheld the sea. Very much to my surprise the cape on which I looked down, safe in the rear of the descending multitude, was occupied by a kind of city.

The houses were not the mere huts of South Sea Islanders, but, though built for the most part of carved and painted wood, had white stone foundations, and were of considerable height. On a rock in the centre of the bay were some stone edifices which I took to be temples or public buildings. The crowd gradually broke up, turning into their own dwellings on the shore, where, by the way, some large masted vessels were drawn up in little docks. But, while the general public, if I may say so, slowly withdrew, the woman with the idol in her arms, accompanied by some elderly men of serious aspect, climbed the road up to the central public buildings.

Moved by some impulse which I could hardly explain, I stealthily followed them, and at last found myself on a rocky platform,

a kind of public square, open on one side to
the sea, and shut in on either hand, and at
the back, by large houses with smooth round
pillars, and decorated with odd coloured
carvings.   There was in the open centre of
the square an object which I recognized as
an altar, with a fire burning on it.   Some
men came out of the chief building, dragging
a sheep, with chains of flowers round its neck.
Another man threw something on the fire,
which burned with a curious smell.   At once
I recognized the savour of incense, against
which (as employed illegally by the Puseyites)
I had often firmly protested in old days at
home.   The spirit of a soldier of the Truth
entered into me; weary as I was, I rushed
from the dusky corner where I had been
hidden in the twilight, ran to the altar, and
held up my hand with my hymn-book as
I began to repeat an address that had often
silenced the papistic mummers in England.
Before I had uttered half a dozen words, the
men who were dragging the sheep flew at me,
and tried to seize me, while one of them
offered a strange-looking knife at my throat.
I thought my last hour had come, and the old
Adam awakening in me, I delivered such a

blow with my right on the eye of the man with the knife, that he reeled and fell heavily against the altar. Then assuming an attitude of self-defence (such as was, alas! too familiar to me in my unregenerate days), I awaited my assailants.

They were coming on in a body when the veil of the large edifice in front was lifted, and a flash of light streamed out on the dusky square, as an old man dressed in red hurried to the scene of struggle. He wore a long white beard, had green leaves twisted in his hair, and carried in his hand a gilded staff curiously wreathed with wool. When they saw him approaching, my assailants fell back, each of them kissing his own hand and bowing slightly in the direction of the temple, as I rightly supposed it to be. The old man, who was followed by attendants carrying torches burning, was now close to us, and on beholding me, he exhibited unusual emotions.

My appearance, no doubt, was at that moment peculiar, and little creditable, as I have since thought, to a minister, however humble. My hat was thrust on the back of my head, my coat was torn, my shirt open, my neck-tie twisted round under my ear, and

C

my whole attitude was not one generally
associated with the peaceful delivery of the
message.   Still, I had never conceived that
any spectacle, however strange and unbecoming, could have produced such an effect
on the native mind, especially in a person
who was manifestly a chief, or high-priest of
some heathen god.   Seeing him pause, and
turn pale, I dropped my hands, and rearranged
my dress as best I might.   The old Tohunga,
as my New Zealand flock used to call their
priest, now lifted his eyes to heaven with an
air of devotion, and remained for some
moments like one absorbed in prayer or
meditation.   He then rapidly uttered some
words, which, of course, I could not understand, whereon his attendants approached me
gently, with signs of respect and friendship.
Not to appear lacking in courtesy, or inferior
in politeness to savages, I turned and raised
my hat, which seemed still more to alarm the
old priest.   He spoke to one of his attendants,
who instantly ran across the square, and
entered the courtyard of a large house,
surrounded by a garden, of which the tall
trees looked over the wall, and wooden
palisade.   The old man then withdrew into

the temple, and I distinctly saw him scatter, with the leafy bough of a tree, some water round him as he entered, from a vessel beside the door. This convinced me that some of the emissaries of the Scarlet Woman had already been busy among the benighted people, a conjecture, however, which proved to be erroneous.

I was now left standing by the altar, the attendants observing me with respect which I feared might at any moment take the blasphemous form of worship. Nor could I see how I was to check their adoration, and turn it into the proper channel, if, as happened to Captain Cook, and has frequently occurred since, these darkened idolaters mistook me for one of their own deities. I might spurn them, indeed; but when Nicholson adopted that course, and beat the Fakirs who worshipped him during the Indian Mutiny, his conduct, as I have read, only redoubled their enthusiasm. However, as events proved, they never at any time were inclined to substitute me for their heathen divinities; very far from it indeed, though their peculiar conduct was calculated to foster in my breast this melancholy delusion.

I had not been left long to my own
thoughts when I marked lights wandering in
the garden or courtyard whither the messenger had been sent by the old priest. Presently
there came forth from the court a man of
remarkable stature, and with an air of serious-
ness and responsibility.   In his hand he carried a short staff, or baton, with gold knobs,
and he wore a thin golden circlet in his hair.
As he drew near, the veil of the temple was
again lifted, and the aged priest came forward,
bearing in his arms a singular casket of
wood, ornamented with alternate bands of
gold and ivory, carved with outlandish figures.
The torch-bearers crowded about us in the
darkness, and it was a strange spectacle to
behold the smoky, fiery light shining on the
men's faces and the rich coloured dresses, or
lighting up the white idol of Apollon, which
stood among the laurel trees at the entrance
of the temple.

III.

THE PROPHECY.

THE priest and the man with the gold circlet
whom I took to be a chief, now met, and,
fixing their eyes on me, held a conversation
of which, naturally, I understood nothing.
I maintained an unmoved demeanour, and,
by way of showing my indifference, and also
of impressing the natives with the superiority
of our civilization, I took out and wound up
my watch, which, I was glad to find, had not
been utterly ruined by the salt water. Meanwhile the priest was fumbling in his casket,
whence he produced a bundle of very ragged
and smoky old bits of parchment and scraps
of potsherds. These he placed in the hands
of his attendants, who received them kneeling. From the very bottom of the casket
he extracted some thin plates of a greyish
metal, lead, I believe, all mouldy, stained, and
ragged. Over these he pored and puzzled for
some time, trying, as I guessed, to make out
something inscribed on this curious substitute
for writing-paper. I had now recovered my

presence of mind, and, thinking at once to astonish and propitiate, I drew from my pocket, wiped, and presented to him my spectacles, indicating, by example, the manner of their employment. No sooner did he behold these common articles of every-day use, than the priest's knees began to knock together, and his old hands trembled so that he could scarcely fix the spectacles on his nose. When he had managed this it was plain that he found much less difficulty with his documents. He now turned them rapidly over, and presently discovered one thin sheet of lead, from which he began to read, or rather chant, in a slow measured tone, every now and then pausing and pointing to me, to my hat, and to the spectacles which he himself wore at the moment. The chief listened to him gravely, and with an expression of melancholy that grew deeper and sadder till the end. It was a strange scene.

I afterwards heard the matter of the prophecy, as it proved to be, which was thus delivered. I have written it down in the language of the natives, spelling it as best I might, and I give the translation which I made when I became more or less acquainted with their very difficult dialect.* It will be seen that the prophecy, whatever its origin, was strangely fulfilled. Perhaps the gods of this people were not mere idols, but evil spirits, permitted, for some wise purpose, to delude their unhappy worshippers.† This, doubtless, they might best do by occasionally telling the truth, as in my instance. But this theory—namely, that the gods of the heathen are perhaps evil and wandering spirits—is, for reasons which will afterwards appear, very painful to me, personally reminding me that I may have sinned as few have done since the days of the early Christians. But I trust this will not be made a reproach to me in our Connection, especially as I have been the humble instrument of so blessed a change in the land of the heathen, there being no more of them left. But, to return to the

* The original text of this prophecy is printed at the close of Mr. Gowles's narrative.

† It has been suggested to me that some travelled priest or conjurer of this strange race may have met Europeans, seen hats, spectacles, steamers, and so forth, and may have written the prophecy as a warning of the dangers of our civilization. In that case the forgery was very cunningly managed, as the document had every appearance of great age, and the alarm of the priest was too natural to have been feigned.

prophecy, it is given roughly here in English.
It ran thus :—" But when a man, having a
chimney pot on his head, and four eyes,
appears, and when a sail-less ship also comes,
sailing without wind and breathing smoke,
then will destruction fall upon the Scherian
island." Perhaps, from this and other ex-
pressions to be offered in a later chapter, the
learned will be able to determine whether the
speech is of the Polynesian or the Papuan
family, or whether, as I sometimes suspect,
it is of neither, but of a character quite
isolated and peculiar.

The effect produced on the mind of the
chief by the prophecy amazed me, as he
looked, for a native, quite a superior and
intelligent person. None of them, however,
as I found, escaped the influence of their
baneful superstitions. Approaching me, he
closely examined myself, my dress, and the
spectacles which the old priest now held in
his hands. The two men then had a hurried
discussion, and I have afterwards seen reason
to suppose that the chief was pointing out the
absence of certain important elements in the
fulfilment of the prophecy. Here was I,
doubtless, "a man bearing a chimney on his

head" (for in this light they regarded my hat), and having "four eyes," that is, including my spectacles, a convenience with which they had hitherto been unacquainted. It was undeniable that a prophecy written by a person not accustomed to the resources of civilization, could not more accurately have described me and my appearance. But the "ship without sails" was still lacking to the completion of what had been foretold, as the chief seemed to indicate by waving his hand towards the sea. For the present, therefore, they might hope that the worst would not come to the worst. Probably this conclusion brought a ray of hope into the melancholy face of the chief, and the old priest himself left off trembling. They even smiled, and, in their conversation, which assumed a lighter tone, I caught and recorded in pencil on my shirt-cuff, for future explanation, words which sounded like *aiskistos aneer, farmakos, catharma*, and *Thargeelyah.* Finally the aged priest hobbled back into his temple, and the chief, beckoning me to follow, passed within the courtyard of his house.

* How terribly these words were afterwards to be interpreted, the reader will learn in due time.

IV.

AT THE CHIEF'S HOUSE.

THE chief leading the way, I followed through the open entrance of the courtyard. The yard was very spacious, and under the dark shade of the trees I could see a light here and there in the windows of small huts along the walls, where, as I found later, the slaves and the young men of the family slept. In the middle of the space there was another altar, I am sorry to say ; indeed, there were altars everywhere. I never heard of a people so religious, in their own darkened way, as these islanders. At the further end of the court was a really large and even stately house, with no windows but a clerestory, indicated by the line of light from within, flickering between the top of the wall and the beginning of the high-pitched roof. Light was also streaming through the wide doorway, from which came the sound of many voices. The house was obviously full of people, and, just before we reached the deep verandah, a roofed space open to the air in front, they began to come

out, some of them singing. They had flowers
in their hair, and torches in their hands. The
chief, giving me a sign to be silent, drew me
apart within the shadow of a plane tree, and
we waited there till the crowd dispersed, and
went, I presume, to their own houses. There
were no women among them, and the men
carried no spears nor other weapons. When
the court was empty, we walked up the broad
stone steps and stood within the doorway. I
was certainly much surprised at what I saw.
There was a rude magnificence about this
house such as I had never expected to find in
the South Sea Islands. Nay, though I am
not unacquainted with the abodes of opulence
at home, and have been a favoured guest
of some of our merchant princes (including
Messrs. Bunton, the eminent haberdashers,
whose light is so generously bestowed on our
Connection), I admit that I had never looked
on a more spacious reception-room, furnished,
of course, in a somewhat savage manner, but,
obviously, regardless of expense. The very
threshold between the court and the reception-
room, to which you descended by steps, was
made of some dark metal, inlaid curiously
with figures of beasts and birds, also in metal

(gold, as I afterwards learned), of various
shades of colour and brightness.

At first I had some difficulty in making out
the details of the vast apartment which lay
beyond. I was almost dizzy with hunger and
fatigue, and my view was further obscured by
a fragrant blue smoke, which rose in soft
clouds from an open fireplace in the middle of
the room. Singular to say, there was no
chimney, merely a hole in the lofty roof,
through which most of the smoke escaped.
The ceiling itself, which was supported by
carved rafters, was in places quite black
with the vapour of many years. The smoke,
however, was thin, and as the fuel on the fire,
and on the braziers, was of dry cedar and
sandal-wood, the perfume, though heavy, was
not unpleasant. The room was partly illumi-
nated by the fire itself, partly by braziers full
of blazing branches of trees; but, what was
most remarkable, there were rows of metal
images of young men (naked, I am sorry to
say), with burning torches in their hands,
ranged all along the side walls.

A good deal of taste, in one sense, had been
expended in making these images, and money
had clearly been no object. I might have

been somewhat dazzled by the general effect, had I not reflected that, in my own country, gas is within reach of the poorest purse, while the electric light itself may be enjoyed by the very beggar in the street. Here, on the contrary, the dripping of the wax from the torches, the black smoke on the roof, the noisy crackling of the sandal-wood in the braziers, all combined to prove that these natives, though ingenious enough in their way, were far indeed below the level of modern civilization. The abominable ceremony of the afternoon would have proved as much, and now the absence of true *comfort*, even in the dwelling of a chief, made me think once more of the hardships of a missionary's career.

But I must endeavour to complete the picture of domestic life in the island, which I now witnessed for the first time, and which will never be seen again by Europeans. The walls themselves were of some dark but glittering metal, on which designs in lighter metal were inlaid. There were views of the chief going to the chase, his bow in his hand ; of the chief sacrificing to idols ; of men and young women engaged in the soul-destroying practice of promiscuous dancing ; there were

wild beasts, lions among others ; rivers, with
fish in them ; mountains, trees, the sun and
moon, and stars, all not by any means ill de-
signed, for the work of natives.   The pictures,
indeed, reminded me a good deal of the ugly
Assyrian curiosities in the British Museum, as
I have seen them when conducting the children of the Bungletonian Band of Hope
through the rooms devoted to the remains of
Bible peoples, such as the Egyptians, Hittites,
and others.

Red or blue curtains, strangely embroidered,
hung over the doors, and trophies of swords,
shields, and spears, not of steel, but of some
darker metal, were fixed on the tall pillars
that helped to prop the roof.   At the top of
the wall, just beneath the open unglazed
spaces, which admitted light and air in the
daytime, and wind and rain in bad weather,
was a kind of frieze, or coping, of some deep
blue material.*   All along the sides of the
hall ran carved seats, covered with pretty
light embroidered cloths, not very different
from modern Oriental fabrics.   The carpets
and rugs were precisely like those of India
and Persia, and I supposed that they must

* I afterwards found it was blue smalt.

have been obtained through commerce. But I afterwards learned that they were, beyond doubt, of native manufacture.

At the further end of the room was a kind of platform, or daïs, on which tables were set with fruit and wine. But much more curious than the furniture of the hall was the group of women sitting by the fire in the centre. There sat in two rows some twenty girls, all busily weaving, and throwing the shuttle from hand to hand, laughing and chattering in low voices. In the midst of them, on a high chair of cedar-wood, decorated with ivory, and with an ivory footstool, sat a person whom, in a civilized country, one must have looked on with respect as a lady of high rank. She, like her husband the chief, had a golden circlet twisted in her hair, which was still brown and copious, and she wore an appearance of command.

At her feet, on a stool, reclined a girl who was, I must confess, of singular beauty. Doto had long fair hair, a feature most unusual among these natives. She had blue eyes, and an appearance of singular innocence and frankness. She was, at the moment, embroidering a piece of work intended, as I afterwards learned with deep pain, for the covering of one of their idols, to whose service the benighted young woman was devoted. Often in after days, I saw Doto stooping above her embroidery and deftly interweaving the green and golden threads into the patterns of beasts and flowers. Often my heart went out to this poor child of pagan tribe, and I even pleased myself with the hope that some day, a reclaimed and enlightened character, she might employ her skill in embroidering slippers and braces for a humble vessel. I seemed to see her, a helpmate meet for me, holding Mothers' Meetings, playing hymn-tunes on the lyre, or the double pipes, the native instruments, and, above all, winning the islanders from their cruel and abominable custom of exposing their infant children on the mountains. How differently have all things been arranged.

But I am wandering from my story. When we reached the group by the fireside, who had at first been unaware of our entrance, the chief's wife gave a slight start, alarmed doubt-less by my appearance. She could never have seen, nor even dreamed of, such a spectacle as I must have presented, haggard, ragged, faint with hunger, and worn with fatigue as I was. The chief motioned to me that I should kneel at his wife's feet, and kiss her hand, but I merely bowed, not considering this a fit moment to protest otherwise against such sacrilegious mummeries. But the woman—her name I learned later was Ocyale—did not take my attitude in bad part. The startled expression of her face changed to a look of pity, and, with a movement of her hand, she directed Doto to bring a large golden cup from the table at the upper end of the room. Into this cup she ladled some dark liquid from a bowl which was placed on a small three-legged stand, or dumb waiter, close to her side. Next she spilt a little of the wine on the polished floor, with an appearance of gravity which I did not understand. It appears that this spilling of wine is a drink offering to their idols. She then offered me the cup, which I was about to taste, when I perceived that the liquor was indubitably *alcoholic !*

A total abstainer, I had, I am thankful to say, strength enough to resist the temptation thus adroitly thrust upon me. Setting down the cup, I pointed to the badge of

D

blue ribbon, which, though damp and colourless, remained faithful to my button-hole.
I also made signs I was hungry, and would
be glad of something to eat. My gestures,
as far as the blue ribbon went, must have
been thrown away, of course, but any one
could understand that I was fainting from
hunger. The mistress of the house called
to one of the spinning girls, who rose and
went within the door opening from the platform at the upper end of the room. She
presently returned with an old woman, a
housekeeper, as we would say, and obviously
a faithful and familiar servant. After some
conversation, of which I was probably the
topic, the old woman hobbled off, laughing.
She soon came back, bringing, to my extreme
delight, a basket with cakes and goat cheese,
and some cold pork in a dish.

I ought, perhaps, to say here that, in spite
of the luxury of their appointments, and their
extraordinary habit of "eating and drinking
all day to the going down of the sun" (as one
of their own poets says), these islanders are
by no means good cooks. I have tasted of
more savoury meats, dressed in coverings of
leaves on hot stones, in Maori *pahs*, or in

New Caledonian villages, than among the comparatively civilized natives of the country where I now found myself. Among the common people, especially, there was no notion of hanging or keeping meat. Often have I seen a man kill a hog on the floor of his house, cut it up, toast it, as one may say, at the fire, and then offer the grilled and frequently under-done flesh to his guests. Invariably the guests are obliged to witness the slaughter of the animal which is to supply their dinner. This slaughter is performed as a kind of sacrifice ; the legs of the beast are the portions of the gods, and are laid, with bits of fat, upon the altars. Then chops, or rather kabobs, of meat are hacked off, spitted, and grilled or roasted at the fire. Consequently all the meat tasted in this island is actually " meat offered to idols."

When I made this discovery the shock was very great, and I feared I was repeating a sin denounced from the earliest ages. But what was I to do? Not the meat only, but the vegetables, the fruit, the grain, the very fish (which the natives never eat except under stress of great hunger), were sacred to one or other of their innumerable idols. I must

eat, or starve myself to death—a form of
suicide. I therefore made up my mind to
eat without scruple, remembering that the
gods of the nations are nothing at all, but the
fancies of vain dreamers, and the invention
of greedy and self-seeking priests.

These scruples were of later growth, after
I had learned that their meals were invariably
preceded by a sacrifice, partly to provide
the food, partly as grace before meat. On
the present occasion I made an excellent
supper, though put to a good deal of incon-
venience by the want of forks, which were
entirely unknown on the island. Finding that
I would not taste the alcoholic liquor, which
the natives always mixed with a large propor-
tion of water, Doto rose, went out, and returned
with a great bowl of ivy-wood, curiously
carved, and full of milk. In this permitted
beverage, as my spirits were rising, I drank
the young lady's health, indicating my grati-
tude as well as I could. She bowed grace-
fully, and returned to her task of embroidery.
Meanwhile her father and mother were deep
in conversation, and paid no attention to
me, obviously understanding that my chief
need was food. I could not but see that the

face of the chief's wife was overclouded, probably with anxiety caused by the prophecy of which I was, or was taken for, the subject.

When my hunger was satisfied, I fell, it seems, into a kind of doze, from which I was wakened by the noise of people rising, moving, and pushing back chairs. I collected my senses, and perceived that the room was almost dark, most of the inmates had gone, and the chief was lighting a torch at one of the braziers. This torch he placed in my hand, indicating, as I understood, that I was to put myself under the guidance of two of the young women who had been spinning. At this I was somewhat perplexed, but followed where they went before me, each of them holding a burning torch. The light flared and the smoke drifted among the corridors, till we came within sound of running water. In a lofty green chamber was a large bath of polished marble, carved with shapes of men armed with pitchforks, and employed in spearing fish. The bath was full of clear water, of somewhat higher than tepid heat, and the stream, welling up in one part, flowed out in another, not splashing or spilling. The young women now

brought flasks of oil, large sponges, such as
are common in these seas, and such articles
of dress as are worn by the men among the
natives. But, to my astonishment, the girls
showed no intention of going away, and it
soon became evident *that they meant to assist
me in my toilet!* I had some difficulty in
getting them to understand the indecorum
of their conduct, or rather (for I doubt if
they understood it after all) in prevailing on
them to leave me. I afterwards learned that
this custom, shocking as it appears to
Europeans, is regarded as entirely right and
usual even by the better class of islanders ;
nor, to do them justice, have I ever heard any
imputations on the morality of their women.
Except among the shepherds and shep-
herdesses in the rural districts, whose conduct
was very regardless, a high standard of
modesty prevailed among the female natives.
In this, I need not say, they were a notable
exception among Polynesian races.

Left to my own devices by the retreat of
the young women, I revelled in the pleasures
of the bath, and then the question arose, How
was I to be clothed ?

I had, of course, but one shirt with me, and

that somewhat frayed and worn. My boots, too, were almost useless from their prolonged immersion in salt water. Yet I could not bring myself to adopt the peculiar dress of the natives, though the young persons had left in the bath-room changes of raiment such as are worn by the men of rank. These garments were simple, and not uncomfortable, but, as they showed the legs from the knees downwards, like kilts, I felt that they would be unbecoming to one in my position.

Almost the chief distinction between civilized man and the savage, is the wearing of trousers. When a missionary in Tongo, and prime minister of King Haui Ha there, I made the absence of breeches in the males an offence punishable by imprisonment. Could I, on my very first appearance among the islanders to-morrow, fly, as it were, in the face of my own rules, and prove false to my well-known and often expressed convictions? I felt that such backsliding was impossible. On mature consideration, therefore, I made the following arrangement.

The garments of the natives, when they condescended to wear any, were but two in number. First, there was a long linen or

woollen shirt or smock, without sleeves, which
fell from the neck to some distance below
the knees. This shirt I put on. A belt is
generally worn, into which the folds of the
smock can be drawn up or "kilted," when the
wearer wishes to have his limbs free for active
exercise. The other garment is simply a
large square piece of stuff, silken or woollen
as it happens in accordance with the weather,
and the rank of the wearer. In this a man
swathes himself, somewhat as a Highlander
does in his plaid, pinning it over the shoulder
and leaving the arms free. When one is
accustomed to it, this kind of dress is not
uncomfortable, and many of the younger
braves carried it with a good deal of grace,
showing some fancy and originality in the
dispositions of the folds. Though attired in
this barbarous guise, I did not, of course,
dispense with my trousers, which, being black,
contrasted somewhat oddly with my primrose-
coloured *ki ton*, as they call the smock, and
the dark violet *clamis*, or plaid. When the
natives do not go bareheaded, they usually
wear a kind of light, soft wideawake, but this
I discarded in favour of my hat, which had
already produced so remarkable an effect on
their superstitious minds.

Now I was dressed, as fittingly as possible in the circumstances, but I felt that my chief need was a bed to lie down upon. I did not wish to sleep in the bath-room, so, taking my torch from the stand in which I had placed it, I sallied forth into the corridors, attired as I have described, and carrying my coat under my arm. A distant light, and the noise of females giggling, which increased most indecorously as I drew near, attracted my attention. Walking in the direction of the sounds, I soon discovered the two young women to whose charge I had been committed by the chief. They appeared to be in high spirits, and, seizing my arms before I could offer any resistance, they dragged me at a great pace down the passage and out into the verandah. Here the air was very fragrant and balmy, and a kind of comfortable "shakedown" of mattresses, covered with coloured blankets, had been laid for me in a corner. I lay down as soon as the sound of the young women's merriment died out in the distance, and after the extraordinary events of the night, I was soon sleeping as soundly as if I had been in my father's house at Hackney Wick.

V.

A STRANGER ARRIVES.

WHEN I wakened next morning, wonderfully
refreshed by sleep and the purity of the air,
I had some difficulty in remembering where I
was and how I came there in such a peculiar
costume. But the voices of the servants in
the house, and the general stir of people
going to and fro, convinced me that I had
better be up and ready to put my sickle into
this harvest of heathen darkness. Little did
I think how soon the heathen darkness would
be trying to put the sickle into me! I made
my way with little difficulty, being guided by
the sound of the running water, to the bath-
room, and thence into the gardens. These
were large and remarkably well arranged in
beds and plots of flowers and fruit-trees. I
particularly admired a fountain in the middle,
which watered the garden, and supplied both
the chief's house and the town. Returning
by way of the' hall, I met the chief, who,
saluting me gravely, motioned me to one of
many small tables on which was set a bowl

of milk, some cakes, and some roasted kid's flesh.

After I had done justice to this breakfast, he directed me to follow him, and, walking before me with his gold-knobbed staff in his hand, passed out of the shady court into the public square. Here we found a number of aged men seated on unpleasantly smooth and cold polished stones in a curious circle of masonry. They were surrounded by a crowd of younger men, shouting, laughing, and behaving with all the thoughtless levity and merriment of a Polynesian mob. They became silent as the chief approached, and the old men rose from their places till he had taken a kind of rude throne in the circle.

For my part, I was obliged to stand alone in their midst, and it seemed that they were debating about myself and my future treatment. First the old priest, whom I had seen on the night before, got up, and, as I fancied, his harangue was very unfavourable to me. He pointed at the inevitable flower-crowned altar which, of course, was in the centre of the market-place, and from the way he shook a sickle he held in his hand I believe that he was proposing to sacrifice me on the spot.

In the midst of his oration two vultures, black with white breasts, flew high over our heads, chasing a dove, which they caught and killed right above the market-place, so that the feathers fell down on the altar. The islanders, as I afterwards discovered, are full of childish superstitions about the flight of birds, from which they derive omens as to future events. The old priest manifestly attempted to make political capital against me out of the interesting occurrence in natural history which we had just observed. He hurried to the altar, caught up a handful of the bleeding feathers, and, with sickle in hand, was rushing towards me, when he tripped over the head of a bullock that had lately been sacrificed, and fell flat on his face, while the sickle flew far out of his hand.

On this the young men, who were very frivolous, like most of the islanders, laughed aloud, and even the elders smiled. The chief now rose with his staff in his grasp, and, pointing first to me and then to the sky, was, I imagined, propounding a different inter-pretation of the omen from that advanced by the old priest. Meantime the latter, with a sulky expression of indifference, sat nursing

his knees, which had been a good deal
damaged by his unseemly sprawl on the
ground. When the chief sat down, a very
quiet, absent-minded old gentleman arose.
Elatreus was his name, as I learned later; his
family had a curious history, and he himself
afterwards came to an unhappy and terrible
end, as will be shown in a subsequent part of
my narrative.

I felt quite at home, as if I had been at
some vestry-meeting, or some committee in
the old country, when Elatreus got up. He
was stout, very bald, and had a way of
thrusting his arm behind him, and of hum-
ming and hawing, which vividly brought back
to mind the oratory of my native land. He
had also, plainly enough, the trick of forgetting what he intended to say, and of
running off after new ideas, a trick very
uncommon among these natives, who are
born public speakers. I flattered myself that
this orator was in favour of leniency towards
me, but nobody was paying much attention
to him, when a shout was heard from the
bottom of the hill on which the square is
built. Everybody turned round, the elders
jumped up with some alacrity for the sake

of a better view on the polished stones
where they had been sitting, and so much
was the business before the meeting forgotten
in the new excitement, that I might have run
away unnoticed, had there been anywhere
to run to. But flight was out of the
question, unless I could get a boat and some
provisions, and I had neither. I was pleased,
however, to see that I was so lightly and
laxly guarded.

The cause of the disturbance was soon
apparent. A number of brown, half-naked,
sturdy sailors, with red caps, not unlike
fezzes, on their heads, appeared, bawling and
making for the centre of the square. They
were apparently carrying or dragging some
person with them, some person who offered
a good deal of resistance. Among the foreign
and unintelligible cries and howls which rang
through the market-place, my heart leaped
up, in natural though unsanctified pleasure, as
I heard the too well-known but unexpected
accents of British profanity.

"Where the (somewhere) are you blooming
sons of beach-combers dragging a Bri'sh
shailor? Shtand off, you ragged set of white-
washed Christy Minstrels, you! Where's the

Bri'sh Conshul's? Take me, you longshore sons of sharks, to the Bri'sh Conshul's! If there's one white man among you let him stand out and hit a chap his own weight."

"Hullo!" suddenly cried the speaker, whom I had recognized as William Bludger, one of the most depraved and regardless of the whole wicked crew of the *Blackbird*,— "hullo, if here isn't old Captain Hymn-book!"—a foolish nickname the sailors had given me.

He was obviously more than half-drunk, and carried in his hand a black rum-bottle, probably (from all I knew of him) not nearly full. His shirt and trousers were torn and dripping ; apparently he had been washed ashore, like myself, after the storm, and had been found and brought into the town by some of the fishing population.

What a blow to all my hopes was the wholly unlooked-for arrival of this tipsy, irreclaimable seaman, this unawakened Bill Bludger! I had framed an ideal of what my own behaviour, in my trying circumstances, ought to be. Often had I read how these islanders possess a tradition that a wonderful white man, a being all sweetness and lucidity, landed in their midst, taught them the knowledge of the arts, converted them to peace and good manners, and at last mysteriously departed, promising that he would return again. I had hopes—such things have happened—that the islanders might take me for this wonderful white man of their traditions, come back according to his promise. If this delusion should occur, I would not at once undeceive them, but take advantage of the situation, and so bring them all into the Bungletonian fold. I knew there was no time to waste. Lutheran, French, or Church of England schemers, in schooners, might even now be approaching the island, with their erroneous and deplorable tenets. Again, I had reckoned, if my hopes proved false, on attaining, not without dignity, the crown of the proto-martyr of my Connection. Beyond occasional confinement in police cells, consequent on the strategic manœuvres of the Salvation Army, none of us had ever known what it was to suffer in the cause. If I were to be the first to testify with my blood, on this unknown soil, at least I could meet my doom with dignity. In any case, I should be remembered, I had reckoned, in the island traditions, either as an isolated and mysterious benefactor, the child of an otherwise unknown race, or as a solitary martyr from afar.

All these vain hopes of spiritual pride were now blown to the wind by Bill Bludger's unexpected appearance and characteristic conduct. No delusions about a divine white stranger from afar could survive the appearance and behaviour of so compromising an acquaintance as William. He was one white stranger too many. There he was, still struggling, shouting, swearing, smelling of rum, and making frantic attempts to reach me and shake hands with me.

" Let bygones be bygones, Captain Hymnbook, your Reverence," he screamed ; "here's your jolly good health and song," and he put his horrible black bottle to his unchastened lips. "Here we are, Captain, two Englishmen agin a lot o' blooming Kanekas ; let's clear out their whole blessed town, and steer for Sydney."

But, perceiving that I did not intend to recognize or carouse with him, William Bludger now changed his tone ; "Yah, you lily-livered Bible-reader," he exclaimed, "what are you going about in *that* toggery for: copying Mr. Toole in *Paw Claudian?*

E

You call yourself a missionary? Jove, you're
more like a blooming play hactor in a penny
gaff! Easy, then, my hearties," he added,
seeing that the fishermen were approaching
him again, with ropes in their hands.
"Avast! stow your handcuffs."

In spite of his oaths and struggles, the
inebriated mariner was firmly bound, hand
and foot, and placed in the centre of the
assembly. I only wished that the natives
had also gagged him, for his language,
though, of course, unintelligible to them, was
profane, and highly painful to me.

Before returning to business, the chiefs
carefully inspected the black bottle, of which
they had dispossessed William Bludger. A
golden vase was produced—they had always
plenty of *them* handy—and the dark fluid was
poured into this princely receptacle, diffusing
a strong odour of rum. Each chief carefully
tasted .the stuff, and I was pained, on gathering, from the expression of their countenances,
that they obviously relished the "fire-water"
which has been the ruin of so many peoples
in these beautiful but benighted seas. However, there was not enough left to go round,
and it was manifestly unlikely that William

Bludger had succeeded in conveying larger supplies from the wreck.

The meeting now assumed its former air of earnestness, and it was not hard to see that the arrival of my unhappy and degraded fellow-countryman had introduced a new element into the debate. Man after man spoke, and finally the chief rose, as I had little doubt, to sum up the discussion. He pointed to myself, and to William Bludger alternately, and the words which I had already noted, *Thargeelyah,* and *farmakoi,* frequently recurred in his speech. His ideas seemed to meet with general approval; even the old priest laid aside his sickle, and beat applause with his hands. He next rose, and, taking two garlands of beautiful flowers from the horns of the altar, placed one wreath on the head of the drunken sailor, who had fallen asleep by this time. He then drew near me, and I had little doubt that he meant to make me also wear a garland, like some woman of rank and fashion at a giddy secular entertainment. Whatever his motive might be I was determined to wear nothing of the kind. But here some attendants grappled and held me, my hat was lifted from my brows, and the

circlet of blossoms was carefully entwined all
round my hat. The head-covering was then
replaced, the whole assembly, forming a circle,
danced around me and the unconscious Bludger, and, finally, the old priest, turning his face
alternately to me and to the sun, intoned a
hymn, the audience joining in at intervals.

My worst fears were, apparently, being
realized. In spite of the compromising appearance and conduct of Bludger, it seemed
beyond doubt that we were both regarded as,
in some degree, divine and sacred. Resistance
on my part was, it will be seen, impossible.
I could not escape from the hands of my tormentors, and I was so wholly ignorant, at that
time, of their tongue, that I knew not how to
disclaim the honours thus blasphemously
thrust upon me. I did my best, shouting, in
English, "I am no *Thargeelyah*. I am no
farmakos," supposing those words to be the
native terms for one or other of their gods.
On this the whole assembly, even the gravest,
burst out laughing, each man poking his
neighbour in the ribs, and uttering what I
took to be jests at my expense. Their behaviour in this juncture, and frequently afterwards, when I attempted to make them tell

me the meaning of the unknown words, and of *catharma* (another expression the chief had used), greatly perplexed me. I had afterwards too good reason to estimate their dreadful lack of the ordinary feelings of humanity at its true value.

However, nothing but laughter (most unfit-ting the occasion) could be got out of the assembled natives. They now began to re-turn to their homes, and Bludger, crowned with flowers that became him but ill, was car-ried off, not, as it seemed to me, without even a reverential demeanour on the part of his escort. Those who surrounded me, a kind of body-guard of six young men, had entirely recovered their composure, and behaved to me with a deference that was astonishing, but reassuring. From this time, I ought to say, though permitted to go where I would, and allowed to observe even their most secret rites, enjoying opportunities such as will never fall to another European, I was never, but once, entirely alone. My worshippers, as they might almost be called, so humble was their demeanour, still kept watchful eyes upon me, as if I were a being so precious that they were jealous of my every movement. It was

now made plain to me, by signs, that I must
wait for some little space before being con-
veyed to my appointed residence.

VI.

A BACKSLIDER.   A WARNING.

WE had not remained long by ourselves in
the square, when the most extraordinary procession which I had ever beheld began to
climb into the open space from the town
beneath.   I do not know if I have made it
sufficiently clear that the square, on the crest
of the isolated hill above the sea, was occupied only by public buildings, such as the
temple, the house of the chief, and a large
edifice used as a kind of town hall, so to
speak.   The natives in general lived in much
smaller houses, many of them little better
than huts, and divided by extremely narrow
and filthy streets, on the slopes, and along the
shores of the bay.

It was from these houses and from all the
country round that the procession, with
persons who fell into its ranks as they came,
was now making its way.   Almost all the

parties concerned were young, boys and girls, or very young men and women, and though their dress was much scantier and less decent than what our ideas of delicacy require, it must be admitted that the general aspect of the procession was far from unpleasing. The clothes and wraps which the men and women wore were of various gay colours, and were, in most cases, embroidered quite skilfully with representations of flowers, fruits, wild beasts, and individuals of grotesque appearance. Every one was crowned with either flowers or feathers.

But, most remarkable of all, there was scarcely a person in this large gathering who did not bring or lead some wild bird or beast. The girls carried young wild doves, young rooks, or the nestlings of such small fowls as sparrows and finches. It was a pretty sight to see these poor uninstructed young women, flushed with the exertion of climbing, and merry, flocking into the square, each with her pet (as I supposed, but the tender mercies of the heathen are cruel) half hidden in the folds of her gown. Of the young men, some carried hawks, some chained eagles, some young vultures. Many were struggling, too,

with wild stags and wild goats, which they
compelled with the utmost difficulty to march
in the ranks of the procession. A number of
young persons merely bore in their hands
such fruits as were in season, obviously fine
specimens, of which they had reason to be
proud.

Others, again, were carrying little young
bears, all woolly, comfortable-looking creatures, while the parent bears, adult bears at
any rate, were brought along, chained, in the
rear. My guards, or adorers, or whatever the
young men who looked after me really
were, led me forward, and made signs to
me that I was to bring up the rear of the
procession—behind the bears, which made no
attempt (as in the case of the prophet) to
take the part of a Minister of the Bungletonian Connection. What a position for one
who would fain have been opening the eyes
of this darkened people to better things!
But, till I had acquired some knowledge of
their language, I felt my only chance was to
acquiesce in everything not positively sinful.
The entrance of a menagerie and horticultural
exhibition into the town—for thus I explained
to myself what was going on before my eyes—

could not be severely censured by the harshest
critic, and I prepared to show my affability
by joining in an innocent diversion and
popular entertainment.

Soon I found that, after all, I was not to be
absolutely last in the advance of this mis-
cellaneous exhibition, nor were the intentions
of the people so harmless as I had imagined.
This was no affair of cottage window gardens,
and a distribution of prizes.

The crowd which had collected in front of
the chief's house opened suddenly, and, in the
throng of people, I detected a movement of
excitement and alarm. Next I saw the horns
of animals mixed with the heads and shoulders
of the multitude, and then an extraordinary
spectacle burst, at full speed, upon my gaze.
Four great wild stags, plunging, rearing, and
kicking, rushed by, dragging a small vehicle
of unusual shape, in which stood, to my
horror, the chief's beautiful daughter, Doto.
The vehicle passed me like a flash of horns
in spite of the attempts of four resolute
men, who clung at the stags' heads to restrain
the impetuosity of these coursers. The
car, I should explain—though I can hardly
expect to be believed—was not unlike the

floor of a hansom cab, from which the seat, the roof, the driver's perch, and everything else should have been removed, except the basis, the wheels, and the splashboard, the part on which we generally find the advertisements of Messrs. Mappin and Webb. On this floor, then, Doto stood erect, holding the reins; her yellow hair had become unbound, and was floating like a flag behind her, and her beautiful face, far from displaying any alarm, was flushed with pleasure and pride. She was dressed in splendid and glittering attire, over which was fastened—so strange were the manners of these islanders—the newly-stripped skin of a great black bear. Thus dragged by the wild deer, Doto passed like a flash through the midst of the men and women, her stags being maddened to fresh excitement by the sight and smell of the bears, and other wild animals. But, eager as were the brutes that dragged the precarious carriage, they were somewhat tamed by the great steepness of the ascent, up which they bounded, to the heights at the back of the town. Up this path, often narrow and excessively dangerous, we all took our way, and finally, after passing through various perilous defiles and skirting many cliffs, we arrived at a level space in front of an ancient temple of one of their heathen gods. It was built like the others in the settlement below, but the white stone had become brown and yellow with time and weather, and the colours, chiefly red and blue, with which the graven images, in contempt of the second commandment, were painted, had faded, and grown very dim.

On the broad platform in front of this home of evil spirits had been piled a great mound of turf, sloping very gradually and smoothly, like the terrace of a well-kept lawn, to the summit, which itself was, perhaps, a hundred feet in circumference. On this was erected a kind of breastwork of trunks of trees, each tree some fifteen feet in length, and in the centre of the circular breastwork was an altar, as usual, under which blazed a fire of great fierceness. From the temple came a very aged woman, dressed in bear skins, who carried a torch. This torch she lit at the blaze under the altar, and a number of the young men, lighting their torches at hers, set fire to the outer breastwork, in which certain open spaces or entrances had been purposely

left. No sooner had the trees begun to catch
fire, which they did slowly, being of green
wood, than the multitude outside, with the
most horrible and piercing outcries, began to
drive the animals which they had brought
with them into the midst of the flames.

The spectacle was one of the most terrible
I ever beheld, even among this cruel and
outlandish people, whose abominable inven-
tions contrasted so strangely with the mild-
ness of their demeanour where their religion
was not concerned. It was pitiful to see the
young birds, many of them not yet able to
fly, flutter into the flames and the stifling
smoke, and then fall, scorched, and twittering miserably. The young lambs and other
domesticated animals were forced in without
much resistance, but the great difficulty was
to urge the wolves, antelopes, and other wild
creatures, into the blaze. The cries of the
multitude, who bounded about like maniacs,
armed with clubs and torches, rose madly
over the strange unusual screams and howls
uttered by the wild beasts in their pain
and terror. Ever and anon some animal
would burst through the crowd, perhaps half
burned, and with its fur on fire, and would be

pursued to a certain distance, after which it was allowed to escape by the sacrificers. As I was watching, with all my hopes enlisted on its side, the efforts of an antelope to escape, I heard a roar which was horrible even in that babel of abominable sights and sounds.

A great black bear, its pelt one sheet of flame, its whole appearance (if I may be permitted to say so) like that of a fiend from the pit, forced its way through the throng, and, bounding madly to the spot where Doto's car stood at a little distance, rose erect on its hind feet, and fixed its claws in the flank of one of the stags, the off-leader. Instantly the team of stags, escaping from the hands of the strong men who stood at their heads, plunged violently down the narrow and dangerous path which led to the city. I shouted to Doto to leap out, but she did not hear or did not understand me.

With a fixed look of horror on her white face, she dropped the useless reins, and the vehicle passed out of sight round a corner of the cliff.

I had but a moment in which to reflect on what might be done to rescue her. In that moment I providentially spied a double-edged

axe which lay beside me on the grass, having
fallen from the hands of one of the natives.
Snatching up this weapon, I rushed to the
edge of the cliff, and looked down. It was
almost a sheer precipice, broken only by
narrow shelves and clefts, on some of which
grass grew, while on others a slight mountain-
ash or a young birch just managed to find
foothold.

Far, far beneath, hundreds of feet below,
I could trace the windings of the path up
which we had climbed.

Instantly my plan was conceived. I would
descend the cliff, risking my life, of course,
but that was now of small value in this hopelessly heathen land, and endeavour to save
the benighted Doto from the destruction to
which she was hastening. Her car must pass
along that portion of the path which lay, like
a ribbon, in the depth below me, unless, as
seemed too probable, it chanced to be upset
before reaching the spot. To pursue it from
behind was manifestly hopeless.

These thoughts flashed through my brain
more rapidly than even the flight of the
maddened red deer ; and scarcely less swiftly,
I began scrambling down the face of the cliff.

It was really a series of almost hopeless leaps
to which I was committed, and the axe, to
which I clung, rather impeded than aided me
as I let myself drop from one rocky shelf to
another, catching at the boughs and roots of
trees to break my fall.   At last I reached the
last ledge before the sheer wall of rock, which
hung above the path.   As I let myself down,
feeling with my feet for any shelf or crack in
the wall, I heard the blare of the stags, and
the rattle of the wheels.   Half intentionally,
half against my will, I left my hold of a tree-
root, and slid, bumping and scratching myself
terribly, down the slippery and slatey face
of the rocky wall, till I fell in a mass on the
narrow road.   In a moment I was on my feet,
the axe I had thrown in front of me, and I
grasped it instinctively as I rose.   It was not
too soon.   The deer were almost on me.
Stepping to the side of the way, where a rock
gave some shelter, I dealt a blow at the
nearest stag, under which he reeled and fell
to the ground, his companion stumbling over
him.   In the mad group of rearing beasts I
smote right and left at the harness, which
gave way beneath my strokes, and the unhurt
stags sped down the glen, and then rushed

into separate corries of the hills. The car was upset, and Doto lay pale and bleeding among the hoofs of the stricken deer.

I dragged her out of the danger to the side of the path. I felt her pulse, which still fluttered. I brought her, in my hat, water from the stream ; and, finally, had the pleasure of seeing her return to life before the first of her friends came, wailing and lamenting, and tearing their hair, down the path.

When they found the girl unwounded, though still weak and faint, their joy knew no bounds, though I too plainly perceived that they were returning thanks to the heathen goddess whose priestess Doto was. As for me, they once more crowned me in the most elaborate, and, I think, unbecoming manner, with purple pandanus flowers. Then, having laid Doto on a litter, they returned in procession to the town, where the girl was taken into the chief's house. As we parted, she held out her hand to me, but instantly withdrew it with a deep sigh. I closely watched her. She was weeping. I had noticed before that all the natives, as much as possible, avoided personal contact with me. This fact, coupled with the reverence which they displayed towards me, confirmed my impression that they regarded me as something supernatural, not of this world, and divine.

To remove this belief was most certainly my duty; but how was it to be done? Alas! I must now admit that I yielded to a subtle temptation, and was led into conduct unworthy of a vessel. Sad to say, as I search the records of my own heart, I am compelled to confess that my real desire was not so much to undeceive the people—for in their bewildering myriads of foolish beliefs one more or less was of small importance—as to recommend myself to Doto. This young woman, though not a member of our Connection, and wholly ignorant of saving Truths, had begun to find favour in my eyes, and I hoped to lead her to the altar; altars, for that matter, being plentiful enough in this darkened land. I should have remembered the words once spoken by a very gracious young woman, the daughter of a pious farmer. "Mother," said she, "I have made up my mind never to let loose my affections upon any man as is not pious, and in good circumstances." Doto was, for an islander, in good

F

circumstances, but who, ah! who, could call
her pious ?

I endeavoured, it is true, to convert her,
but, ah! did I go to work in the right way?
Did I draw, in awful colours, the certain
consequences of ignorance of the Truth?
Did I endeavour to strike a salutary terror
into her heathen heart ?

No ; such would have been a proper course
of conduct, but such was not mine! I weakly
adopted the opposite plan—that used by the
Jesuits in their dealings with the Chinese
and other darkened peoples. I attempted,
meanly attempted (but, as may be guessed,
with but lim.' 'd ...:cess), to give an orthodox
Nonconformist character to the observances
of Doto's religion. For example, instead of
thundering, as was my duty, at her worldly
diversions of promiscuous dancing, and ball
play, I took a part in these secular pursuits,
fondly 'persuading myself that my presence
discouraged levity, and was a check upon unseemly mirth.

Thus, among the young native men and
maidens, in the windings of the mazy dance,
might have been seen disporting himself, a
person of stalwart form, whose attire still

somewhat faintly indicated his European
origin and sacred functions. A hymn-book
in my hand instead of a rattle (used by the
natives), I capered gaily through their midst.
Often and often I led the music, instructing
my festive flock in English hymns, which,
however, I adapted to gay and artless
melodies, such as " There's some one in de
house wid Dinah !" or " Old Joe kicking up
behind and afore !"

This kind of entertainment was entirely
new to the natives, who heartily preferred
it to their own dull music, resembling what
are called, I believe, "Gregorians," by a
bloated and Erastian establishment.

So far, then, I may perchance trust that
my efforts were not altogether vain, and the
seed thus sown may, in one or two cases,
have fallen on ground not absolutely stony.
But, alas ! I have little room for hope.

I pursued my career of unblushing "economy"—as the Jesuits say, meaning, alas !
economy of plain truth speaking—and of
heathen dissipation. Few were the dances
in which I did not take a part, sinking so low
as occasionally to oblige with a hornpipe.
My blue ribbon had long ago worn out, and

with it my strict views on Temperance. I
acquired a liking for the strange drink of the
islanders—a thick wine and water, sometimes
mixed with cheese and honey.   In fact, I was
sliding back — like the unfortunate Fanti
missionary, John Creedy, M.A., whose case,
as reported by precious Mr. Grant Allen, so
painfully moved serious circles—I was sliding
back to the level of the savagery around me.
May these confessions be accepted in the same
spirit as they are offered; may it partly palliate
my guilt that I had apparently no chance of
escape from the island, and no hope beyond
that of converting the natives and marrying
Doto. I trusted to do it, not (as of old) by
open and fearless denunciation, but by slowly
winning hearts, in a secular and sportive
capacity, before gaining souls.

Even so have I seen young priests of the
prelatical Establishment aim at popularity by
playing cricket with liberal coal-miners of
sectarian persuasions. They told me they were
" in the mission field," and one observed that
his favourite post in the field was third man.
I know not what he meant. But to return
to the island.

My career of soul-destroying " amusement "

(ah, how hollow!) was not uninterrupted by warnings. Every now and again the mask was raised, and I saw clearly the unspeakable horrors of heathen existence.

For example, in an earlier part of this narrative, I have mentioned an old heathen called Elatreus, a good-natured, dull, absent-minded man, who reminded me of a respectable British citizen. How awful was *his* end, how trebly awful when I reflect how nearly I—but let me not anticipate. Elatreus was the head, and eldest surviving member of a family which had a singular history. never could make out what the story was, but, in consequence of some ancient crime, the chief of the family was never allowed to enter the town hall. The penalty, if he infringed the law, was terrible. Now it chanced one day that I was wandering down the street, my hands full of rare flowers which I had gathered for Doto, and with four young doves in my hat. It was spring, and at that season the young persons of the island expected to receive such gifts from their admirers. I was also followed by eleven little fawns, which I had tamed for her, and four young whelps of the bear. At the same

time, in the lightness of my foolish heart,
I was singing a native song, all about one
Lityerses, to the tune of " Barbara Allen."

At this moment, I observed, coming out of
a side street, old Elatreus. He was doddering
along, his hands behind his back, and his nose
in the air, followed by a small but increasing
crowd of the natives, who crept stealthily
behind at a considerable distance. I paused
to watch what was happening.

Elatreus entered the main street, and
lounged along till he came opposite the town
hall, on which some repairs were being made.
The door stood wide open. He gazed at it,
in a vacant but interested way, and went up
the steps, where he stood staring in an absent-
minded, vacant kind of fashion. I could see
that the crowd watching him from the corner
of the side street was vastly excited.

Elatreus now passed his hand across his
brow, seemed vastly puzzled, and yawned.
Then he slowly entered the town hall. With
a wild yell of savage triumph the mob rushed
in after him, and in a few moments came
forth again, with Elatreus bound and mana-
cled. Some one sped away, and brought
the old priest, who carried the sickle. He

appeared full of joy, and lustily intoned—for they have this Popish custom of intoning—-an unintelligible hymn. By this time Elatreus had been wreathed and crowned with flowers, and the rude multitude for this purpose seized the interesting orchids which I had gathered for my Doto. They then dragged the old man, pitifully lamenting, to the largest altar in the centre of the square.

Need I say what followed? The scene was too awful. With a horrible expression of joy the priest laid the poor wretch on the great stone altar, and with his keen sickle—but it is too horrible! . . . This was the penalty for a harmless act, forbidden by a senseless law, which Elatreus—a most respectable man for an idolater—had broken in mere innocent absence of mind.

Alas! among such a people, how could I ever hope, alone and unaided, to effect any truly regenerating work?

Yet I was not wholly discouraged ; indeed, my *infatuation* for Doto made me overlook much profligate behaviour that I do not care to mention in a tract which may fall into the hands of the young. One other example of the native barbarity, however, I must narrate.

A respected couple in the vicinity had long been childless. At length their wishes were crowned with success, and a little baby girl was born to them. But the priest, who had curious ideas of his own, insisted on consulting, as to this child, a certain witch, a woman who dwelt apart in a cave where there was a sulphurous hot-water spring, surrounded by laurel bushes, regarded as sacred by the benighted islanders. This spring, or the fumes that arose from it, was supposed to confer on the dweller in the cave the gift of prophecy. She was the servant of Apollon, and was credited with possessing a spirit of divination. The woman, after undergoing, or simulating, an epileptic attack, declared, in rhythmical language, that the babe must not be allowed to live. She averred that it would "bring destruction on Scheria," the native name for the island, which I have styled Boothland, in honour of the Salvation Army. This was enough for the priests, who did not actually slay the infant, but exposed it on the side of a mountain, where the beasts and birds were likely to have their way with it.

Now it chanced that I had climbed the hill-top that day to watch for a sail, for I never quite lost hope of being taken away by some British or continental vessel. My attendants, for a wonder, were all absent at some feast—Carneia, I think they called it—of their heathen gods. The time was early summer; it only wanted a fortnight of the date, as far as I could reckon, at which I had first been cast on the island, a year before.

As I descended the hillside, pleased, I must own, by the warm bright sunlight, the colour of the sea, and the smell of the aromatic herbs,—pleased, and half forgetful of the horrid heathenism that surrounded me, I heard a low wail as of an infant. I searched about, in surprise, and came on a beautiful baby, in rich swaddling bands, with a gold signet ring tied round its neck. Such an occurrence was not very unusual, as the natives, like most savages, were in the habit of keeping down the surplus population, by thus exposing their little ones. The history of the island was full of legends of exposed children, picked up by the charitable (there was, oddly enough, no prohibition against this), and afterwards recognized and welcomed by their families. As any Englishman would have done, I lifted the dear little thing in my arms, and, a happy thought occurring to me, carried it off as a present to Doto, who doted on babies, as all girls do. The gift proved to be the most welcome that I had ever offered, though Doto, as usual, would not accept it from my hands, but made me lay it down beside the hearth, which they regarded as a sacred place. Even if an enemy reached the hearth of his foe, he would, thenceforth, be quite safe in his house. Doto then picked up the child, warmed and caressed it, sent for milk for its entertainment, and was full of pleasure in her new pet.

She was a dear good girl, Doto, in spite of her heathen training.*

Strangely enough, as I thought at the time, she burst out weeping when I took my leave of her, and seemed almost as if she had some secret to impart to me. This, at least, showed an interest in me, and I walked to my home with high presumptuous thoughts.

As I passed a certain group of rocks, in a lonely uncultivated district, while the grey of evening was falling, I heard a low whistle.

---

* I have never been able to understand Mr. Gowles's infatuation for this stuck-up creature, who, I am sure, gave herself airs enough, as any one may see.—MRS. GOWLES.

The place had a bad reputation, being thought to be haunted. Perhaps I had unconsciously imbibed some of the superstitions of the natives, for I started in alarm.

Then I heard an unmistakably British voice cry, in a suppressed tone, "Hi!"

The underwood rustled, and I beheld, to my astonishment, the form, the crawling and abject form, of William Bludger!

Since the day of his landing we had never once met, William having been sent off to a distant part of the island.

"Hi!" he said again, and when I exclaimed, naturally, "Hullo!" he put his finger on his lips, and beckoned to me to join him. This I did, and found that he was lurking in a cavern under the group of grey weather-worn stones.

When I entered the cave, Bludger fell a-trembling so violently that he could not speak. He seemed in the utmost alarm, his face quite ashen with terror.

"What is the matter, William Bludger?" I asked; "have you had a Call, or why do you thrust yourself on me?"

"Have *you* sich a thing as a chaw about ye?" he asked in tremulous accents. "I'm

that done ; never a drop has passed my lips
for three days, strike me dead ; and I'd give
anything for a chaw o' tobacco. A sup of
drink you have *not* got, Capt'n Hymn-book,
axing your pardon for the liberty ? "

"William," I said, " even in this benighted
island, you set a pitiful example. You have
been drinking, sir ; you are reaping what you
have sown ; and only temperance, strict, un-
deviating total abstinence rather, can restore
your health."

"So help me !" cried the wretched man,
"except a drop of Pramneian * I took, the
morning I cut and run,—and that was three
days ago,— nothing stronger than castor-oil
berries have crossed my lips. It ain't that,
sir ; it ain't the drink. It's—it's the *Thar-*
geelyah. Next week, sir, they are going to
roast us—you and me—flog us first, and roast
us after. Oh Lord ! Oh Lord ! "

---

* This was the name of a native vintage.

VII.

FLIGHT.

"FLOG us first, and roast us afterwards." I repeated mechanically the words of William Bludger. "Why, you must be mad ; they are more likely to fall down and worship us,— *me* at any rate."

"No, Capt'n," replied William ; "that's your mistake. They say we're both *Cathar-mata ;* that's what they call us ; and you're no better than me."

"And what are *Catharmata ?*" I inquired, remembering that this word, or something like it, had been constantly used by the natives in my hearing.

"Well, Capt'n, it means, first and foremost, just the off-scourings of creation, the very dust and sweepings of the shop," answered Bludger, who had somehow regained his confidence. To have a fellow-sufferer, and to see the pallor which, doubtless, overspread my features, was a source of comfort to this hardened man. At the same time I confess that, if William Bludger alone had been destined to suffer, I could have contemplated the decree with Christian resignation.

"I speak the beggars' patter pretty well now," Bludger went on; "and I see *Cathar-mata* means more than just mere dirt. It means two unlucky devils."

"William?" I exclaimed.

"It means, saving your presence, two poor coves, as has no luck, like you and me, and that can be got rid of once a year, at an entertainment they call the *Thargeelyah,* I dunno why, a kind o' friendly lead. They choose fellows as either behaves ill, or has no friends to make a fuss about them, and they gives them three dozen, or more, and takes them down to the beach, and burns them alive over a slow fire. And then they toss the ashes out to sea, and think all the bad luck goes away with the tide. Oh, I never was in such a hole as this!"

Bludger's words made me shudder. I had never forgotten the hideous sacrifice, doubt-less the *Thargeelyah,* as they called it, that greeted me when I was first cast ashore on the island. To think that I had only been saved that I might figure as a victim of some of their heathen gods!

Oh, now the thought came back to me with a bitter repentance, that if I had only converted all the islanders, they would never have dreamed of sacrificing me in honour of a mere idol! Why had I been so lukewarm, why had I backslidden, why had I endeavoured to make myself agreeable by joining in promiscuous dances, when I should have been thundering against Pagan idolatry, holy water, idols, sacrifices, and the whole abominable system of life on the island? True, I might have goaded them into slaying me; I might have suffered as a martyr; but, at the least, I would have deserved the martyr's crown. And now I was to perish at the stake, without even the precious consolation of being a real martyr, and was to be flogged into the bargain.

I gave a hollow groan as these reflections passed through my mind, and this appeared to afford William Bludger some consolation.

"You don't seem to like it yourself, Capt'n; what's your advice? We're both in the same boat; leastways I wish we *were* in a boat; anyhow we're both in the same hole."

There was no denying this, and it was high time to mature some plan of escape. Already

I must have been missed by my attendants, my gaolers rather, who would have returned from their festival, and would be looking for me everywhere.

I bitterly turned over in my mind the facts of our situation; "ours," for, as a just punishment of my remissness, I was in the same quandary as a drunken, dissipated sailor before the mast.

If William had but possessed a sweet and tuneful voice (often a gift found in the most depraved natures), and if *I* had been able to borrow a harmonium on wheels, I would not, even now, have despaired of converting the whole island in the course of the week. As remarkable feats have been performed, with equal alacrity, by precious Messrs. Moody and Sankey, and I am informed that expeditious conversions are by no means infrequent among politicians. But it was vain to think of this resource, as William had no voice, and knew no hymns, while I had no means of access to a perambulating harmonium.

"I'll tell you what it is, sir," said Bludger; "I have a notion."

"Name it, William," I replied, my heart

and manner softened by community in suffering and terror.

"Well, if I were you, sir, I would not go home to-night at all; I'd stop where you are. The beggars won't find you, let them hunt as they like; they daren't come near this place, bless you, it's an 'Arnt;" by which he meant that it was haunted.

"Well," said I, "but how should we be any better off to-morrow morning?"

"That's just it, sir," said Bludger. "We'll be up with the first stroke of dawn, nip down to the harbour, get on board a boat, and be off before any of them are stirring."

"But, even if we manage to secure a boat," I said, "what about provisions, and where are we to sail for?"

"Oh, never mind that," said Bill; "we can't be worse off than we are, and I'll slip out to-night, and lay in some prog in the town. Also some grog, if I can lay my hands on it," he added, with an unholy smile.

"No, William," I murmured; "no grog; our lives depend on our sobriety."

"Always a-preaching, the old tub-thumper," I heard William say to himself; but he made no further reference to the subject.

It was now quite dark, and we lay whispering, in the damp hollow under the great stone.
Our plan was to crawl away at the first blush
of dawn, when men generally sleep most
soundly ; that William should enter one of the
unguarded houses (for these people never
stole, and did not know the meaning of the
word " thief"), that he should help himself to
provisions, and that meanwhile I should have
a boat ready to start in the harbour.

This larcenous but inevitable programme
we carried out, after waiting through dreadful
hours of cold and shivering anxiety.   Every
cry of a night bird from the marsh or the
wood sent my heart into my mouth.   I
felt inconceivably mean and remorseful, my
vanity having received a dreadful shock from
the discovery that, far from being a god, I
was to be a kind of burnt-offering.

At last the east grew faintly grey, and we
started, not keeping together, but Bludger
marching cautiously in my rear, at a considerable distance.   We only met one person,
a dissipated young man, who, I greatly fear,
had been paying his court to a shepherdess
in the hills.   When he shouted a challenge, I
replied, *Erastes eimi*, which means, I am sorry

to say, " I am a lover," and implied that I,
also, had been engaged in low intrigue.
" Farewell, with good fortune," he replied,
and went on his way, singing some catch
about Amaryllis, who, I presume, was the
object of his unhallowed attentions.

We slipped into the silent town, unwalled
and unguarded as it was, for as one of their
own poets had said, " We dwell by the wash
of the waves, far off from toilsome men, and
with us are no folk conversant." They were
a race that knew war only by a vague tradition, that they had dwelt, at some former age,
in an island, perhaps New Zealand, where
they were subject to constant annoyance from
Giants,—a likely story. Thence they had
migrated to their present home, where only
one white man had ever been cast away—one
Odysseus, so their traditions declared—before
our arrival. Him, however, they had treated
hospitably, very unlike their contemplated
behaviour to Bludger and me.

I am obliged to make this historical
digression that the reader may understand
how it happened, under Providence, that we
were not detected in passing through the
town, and how Bludger successfully accom-

plished what, I fear, was by no means his first burglary.

We parted at the chief's house, Bill to secure provisions, and I to unmoor a boat, and bring her round to a lonely bay on the coast, where my companion was to join me.

I accomplished my task without the slightest difficulty, selected a light craft,— they did not use canoes, but rowed boats like coracles,—and was lying at anchor, moored with a heavy stone, in the bay.

The dawn was now breaking in the most beautiful colours—gold, purple, crimson, and green—across the sea. All nature was still, save for the first pipe of awakening birds. There was a delicate fragrance in the air, which was at once soft and keen, and, as I watched the red sunlight on the high cliffs, and on the smooth trunks of the palm trees, I felt, strange to say, a kind of reluctance to leave the island.

The people, apart from their cruel and abominable religion, were the gentlest and most peaceful I have ever known. They were beautiful to look upon, so finely made and shapely that I have never seen their like. Their language was exquisitely sweet and

melodious, and though, except hymns, I do
not care for poetry, yet I must admit that
some of their compositions in verse were
extremely pleasing, though they were ignorant of the art of rhyme. All about them
was beautifully made, and they were ignorant
of poverty. I never saw a beggar on the
island; and Christians, unhappily, do not
share their goods with each other, and with
the poor, so freely as did these benighted
heathens. Often have I laboured to make
them understand what our Pauper Question
means, but they could not comprehend me.

"How can a man lack home, and food, and
fire?" they would say; "do people not love
each other in your country?"

I explained that we love each other *as
Christians*, but this did not seem to enlighten
their benighted minds. On the other hand,
it is true that they settle their population
question by strangling or exposing the
majority of their infant daughters.

Rocked on the smooth green swell of
the sea, beneath the white rocks, I was
brooding over these and many other matters,
when I heard sudden and violent movements
in the deep vegetation on the hillside. The

laurel groves were stirred, and Bill Bludger, with a basket in his hand, bounded down the slope, and swam for dear life to the boat.

"They're after me," he cried ; and at that moment an arrow quivered in the side of the boat.

I helped William on board as well as I might, under a shower of arrows from the hill-top, most of which, owing to the distance, were ill directed and fell short, or went wide.

Into the boat, at last, I got him, and thrusting an oar in his direction, I said, "Pull for your life," and began rowing. To my horror, the boat made no way, but kept spinning round. A glance in the bow showed me what was the matter : *William Bludger was hopelessly intoxicated !* He had got at the jars of wine in the chief's cellar,—*thala-mos*, they call it,—and had not taken the precaution of mixing the liquor with water, as the natives invariably do when they drink. The excitement of running had sent the alcoholic fumes direct to his brain, and now he lay, a useless and embarrassing cargo, in the bows. Meanwhile, the shouts of the natives rang nearer and louder, and I knew that boats would soon be launched for our

capture. I thought of throwing Bludger
overboard, and sculling, but determined not
to stain what might be my last moments
with an act of selfishness. I therefore pulled
hard for the open sea, but to no avail. On
every side boats crowded round me, and I
should probably have been shot, or speared,
but for the old priest, who, erect in the bows
of the largest vessel, kept yelling that we
were to be taken alive.

Alas! I well knew the secret of his cruel
mercies.

He meant to reserve us for the sacrifice.

VIII.

SAVED!

WHY should I linger over the sufferings of
the miserable week that followed our capture?
Hauled back to my former home, I was
again made the object of the mocking reverence of my captors. Ah, how often, in my
reckless youth, have my serious aunts warned
me that I "would be a goat at the last"!
Too true, too true ; now I was to be a scape-
goat, to be driven forth, as these ignorant and

strangely perverted people believed, with the sins of the community on my head, those sins which would, according to their *miserable superstition*, be expiated by the death, and consumed away by the burning, of myself and William Bludger!

The week went by, as all weeks must, and at length came the solemn day which they call *Thargeelyah*, the day more sacred than any other to their idol, Apollon. Long before sunrise the natives were astir; indeed, I do not think they went to bed at all, but spent the night in hideous orgies. I know that, tossing sleepless through the weary hours, I heard the voices of young men and women singing on the hillsides, and among the myrtle groves which are holy to the most disreputable of their deities, a female, named *Aphrodighty*. Harps were twanging too, and I heard the refrain of one of the native songs, " To-night they love who never loved before; to-night let him who loves love all the more." The words have unconsciously arranged themselves, even in English, as poetry; those who know Thomas Gowles best, best know how unlikely it is that he would willingly dabble in the worldly art of

verse-fashioning. Think of my reflections
with a painful, shameful, and, above all,
undeserved death before me, while all the
fragrant air was ringing with lascivious merriment. My impression is that, as all the sins
of the year were, in their opinion, to be got
rid of next day, and tossed into the sea with
the ashes of Bludger and myself, the natives
had made up their minds—an eligible opportunity now presenting itself—to be *as wicked
as they knew how.* Alas! though I have not
dwelt on this painful aspect of their character,
they "knew how" only too well.

The sun rose at last, and flooded the island,
when I perceived that, from every side,
crowds of revellers were pressing together
to the place where I lay in fetters. They
had a wild, dissipated air, flowers were
wreathed and twisted in their wet and dewy
locks, which floated on the morning wind.
Many of the young men were merely dressed
—if "dressed" it could be called—in the
skins of leopards, panthers, bears, goats, and
deer, tossed over their shoulders. In their
hands they all held wet, dripping branches
of fragrant trees, many of them tipped with
pine cones, and wreathed with tendrils of the

vine. Others carried switches, of which I
divined the use only too clearly, and the
women were waving over their heads tame ser-
pents, which writhed and wriggled hideously.
It was an awful spectacle!

I was dragged forth by these revellers;
many of them were intoxicated, and, in a
moment—I blush even now to think of it—
I was stripped naked! Nothing was left
to me but my hat and spectacles, which, for
some religious reason I presume, I was,
fortunately, allowed to retain. Then I was
driven with blows, which hurt a great deal,
into the market-place, and up to the great
altar, where William Bludger, also naked,
was lying more dead than alive.

"William," I said solemnly, "what cheer?"

He did not answer me. Even in that
supreme moment it was not difficult to
discern that William had been looking on
the wine when it was red, and had not con-
fined himself to mere ocular observation. I
tried to make him remember he was an
Englishman, that the honour of our country
was in our· hands, and that we should die
with the courage and dignity befitting our
race. These were strange consolations and

exhortations for *me* to offer in such an extremity, but, now it had come to the last pass, it is curious what mere worldly thoughts hurried through my mind.

My words were wasted: the natives seized William and forced him to his feet. Then, while a hymn was sung, they put chains of black and white figs round our necks, and thrust into our hands pieces of cheese, figs, and certain peculiar herbs. This formed part of what may well be called the "Ritual" of this cruel race. May Ritualists heed my words, and turn from the errors of their ways!

Too well I knew all that now awaited us. All that I had seen and shuddered at, on the day of my landing on the island, was now practised on self and partner. *We* had to tread the long paved way to the distant cove at the river's mouth; we had to endure the lashes from the switches of wild fig. The priestess, carrying the wooden idol, walked hard by us, and cried out, whenever the blows fell fewer or lighter, that the idol was waxing too heavy for her to bear. Then they redoubled their cruelties.

It was a wonderfully lovely day   In the

blue heaven there was not a cloud. We had reached the river's mouth, and were fast approaching the stakes that had already been fixed in the sands for our execution; nay, the piles of green wood were already being heaped up by the young men. There was, there could be, no hope, and, weary and wounded, I almost welcomed the prospect of death, however cruel.

Suddenly the blows ceased to shower on me, and I heard a cry from the lips of the old priest, and, turning about, I saw that the eyes of all the assembled multitude were fixed on a point on the horizon.

Looking automatically in the direction towards which they were gazing, I beheld—oh joy, oh wonder!—I beheld a long trail of cloud floating level with the sea! It was the smoke of a steamer!

"Too late, too late," I thought, and bitterly reflected that, had the vessel appeared but an hour earlier, the attention of my cruel captors might have been diverted to such a spectacle as they had never seen before.

But it was *not* too late.

Perched on a little hillock, and straining his gaze to the south, the old priest was speaking loudly and excitedly. The crowd deserted us, and gathered about him.

I threw myself on the sand, weary, hopeless, parched with thirst, and racked with pain. Bludger was already lying in a crumpled mass at my feet. I think he had fainted.

I retained consciousness, but that was all. The fierceness of the sun beat upon me, the sky and sea and shore swam before me in a mist. Presently I heard the voice of the priest, raised in the cadences which he favoured when he was reading texts out of their sacred books, if books they could be called. I looked at him with a faint curiosity, and perceived that he held in his hands the wooden casket, adorned with strangely carved bands of gold and ivory, which I had seen on the night of my arrival on the island.

From this he had selected the old grey scraps of metal, scratched, as I was well aware, with what they conceived to be ancient prophecies.

I was now sufficiently acquainted with the language to understand the verses which he was chanting, and which I had already heard, without comprehending them. They ran thus in English :

"But when a man, having a chimney pot on his head, and four eyes, appears in Scheria, and when a ship without sails also comes, sailing without wind, and breathing smoke, then shall destruction fall on the island."

He had not ended when it was plain, even to those ignorant people, that the prophecy was about to be fulfilled. From the long, narrow, black line of the steamer, which had approached us with astonishing speed, "sailing without wind, and breathing smoke," there burst six flashes of fire, followed by a peal like thunder, and six tall fountains, as the natives fancied, of sea-water rose and fell in the bay, where the shells had lighted.

It was plain that the commander of the vessel, finding himself in unknown seas, and hard by an unvisited country, was determined to strike terror and command respect by this salute.

The noise of the broadside had scarcely died away, when the natives fled, disappeared like magic, leaving many of their garments behind them.

They were making for their town, which was concealed from the view of the rapidly nearing steamer. From her mast I could now see, flaunting the slight breeze, the dear old Union Jack, and the banner of the Salvation Navy! *

My resolution was taken in a moment. Bludger had now recovered consciousness, and was picking up heart. I thrust into his hands one of the branches with which we had been flogged, fastened to it a cloak of one of the natives, bade him keep waving it from a rocky promontory, and, rushing down to the sea, I leaped in, and swam with all my strength towards the vessel. Weak as I was, my new hopes gave me strength, and presently, from the crest of a wave, I saw that the people of the steamer were lowering a boat, and rowing towards me.

In a few minutes they had reached me, my countrymen's hands were in mine. They dragged me on board; they pulled back to their vessel; and I stood, entirely undressed, on the deck of a British ship!

So long had I lived among people heedless of modesty that I was rushing, with open arms,

* Mr. Gowles was an ardent Liberal, but at the time when he wrote, the Union Jack had not been denounced by his great leader. We have no doubt that, at a word from Mr. Gladstone, he would have sung, *Home Rule, Hibernia!*—ED. *Wandering Sheep.*

towards the officer on the quarter-deck, who was dressed as a bishop, when I heard a scream of horror. I turned round in time to see the bishop's wife fleeing precipitately to the cabin, and driving her children and governess in front of her.

Then all the horror of the situation flooded my heart and brain, and I fell fainting on the quarter-deck.

When I recovered my consciousness, I found myself plainly but comfortably dressed in the ordinary costume, except the hat, which lay beside me, of a dean in the Church of England. My wounds had been carefully attended to, William Bludger had been taken on board, and I was surrounded by the kind faces of my benefactors, including the bishop's consort. My apologies for my somewhat sudden and unceremonious intrusion were cut short by the arrival of tea and a slight collation suitable for an invalid. In an hour I was walking the quarter-deck with the bishop in command of the *William Wilberforce*, armed steam yacht, of North Shields, fitted out for the purposes of the Salvation Navy. From the worthy prelate in command of the *William Wilberforce*, I learned much concern-

ing his own past career and the nature of his
enterprise, as I directed the navigation of the
vessel through the shoals and reefs which lay
about the harbour of the island.

The bishop (a purely brevet title) would
refresh his memory, now and then, from a
penny biography of himself with which he
was provided, and the following, in brief, is a
record of his life and adventures :—

Thomas Sloggins (that was his name),
from his earliest infancy, had been possessed
with a passion for *doing good to others*, a passion, alas ! but too rarely reciprocated. I pass
over many affecting details of his adventures
as a ministering child : how he endeavoured
to win his father from tobacco by breaking
his favourite pipes ; how he strove to wean
his elder brother from cruel field-sports, by
stuffing the joints of his fishing-rod with
gravel ; with many other touching incidents.

Being almost entirely uneducated, young
Sloggins, when he reached man's estate, conceived that he would most benefit his fellow-
creatures by combining the professions of the
pulpit and the press—by preaching on Sun-
days and at odd times, while he acted as
outdoor reporter to *The Rowdy Puritan* on

II

every lawful day. Being a man of great earnestness and enterprise, he soon rose in the ranks of the Salvation Navy; and at one time commanded an evangelical barge on the benighted canals of our country. Finally, he made England almost too hot to hold him, by the original forms of his benevolence, while, at the same time, he acquired the utmost esteem and confidence of many wealthy philanthropists and excellent, if impulsive, ladies. These good people provided him with that well-equipped and armed steam yacht, the *William Wilberforce*, which he manned with a crew of converted characters (they certainly looked as if they must have needed a great deal of converting), and he had now for months been cruising in the South Pacific. A local cyclone had driven the *William Wilberforce* out of her reckoning, and hence the appearance of that vessel in the very nick of time to achieve my rescue.

When the bishop had finished his story, I briefly recapitulated to him my own adventures, and we agreed that the conversion of the island must be our earliest task. To begin with, we steered into the harbour, where a vast multitude of the natives were

assembled in arms, and awaited our approach
with a threatening demeanour. Our landing
was opposed, but a few well-directed volleys
from a Gardiner gun (which did not jam)
caused the hostile force to disperse, and we
landed in great state. Marching on the
chief's house, we were received with an abject
submission that I had scarcely expected.
The people were absolutely cowed, more by
the fulfilment of the prophecy, I think, than
even by the execution done by our Gardiner
machine gun. At the bishop's request, I
delivered a harangue in the native tongue,
declaring that we only required the British
flag to be hoisted on the palace, and the
immediate disendowment of the heathen
church as in those parts established. I was
listened to in uneasy silence ; but my demand
for lodgings in the palace was acceded to ;
and, in a few hours, the bishop, with his wife
and children, were sumptuously housed under
the roof of the chief. The ladies of the
chief's family showed great curiosity in
watching and endeavouring to converse with
our friends. I was amused to see how soon
the light-hearted islanders appeared to forget
their troubles and apprehensions. Doto, in

particular, became quite devoted to the prelate's elder daughter (the youngest of the bishop's family was suffering from measles), and would never be out of her company. Thus all seemed to fare merrily; presents were brought to us—flowers, fruit, the feathers of rare birds, and ornaments of native gold were literally showered upon the ladies of the party. The chief promised to call a meeting of his counsellors on the morrow, and all seemed going on well, when, alas! measles broke out in the palace. The infant whom I had presented to Doto—the infant whom I had found on the mountain side—was the first sufferer. Then Doto caught the disease herself, then her mother, then the chief. In vain we attempted to nurse and tend them ; in vain we expended the contents of the ship's medicine chest on the invalids. The malady having, as it were, an entirely new field to work upon, raged like the most awful pestilence. Through all ranks of the people it spread like wild-fire ; many died, none could be induced to take the most ordinary precautions. The natives became, as it were, mad under the torments of fever and the burning heat of the unaccustomed malady ;

they rushed about, quite unclad, for the sake of the deceptive coolness, and hundreds of them cast themselves into the sea and into the river.

It was my sad lot to see my dear Doto die—the first of the sufferers in the palace to succumb to the disease. Meanwhile, the bishop and myself being entirely absorbed in attendance on the sick, the crew of the *William Wilberforce*, I deeply regret to say, escaped from all restraint, and forgot what was due to themselves and their profession. They revelled with the most abandoned of the natives, and disease and drink ravaged the once peaceful island. Every sign of government and order vanished. The old priest built a huge pile of firewood, and laying himself there with the images of the gods, set fire to the whole, and perished with his own false religion.

After this event, the island ceased to be a safe residence for ourselves. Among the mountains, as I learned, where the pestilence had not yet penetrated, the shepherds and the wilder tribes were gathering in arms. One night we stole on board the *William Wilberforce*, leaving the city desolate, filled with the smoke of funeral pyres, and the wailing of men and women. There was a dreadful sultry stillness in the air, and all day long wild beasts had been dashing madly into the sea, and the sky had been obscured by flights of birds. On all the crests of the circle of surrounding hills we saw, in the growing darkness, the beacons and camp fires of the insurgents from the interior. Just before the dawn the *William Wilberforce* was attacked by the whole mass of the natives in boats and rafts. But we had not been unprepared for this movement, nor were the resources of science unequal to the occasion. We had surrounded the *William Wilberforce* with a belt, or cordon, of torpedoes, and as each of the assaulting boats touched the boom, a terrible explosion shook the water into fountains of foam, and the waves were strewn with scalded, wounded, and mutilated men. Meanwhile, we bombarded the city and the harbour, and the night passed amid the most awful sounds and sights—fire, smoke, yells of anger and pain, cries of the native leaders encouraging their men, and shouts from our own people, who had to repel the boarders when the boom

was at last forced, with pikes and cutlasses.
Just before the dawn a strange thing happened.
A great glowing coal, as it seemed, fell with
a hissing crash on the deck of the *William
Wilberforce*, and others dropped, with a
strange sound and a dreadful odour of burning, in the water all around us. Had the
natives discovered some mode of retaliating
on our use of firearms?

I looked in the direction of their burning
city, and beheld, on the sharp peak of the
highest mountain (now visible in the grey
morning light), an object like a gigantic pine-
tree of fire. The blazing trunk rose, slim and
straight, from the mountain crest, and, at a
vast height, developed a wilderness of burning
branches. Fearful hollow sounds came from
the hill, its sides were seamed with racing
cataracts of living lava, of coursing and leap-
ing flames, which rolled down with incredible
swiftness and speed towards the doomed city.
Then the waters of the harbour were smitten
and shaken, and the *William Wilberforce*
rocked and heaved as in the most appalling
storm, though all the winds were silent, while
a mighty wave swept far inland towards the
streams of fire. There was no room for

doubt; a volcanic eruption was occurring, and a submarine earthquake, as not uncommonly happens, had also taken place. Our only hope was in immediate flight. Presently steam was got up, and we steamed away into the light of the glowing east, leaving behind us only a burning island, and a fire like an ugly dawn flaring in the western sky.

When we returned in the evening, Boothland—as I may now indeed call it, for Scheria has ceased to be—was one black smoking cinder.

Hardly a tree or a recognizable rock remained to show that this had once been a peaceful home of men. The oracle, or prophecy of the old priest, had been horribly, though, of course, quite accidentally, fulfilled.

＊　　　＊　　　＊　　　＊　　　＊

Little remains to be told. On my return home, I chanced to visit the British Museum, and there, much to my surprise, observed an old piece of stone, chipped with the characters, or letters, in use among the natives of Scheria.

"Why," said I, reading the words aloud, "these are the characters which the natives employed on my island."

" These ? " said the worthy official who accompanied me. "Why, these are the most archaic Greek letters which have yet been discovered : inscriptions from beneath the lava beds of Santorin."

"I can't help that," I said. "The Polynesians used them too ; and you see I can read them easily, though I don't know Greek."

I then told him the whole story of my connection with the island, and of the unfortunate results of the contact between these poor people and our superior modern civilization.

I have rarely seen a man more affected by any recital than was the head of the classical department of the Museum by my artless narrative. When I described the sacrifice I saw on landing in the island, he exclaimed, "Great Heavens! the Attic Thargelia." He grew more and more excited as I went on, and producing a Greek book, " Pausanias," he showed me that the sacrifice of wild beasts was practised sixteen hundred years ago in honour of Artemis Elaphria. The killing of old Elatreus for entering the town hall reminded him of a custom in Achæa Pthiotis. When I had finished my tale, he burst out into violent and libellous language. "You have destroyed," he said, "with your miserable modern measles and Gardiner guns, the last remaining city of the ancient Greeks. The winds cast you on the shore of Phæacia, the island sung by Homer; and, in your brutal ignorance, you never knew it. You have ruined a happy, harmless, and peaceful people, and deprived archæology of an opportunity that can never, never return!"

I do not know about archæology, but as for "harmless and peaceful people," I leave it to my readers to say whether the islanders were anything of the sort.

I learn that the Government has just refused to give the Museum a grant of five thousand pounds to be employed in what are called "Excavations in Ancient Phæacia," diggings, that is, in Boothland.

With so many darkened people still ignorant of our enlightened civilization, I think the grant would be a shameful waste of public money.*

* From *Wandering Sheep*.

We publish the original text of the prophecy repeatedly alluded to by Mr. Gowles. The learned say that no equivalent occurs for the line about his "four eyes," and it is insinuated, in a literary journal of eminence, that Mr. Gowles pilfered the notion from Good's glass eye, in a secular romance, called *King Solomon's Mines*, which Mr. Gowles, we are sure, never heard of in his life.—ED.

THE PROPHECY.

’Αλλ’ ὅτε καπνοδόχον τις ἔχων περὶ κράατος αὐλὸν
καὶ νηῦς πυρίπεμπτος ἄτερ πτερύγων ἀνεμώκεων
ἴξεται εἰς ’Απίην χέρσον διὰ λαῖτμα θαλάσσης,
δὴ τοτε πουλυβότειραν ἐπὶ χθόνα λοιμὸς ἱκάνει
ξὺν δέ τε τῷ πτόλεμος, τότε δὴ θεοὶ ἐκλείψουσιν
ἐξ ἑδράνων, τάτ’ ὀλεῖται αἰστωθέντα κατ’ ἄκρης.

THE LAST ADVENTURE OF DON QUIXOTE

Kenneth Morris

THE LAST ADVENTURE OF DON QUIXOTE

CIDE HAMETE BENENGELI relates this; though I cannot tell how he came by it. Indeed, it would be hard to say. All else he wrote was attested by numberless witnesses; but who could give testimony as to this? Perhaps it was for such a reason that his illustrious translator, having a passion for exactitude above all things, concluded to omit it from the Castilian version. Though again, it may have been among the many passages that were scissored out, as he tells us, by the authorities; or he may have felt in it an inferiority of style, and been too much the artist to allow it in. Yet I think it but fair to the patient and accurate Cide that it should come to light at last; and let the critics judge for themselves!

It seems, then, that the book as we have it closes too soon. Don Quixote rose from his sick-bed cured, and something more than that. He had been very ill, certainly; now, it pertained to the marvellous how little ill he felt. In all the long length of his body there was not so much as one ache or pain—unless one might speak of the ache of bounding and glowing health; while as for his mind——

He realized a curious clarity in it, quite unknown to him before. Of old—you know—he had always been troubled with a kind of—how shall I express it?—uncertainty—a sense of being haunted by shams. There had been, as it were, a wraith on the borders of his consciousness: one Alonso Quixano, called *the Good*: whose quiet prosaic life had somehow mingled its drab cotton with the rich silks and gold of his own. The powers of some enchanter had been wont to prevail against him, poisoning with a subtle confusion the truth of things. A giant or a paynim emperor with his hosts, heroically encountered, would loom up suddenly to mock him, on some fantastic plane of vision, as no more than a wretched windmill or a shepherd with his flocks; there had been times when, through the reality of glorious Rozinante, a lean miserable hack had trembled into view—an illusion, if ever there was one; and when Mambrino's magical helmet had seemed a barber's basin. There had been moments when to be God's Knight Errant had appeared a mirage, an unattainable splendour; and all attempts to come up with it a forlorn hope. One rode atilt at one's objective, but as in a dream stumbled and fumbled over irrelevancies; the atmosphere became as wet wool or as treachery about one; progress so to say evaporated: until, like a drunkard or a dreamer, one staggered at last into inevitable thwackings and ignominy.

Not that he had ever broken the faith of his calling, or given an inch to doubt. He had known that that tremendous thing the Glory of Service, or Knight Errantry, did exist: as surely as the rainbow of heaven, as the flames of sunset and dawn, it was *there*; and one might come to plunge one's being in it: one might attain. But there was a world of deceits to fight one's way through first. And if he had never despaired, it was also true that the bright reality of hope had become a little unfamiliar to him. He knew he had been feeding his faith from the stores of his conscious will: had had to provide for it himself. No manna of the spirit had fallen for it from heaven; nor ravens had brought it food, as they did to Elijah of old. He had not really hoped, but had only made himself hope—until now.

But now all was different; and he did not even hope, but *knew*. Master Notary had made his will, and the Curate had taken his confession: of which matters, though one would have supposed them solemn enough, he took the smallest account. Sancho, he recollected, had besought him with much blubbering not to be so injudicious as to die—whatever that might mean. It was somewhere about then that the turn had come in the tide of his affairs: he must have fallen asleep for a little, to wake thus a new man; with the perfect assurance that, going forth now, nothing but victories and serious work awaited him. So he looked on his surroundings, as on the recent past, with the detachment of a mind keyed to higher things. The people in the house seemed to him, as he passed out, shadowy and half unreal. He commended them to God perfunctorily—really, perhaps only in his thoughts: he was going upon a grand adventure, and knew too well they would not be interested. They hardly answered him—that is, if indeed he spoke. There was the house-keeper, good soul,—very busy about something, and apparently weeping the while; there was his niece, red-eyed and mouse-like quiet; Bachelor Samson Carrasco; the Curate; and Master Nicholas the Barber: the last-named three in consultation seemingly, and melancholy enough by the look of them—but unreal, unreal. Sancho, in the kitchen, he noticed as he passed its open door, blubbering over a very hearty meal. He would have had some kind of connexion with that Sancho, he sup-posed;—or was it merely that the fat shrewd fellow had borne the same name as his, Don Quixote's squire? But all that belonged to the foreclosed period of enchantments, and was not to be peered at too closely. It hardly mat-tered; since the day of real things had come. In the same vague manner he noticed the general air of dejection, and wondered what its cause might be—but not much, for the business ahead was too insistent in its call.

He went out to the stable; and—there was, indeed, a lean miserable hack at the manger: a wretched horse-skin hung on bones and propped up on four caricatures of legs at the corners: just such a thing as he had been condemned, when the enchanter's power prevailed against him, to imagine Rozinante to be. But there also, beside that mockery of Knight Errantry's companion, the Horse, stood the real Rozinante, all fire and gentleness and beauty: limbs made for speed and endurance, glossy skin, hoofs like shells from the sea, proud mien and arching neck:

Rozinante, of the unique renown, veritably surpassing (and by far) Bucephalus of old or the Cid's own Babieca. The beautiful creature whinnied him a welcome: with a note of triumph, as knowing how glad a season had come. As for the hack, it lacked but the strength to grow restive at sight of that knightly man in his splendid armour;—for in armour Don Quixote was, though without memory, exactly, how he came to be so clad; in armour he was: not to linger over it too tediously, all panoplied, like Don Apollo of the Heavens, in burnished radiance and rubicund gold.

To him there came Sancho Panza: not the man he had but now left blubbering and guzzling in the kitchen, but the true Sancho at last, the right squire for a knight errant. 'Is it your highness's will to ride forth?' said this Sancho. 'It is, good friend,' said Don Quixote; 'since now the day has come when we are to meet the grand adventure, and win vast empires for the glory of knight errantry.' He must, I think, have forgotten the lady Dulcinea del Toboso; or surely would have mentioned her here. 'As God wills,' said Sancho; and without more words saddled the beautiful Rozinante and led him forth. On the road a mule was waiting, excellently caparisoned: having held the stirrup for his master, and seen him duly a-horseback, the squire mounted the mule, and together they rode forward.

Not, however, upon the familiar (and famous) Campo de Montiel; but through vast regions unlike any in La

Mancha. In front there were the dim bluenesses of immense distance; on this side topless precipices soared dizzily into the heavens above; on that, fathomless abysses that hid the far world beneath their carpeting of cloud. There were prodigious valleys, wide as the world; there were august mountains towering afar in faint turquoise and purple, about whose peaks in the sweetness of the evening clustered the large white flames of the stars. A keen ecstasy and lightness encompassed Don Quixote, limbs and mind and spirit; his soul was nourished with wonder and inspiration, in tutelage to the mountains and to the fires of heaven. Neither weariness nor need of food or drink overtook him; that gigantic beauty momently renewed and increased his strength.

He rode forward, conversing at whiles with his squire on the deeds of knighthood; calm wonderful words came to his lips; noble and beautiful were the replies he had from his companion. Long journeying elapsed before it came to his mind that the name of Sancho was somehow inappropriate for that one. He had listened to grave utterances of poetry and wisdom, at first without heeding their unwontedness, then with a growing surprise; until certainty at last took him that he never had been squired by such a one before. He turned his glance wonderingly from the infinity before him, to behold the most kingly of men riding at his side.

'Señor,' said he, drawing rein.

'Take it not ill, Señor Don Quixote,' said the other,

' that I ride beside your highness through these regions as your squire. My master, having taken account of your deeds and fame in La Mancha, and noted that that region deserved you little, desires that you shall visit his court; furthermore, he has set apart for you, if your grace will honour him by accepting it, command of a wide dangerous region in his dominions; since he knows your ability to win victories against the most stubborn of his foes. The way is long, however, and not easy to find; and therefore he sent me to escort you to his palace.'

' *Caballero*,' said Don Quixote, ' for this lofty graciousness thanks must be given in deeds rather than in words. My sword and my lance are henceforth at your great monarch's disposal.'—So they rode forward; but it did not occur to Don Quixote at that time to make inquiry as to the names and titles of his squire.

Vaster and vaster grew the mountains; wider the valleys as they advanced. Along the lips of chasms where blue infinity fell endlessly below them; by the shores of night-blue waters strewn with a million trembling flame-splashes of gold; night and day, night and day they rode on; and ever the consciousness of immortal strength, the serenity of pure being, grew in the spirit and limbs of the knight. In what Spain were these cosmic mountains ? Had any Amadis of Wales [1] or Palmerin of England, ridden through them before ?

They came, early of an evening, to the top of a barren

[1] Amadis de Gaula is properly so translated, and not as ' of Gaul'.

pass where the road branched: one way leading to the right high up along the mountain-side, the other sweeping clean down into the valley. Far off, shining like a huge coronet in the sunset, gleamed a city with many gem-bright cloud-soft towers and minarets; it shone beyond the immensity of the valley—beyond and above ranges and ranges of snow-capped mountains all velvet blue and dark and pale purple below their snows, whose austerity it crowned. 'It is the high metropolis of my sovereign,' said the squire.

'What dark army is that, which moves in the valley?' said Don Quixote. 'Whose grim castle is that, yonder in its depths to the southward?'

'It is the army of my king's enemies,' said the other anxiously and with a sigh. 'The castle is their chief stronghold; thence their leader, a great insurgent baron, works huge oppressions against the world.'

The soul of Don Quixote swelled into grandeur within him. 'Señor,' he said, 'I little thought the opportunity would be granted me so early to prove the truth of my new allegiance.'

'Do not think of it, Señor Don Quixote, I beseech you! Taking this road to the right, we shall avoid them and act prudently; it is to be considered that they are numberless and puissant. Nay, nay indeed! My royal master would never forgive me, should the smallest harm befall your grace! It will be yours presently to ride against them at the head of armies; but now——'

Ta ! he spoke to *Don Quixote* ! The soul of that great man was as little to be shaken as the mountains, as luminous as the morning sun. He bowed with a very haughty gesture: ' Señor,' he said, ' I have the honour of knight errantry to think of '; and with the word, couched lance, spurred steed, and away.

Down the slope thundered glorious Rozinante; with less danger of stumbling than the renowned Pegasus of antiquity charging through the middle air. Enchantment could prevail nothing against him now; right into the grim host flashed the golden figure of him; lance did its work, breaking the outermost ranks, and was gone; and in his hand instead flashed a falchion out of the mythologies. A roar of consternation arose in front, and he heard his own name carried to the horizons: *Don Quixote of La Mancha ! Alas, it is Don Quixote !* Borne on still by the impetus of his charge, he hacked and hewed to left and right; nought in mind but the ideals of his profession and the gloomy standard, held aloft by giants, towards which he had aimed his horse from the first. They receded; then gathered and surged in on him; but he fought on and on. The force of his charge was spent; but he fought forward. Blows rained upon his shield and upon his armour; it began to go hard with him . . . and through all the ardour of the conflict a certain sound came to him: the patter and bleating of a thousand sheep on the road; sheep coming up behind him; he could hear the cries of the shepherd,

the *yap ! yap !* of the sheepdogs; and it appeared to him
that enchantment was making head against him again;
and lo, with the very sigh that escaped him upon that
thought, the patter and baaing and the barking became the
triumphant shouting of his name: *For Don Quixote of
La Mancha ! For the Tenth Worthy of the World !* and up
from behind a great host in armour swept to his aid, and
at their head (he recognized) the valiant knight Pentapolin
of the Naked Arm; and they drove back the enemy,
and left Don Quixote alone for a moment on the field ;
so that he took breath, and recovered, and with a word
to Rozinante charged again; but what had become of
the army of Pentapolin he was not aware.

And now he charged into the centre, and grasped, after
many deeds of prowess, at the standard pole; and fought
and reeled and struggled; and the great dark champions
were about him like swarming bees about their queen;
so that he made no headway, nor succeeded to drag away
the standard pole; yet held it and would not part with it;
and so, rocking to and fro, that mêlée surged; Don
Quixote in the midst, heroically combating . . . and
rejoicing, thinking that——

Enchantment again; and he might not be free from
it; for he heard the creak, creak, clang of the sails as
they went round; the groaning and complaining of the
mill-wheels; and it was a miracle . . . for he beheld
them, from this side and from that; the windmills, gigantic, lumbering across the plain; not stationary as of

old to be attacked, but advancing . . . and turning, *creak*, *creak*, *clang* . . . and then a roar from them, and a shouting of his name: *Don Quixote de La Mancha! Por Dios y Don Quixote!*—and the windmills, behold, they were giants; all in white and silver armour; and they advanced upon those who were slaying Don Quixote, and with a great roar drove them off; so that my knight had breathing time again; and then that great host of giants passed like a sighing of the wind; and anew Don Quixote used his regained strength to advance.

And now he drove them across the plain in confusion, and helter-skelter in at the gates of their stronghold; and rode on pell-mell pursuing them; and had the standard at last at the gates; and thundered with his mace—but how the mace came in his hand he knew not—upon the portcullis as it fell clanging and locked, so that it shook and was loosened, and was within a little of breaking. Then Don Quixote heard from the far hills a bugle calling; and suddenly the air was loud with a rushing of myriad wings behind. Then rose up one before him flammivomous and horrible, vast and grim as the mountains, bearing a club whose fall should powder the granite mountains where they are firmest, and a brand that shed midnight and ghastly flame and stench; and between his attack and Don Quixote, a sudden sword flashed like the daybreak, and a splendour broke like the noonday sun; and the portcullis was shattered, the gate was down; and the dark lord driven out, and a host swept in with Don Quixote all golden armoured and golden aureoled, and their armour strangely and beautifully adorned with pinions; and so that stronghold was taken.

But at Don Quixote's side stood the one whose sword but now had saved him; and it was the man who had squired him on his journey.

'Señor,' said Don Quixote, 'to whom am I honoured to owe my deliverance?'

'*Caballero*,' said the other, 'let your grace make nothing of the deliverance. I am, in truth, the Captain-general of the war hosts of my sovereign; and hence qualified to appreciate the greatness of your feat. I am styled, Michael of the Flaming Sword.'

Side by side in pleasant converse they rode forward then to the palace gates of their sovereign: Don Quixote of La Mancha and Don Michael Archangel: each wondrously pleased with the nobility and high bearing of his companion.

SAME TIME, SAME PLACE

Mervyn Peake

SAME TIME, SAME PLACE

By MERVYN PEAKE

That night, I hated father. He smelt of cabbage. There was cigarette ash all over his trousers. His untidy moustache was yellower and viler than ever with nicotine, and he took no notice of me. He simply sat there in his ugly armchair, his eyes half closed, brooding on the Lord knows what. I hated him. I hated his moustache. I even hated the smoke that drifted from his mouth and hung in the stale air above his head.

And when my mother came through the door and asked me whether I had seen her spectacles, I hated her too. I hated the clothes she wore ; tasteless and fussy. I hated them deeply. I hated something I had never noticed before ; it was the way the heels of her shoes were worn away on their outside edges—not badly, but appreciably. It looked mean to me, slatternly, and horribly human. I hated her for being human—like father.

She began to nag me about her glasses and the thread-bare condition of the elbows of my jacket, and suddenly I threw my book down. The room was unbearable. I felt suffocated. I suddenly realised that I must get away. I had lived with these two people for nearly twenty-three years. I had been born in the room immediately overhead. Was this the life for a young man ? To spend his evenings watching the smoke drift out of his father's mouth and stain that decrepit old moustache, year after year—to watch the worn away edges of my mother's heels —the dark brown furniture and the familiar stains on the chocolate coloured carpet ? I would go away ; I would shake off the dark, smug mortality of the place. I would forgo my birthright. What of my father's business into which I would step at his death ? What of it ? To hell with it.

I began to make my way to the door but at the third step I caught my foot in a ruck of the chocolate coloured carpet and in reaching out my hand for support, I sent a pink vase flying.

Suddenly I felt very small and very angry. I saw my mother's mouth opening and it reminded me of the front door and the front door reminded me of my urge to escape—to where ? To where ?

I did not wait to find an answer to my own question, but, hardly knowing what I was doing, ran from the house.

The accumulated boredom of the last twenty-three years was at my back and it seemed that I was propelled through the garden gate from its pressure against my shoulder blades.

The road was wet with rain, black and shiny like oilskin. The reflection of the streetlamps wallowed like yellow jellyfish. A bus was approaching—a bus to Piccadilly, a bus to the never-never land—a bus to death or glory.

I found neither. I found something which haunts me still.

The great bus swayed as it sped. The black street gleamed. Through the window a hundred faces fluttered by as though the leaves of a dark book were being flicked over. And I sat there, with a sixpenny ticket in my hand. What was I doing ! Where was I going ?

To the centre of the world, I told myself. To Piccadilly Circus, where anything might happen. What did I *want* to happen ?

I wanted life to happen ! I wanted adventure ; but already I was afraid. I wanted to find a beautiful woman. Bending my elbow I felt for the swelling of my biceps. There wasn't much to feel. ' O hell,' I said to myself, ' O damnable hell : this is *awful*.'

I stared out of the window, and there before me was the Circus. The lights were like a challenge. When the bus had curved its way from Regent Street and into Shaftesbury Avenue, I alighted. Here was the jungle all about me and I was lonely, The wild beasts prowled around me. The wolf packs surged and shuffled. Where was I to go? How wonderful it would have been to have known of some apartment, dimly lighted; of a door that opened to the secret knock, three short ones and one long one—where a strawberry blonde was waiting—or perhaps, better still, some wise old lady with a cup of tea, an old lady, august and hallowed, and whose heels were not worn down on their outside edges.

But I knew nowhere to go either for glamour or sympathy. Nowhere except The Corner House.

I made my way there. It was less congested than usual. I had only to queue for a few minutes before being allowed into the great eating-palace on the first floor. Oh, the marble and the gold of it all! The waiters coming and going, the band in the distance—how different all this was from an hour ago, when I stared at my father's moustache.

For some while I could find no table and it was only when moving down the third of the long corridors between tables that I saw an old man leaving a table for two. The lady who had been sitting opposite him remained where she was. Had she left, I would have had no tale to tell. Unsuspectingly I took the place of the old man and in reaching for the menu lifted my head and found myself gazing into the midnight pools of her eyes.

My hand hung poised over the menu. I could not move for the head in front of me was magnificent. It was big and pale and indescribably proud—and what I would now call a greedy look, seemed to me then to be an expression of rich assurance; of majestic beauty.

I knew at once that it was not the strawberry blonde of my callow fancy that I desired for glamour's sake, nor the comfort of the tea-tray lady—but this glorious creature before me who combined the mystery and exoticism of the former with the latter's mellow wisdom.

Was this not love at first sight? Why else should my heart have hammered like a foundry? Why should my hand have trembled above the menu? Why should my mouth have gone dry?

Words were quite impossible. It was clear to me that she knew everything that was going on in my breast and in my brain. The look of love which flooded from her eyes all but unhinged me. Taking my hand in hers she returned it to my side of the table where it lay like a dead thing on a plate. Then she passed me the menu. It meant nothing to me. The hors d'oeuvres and the sweets were all mixed together in a dance of letters.

What I told the waiter when he came, I cannot remember, nor what he brought me. I know that I could not eat it. For an hour we sat there. We spoke with our eyes, with the pulse and stress of our excited breathing—and towards the end of this, our first meeting, with the tips of our fingers that in touching each other in the shadow of the teapot, seemed to speak a language richer, subtler and more vibrant than words.

At last we were asked to go—and as I rose I spoke for the first time. " Tomorrow ?" I whispered. " Tomorrow ?" She nodded her magnificent head slowly. " Same place ? Same time ?" She nodded again.

I waited for her to rise, but with a gentle yet authoritative gesture she signalled me away.

It seemed strange, but I knew I must go. I turned at the door and saw her sitting there, very still, very upright. Then I descended to the street and made my way to Shaftesbury Avenue, my head in a whirl of stars, my legs weak and trembling, my heart on fire.

I had not decided to return home, but found nevertheless that I was on my way back—back to the chocolate coloured carpet, to my father in the ugly arm chair—to my mother with her worn shoe heels.

When at last I turned the key it was near midnight. My mother had been crying. My father was angry. There were words, threats and entreaties on all sides. At last I got to bed.

The next day seemed endless but at long last my excited fretting found some relief in action. Soon after tea I boarded the west-bound bus. It was already dark but I was far too early when I arrived at the Circus.

I wandered restlessly here and there, adjusting my tie at shop windows and filing my nails for the hundredth time.

At last, when waking from a day dream as I sat for the fifth time in Leicester Square, I glanced at my watch and found I was three minutes late for our tryst.

I ran all the way panting with anxiety but when I arrived at the table on the first floor I found my fear was baseless. She was there, more regal than ever, a monument of womanhood. Her large, pale face relaxed into an expression of such deep pleasure at the sight of me that I almost shouted for joy.

I will not speak of the tenderness of that evening. It was magic. It is enough to say that we determined that our destinies were inextricably joined.

When the time came for us to go I was surprised to find that the procedure of the previous night was once more expected of me. I could in no way make out the reason for it. Again I left her sitting alone at the table by the marble pillar. Again I vanished into the night alone, with those intoxicating words still on my lips. " Tomorrow . . . tomorrow . . . same time . . . same place . . ."

The certainty of my love for her and hers for me was quite intoxicating. I slept little that night and my restlessness on the following day was an agony both for me and my parents.

Before I left that night for our third meeting, I crept into my mother's bedroom and opening her jewel box I chose a ring from among her few trinkets. God knows it was not worthy to sit upon my loved-one's finger, but it would symbolise our love.

Again she was waiting for me although on this occasion I arrived a full quarter of an hour before our appointed time. It was as though, when we were together, we were hidden in a veil of love—as though we were alone. We heard nothing else but the sound of our voices, we saw nothing else but one another's eyes.

She put the ring upon her finger as soon as I had given it to her. Her hand that was holding mine tightened its grip. I was surprised at its power. My whole body trembled. I moved my foot beneath the table to touch hers. I could find it nowhere.

When once more the dreaded moment arrived, I left her sitting upright, the strong and tender smile of her farewell remaining in my mind like some fantastic sunrise.

For eight days we met thus, and parted thus, and with every meeting we knew more firmly than ever, that whatever the difficulties that would result, whatever the forces against us, yet it was now that we must marry, now, while the magic was upon us.

On the eighth evening it was all decided. She knew that for my part it must be a secret wedding. My parents would never countenance so rapid an arrangement. She understood perfectly. For her part she wished a few of her friends to be present at the ceremony.

" I have a few colleagues," she had said. I did not know what she meant, but her instructions as to where we should meet on the following afternoon put the remark out of my mind.

There was a registry office in Cambridge Circus, she told me, on the first floor of a certain building. I was to be there at four o'clock. She would arrange everything.

" Ah, my love," she had murmured, shaking her large head slowly from side to side, " how can I wait until then ?" And with a smile unutterably bewitching, she gestured for me to go, for the great memorial hall was all but empty.

For the eighth time I left her there. I knew that women must have their secrets and must be in no way thwarted in regard to them, and so, once again I swallowed the question that I so longed to put to her. Why, O why had I always to leave her there—and why, when I arrived to meet her—was she always there to meet me ?

On the following day, after a careful search, I found a gold ring in a box in my father's dressing table. Soon after three, having brushed my hair until it shone like sealskin I set forth with a flower in my b ton' le and a suitcase of belongings. It was a beautiful day with no wind and a clear sky.

The bus fled on like a fabulous beast, bearing me with it to a magic land.

But alas, as we approached Mayfair we were held up more than once for long stretches of time. I began to get restless. By the time the bus had reached Shaftesbury Avenue I had but three minutes in which to reach the Office.

It seemed strange that when the sunlight shone in sympathy with my marriage, the traffic should choose to frustrate me. I was on the top of the bus and having been given a very clear description of the building, was able, as we rounded at last in Cambridge Circus, to recognise it at once. When we came alongside my destination the traffic was held up again and I was offered the perfect opportunity of dis-embarking immediately beneath the building.

My suitcase was at my feet and as I stooped to pick it up I glanced at the windows on the first floor—for it was in one of those rooms that I was so soon to become a husband.

I was exactly on a level with the windows in question and commanded an unbroken view of the interior of a first floor room. It could not have been more than a dozen feet away from where I sat.

I remember that our bus was hooting away, but there was no movement in the traffic ahead. The hooting came to me as through a dream for I had become lost in another world.

My hand was clenched upon the handle of the suitcase. Through my eyes and into my brain an image was pouring. The image of the first floor room.

I knew at once that it was in that particular room that I was expected. I cannot tell you why, for during those first few moments I had not seen her.

To the right of the stage (for I had the sensation of being in a theatre) was a table loaded with flowers. Behind the flowers sat a small pin-striped registrar. There were four others in the room, three of whom kept walking to and fro. The fourth, an enormous bearded lady, sat on a chair by the window. As I stared, one of the men bent over to speak to her. He had the longest neck on earth. His starched collar was the length of a walking stick, and his small bony head protruded from its extremity like the skull of a bird. The other two gentlemen who kept crossing and re-crossing were very different. One was bald. His face and cranium were blue with the most intricate tattooing. His teeth were gold and they shone like fire in his mouth. The other was a well-dressed young man, and seemed normal enough until, as he came for a moment closer to the window I saw that instead of a hand, the cloven hoof of a goat protruded from the left sleeve.

And then suddenly it all happened. A door of their room must have opened for all at once all the heads in the room were turned in one direction and a moment later a something in white trotted like a dog across the room.

But it was no dog. It was vertical as it ran. I thought at first that it was a mechanical doll, so close was it to the floor. I could not observe its face, but I was amazed to see the long train of satin that was being dragged along the carpet behind it.

It stopped when it reached the flower-laden table and there was a good deal of smiling and bowing and then the man with the longest neck in the world placed a high stool in front of the table and, with the help of the young man with the goat-foot, lifted the white thing so that it stood upon the high stool. The long satin dress was carefully draped over the stool so that it reached to the floor on every side. It seemed as though a tall dignified woman was standing at the civic altar.

And still I had not seen its face, although I knew what it would be like. A sense of nausea overwhelmed me and I sank back on the seat, hiding my face in my hands.

I cannot remember when the bus began to move. I know that I went on and on and on and that finally I was told that I had reached the terminus. There was nothing for it but to board another bus of the same number and make the return journey. A strange sense of relief had by now begun to blunt the edge of my disappointment. That this bus would take me to the door of the house where I was born gave me a twinge of homesick pleasure. But stronger was my sense of fear. I prayed that there would be no reason for the bus to be held up again in Cambridge Circus.

I had taken one of the downstairs seats for I had no wish to be on an eyelevel with someone I had deserted. I had no sense of having wronged her but she had been deserted nevertheless.

When at last the bus approached the Circus, I peered into the half darkness. A street lamp stood immediately below the registry office. I saw at once that there was no light in the office and as the bus moved past I turned my eyes to a group beneath the street lamp. My heart went cold in my breast.

Standing there, ossified as it were into a malignant mass—standing there as though they never intended to move until justice was done—were the five. It was only for a second that I saw them but every lamp-lit head is for ever with me—the long necked man with his bird skull head, his eyes glinting like chips of glass ; to his right the small bald man, his tattooed scalp thrust forward, the lamplight gloating on the blue markings. To the left of the long-necked man stood the youth, his elegant body relaxed, but a snarl on his face that I still sweat to remember. His hands were in his pockets but I could see the shape of the hoof through the cloth. A little ahead of these three stood the bearded woman, a bulk of evil—and in the shadow that she cast before her I saw in that last fraction of a second, as the bus rolled me past, a big whitish head, very close to the ground.

In the dusk it appeared to be suspended above the kerb like a pale balloon with a red mouth painted upon it—a mouth that, taking a single diabolical curve, was more like the mouth of a wild beast than of a woman.

Long after I had left the group behind me—set as it were for ever under the lamp, like something made of wax, like something monstrous, long after I had left it I yet saw it all. It filled the bus. They filled my brain. They fill it still.

When at last I arrived home I fell weeping upon my bed. My father and mother had no idea what it was all about but they did not ask me. They never asked me.

That evening, after supper, I sat there, I remember, six years ago in my own chair on the chocolate coloured carpet. I remember how I stared with love at the ash on my father's waistcoat, at his stained moustache, at my mother's worn away shoe heels. I stared at it all and I loved it all. I needed it all.

Since then I have never left the house. I know what is best for me.

—Mervyn Peake

That First Affair

J[ohn] A[mes] Mitchell

That First Affair

IT is bad enough to be alone in a big house, and there is yet more solitude, the poets tell us, in being alone in a great city; but the hero of this simple scandal was alone on the surface of the earth, the only man, absolutely single and unique, — solitary, — all by himself.

Of course there were animals, but no record exists of dog or cat or parrot; and what hope for boon companionship with the mylodon, the ichthyosaurus, or the ornithiohnites giganteus?

But, worst of all, he had no memories, for he started already brought up. He had never been a boy. Selkirk and other solitaries, either in heart or trousers' pocket, bore memories of mother, or proof of maiden's love; but this young man knew not mother, maid, or memories, and had never seen a pair of trousers.

His education was limited, as history had not yet begun. Botany was trying her first experiments. Reading, writing, and geography were still unborn; and, thus far, no vulgar fractions had shed their blight upon a peaceful earth. However, being the first of the kind, and never having seen his like, he probably regarded this as the usual condition of affairs; the proper thing, in fact. But the goings on of other animals could not fail to start him on 'a line of thought that was sure to be upsetting. They were pairing off in twos, and with their individual families seemed to get the upper hand

of an unpleasant isolation that threatened to make his own existence a
melancholy failure. And doubly de-
pressing was the gradual discovery that
while among the other animals there
were at least two of a kind, thus ren-
dering these partnerships an easy business, for him there seemed no such
hope. Day after day he searched, but
found no biped similar to himself.
Meeting, one tranquil eve, a palæotherium with his bride, he asked the
happy groom where he found his mate,
and if, in that locality, there were
brides in human shape. " No," the
palæotherium answered, " I have seen
them nowhere ; but off to the south I
passed maidens of the gorilla family
who walk on their hind legs and use
their front paws just as you do ; and
they also bear a certain resemblance in
physiognomy."

" Yes ; I know those maidens," re
plied the solitary one ; " but somehow
they fail to fascinate me. They are

5

hasty-tempered and too muscular. I
should never be master in my own
house; and they are such restless climb-
ers! No; home would not be home
with those girls."

Two squirrels, newly wedded, threw
nuts at him as he wandered melancholy
by, and twitted him on living by himself. "Get a girl," cried the groom,
"and go to housekeeping. There's
nothing like it, really!"

And later a mastodon, hurrying pon-
derously, yet joyfully along, with an
enormous bunch of flowers in his trunk,
nearly trampled the disconsolate bachelor beneath his feet.

"I beg your pardon!" he exclaimed.
"I came within an ace of walking on
you."

"I wish you had."

"Why, what has happened?"

"Oh, nothing has happened, and
nothing ever will!"

The big traveller failed to understand,
but his business that morning was too

interesting for delays. Being of a sympathetic nature, however, he made one attempt at consolation.

"Let me put you on my back, and I'll take you to my wedding. You shall be best man."

The invitation was declined, but incidents of this kind only increased the bitterness of a lonely spirit, and aggravated a situation already painful. The most dismal hours of all were during those regular intervals when the light went out, leaving the earth in darkness. This joyless condition lasted many hours, and was only alleviated by a smaller and much colder luminary than the sun, which, as the lone one gazed upon it, filled him with uncontrollable longings. The evening zephyrs breathed exasperating secrets, always of a tender and mysterious nature. And during these dusky hours the frogs and turtles intensified his woe by their vociferous courtships.

But a surprise was awaiting him, and

7

it came in a novel way. Early one
morning, as he lay upon the grass, conversing with a skylark who was hunting
worms for his family breakfast, the bird
remarked, —

"I suppose you feed your little ones
on quite different food."

"I have no little ones."

"Oh, too bad! All dead?"

"No; I never had any."

"Your wife's alive?"

"Never had any."

"So you're a bachelor! Well, it's
a shame for such a good-looking chap
to go to waste. You ought to marry,
and do it while you're young."

The youth sat up and shook his hair
from his face with an angry movement.

"I would if I could, and quick
enough!"

The lark laughed. "Would if you
could! Why, any girl would have you."

"But there isn't any girl."

"Oh, fiddle!"

"But there isn't, and never has been!"

The bird looked earnestly at him, and came a little nearer. "That is a serious oversight," he said impressively, his head to one side.

"Serious! I should say it was!"

"Look here," said the lark, in a lower tone and coming closer still, "there have been several important errors in this creation, and the one you mention just caps the climax. While of little importance to the world at large, I can see that for you, personally, it is terribly aggravating. Now, I won't mention names, but there are several creatures hereabouts that should never be allowed in a first-class garden. It all comes from a reprehensible carelessness in the supervision."

"That's just what I think," said the young man.

"If, for instance," continued the skylark, "there were fewer mosquitoes and more girls, it would be a far more attractive garden."

" Would n't it, though ! "

" And suppose all the mosquitoes were girls, what a different kind of a time you would have ! "

" Don't talk about it; " and the youth rolled over upon the turf and muttered all the wicked words he knew.

The sympathy of the skylark was aroused, also his anger, and he exclaimed, " What's the use of a man without a girl ? "

" None ! "

" Why, you have no home ! "

" No; I sleep in a new one every night."

" Now, marriage is rife in this garden, and I can't imagine why you should be shut out. You are as good as the rest of us, at least, you appear so."

There was a silence, during which both were thinking. It was broken by the lark, who said, in a reflective tone, —

" It must be a mistake : just a stupid blunder. There's nothing to punish you for. You have n't led a fast life, have you, or been bad in any way ? "

" A fast life ! " exclaimed the man, " fast on what ? There is no one to gamble with ; I never saw a woman ; there 's nothing to drink but water, and I am only a week old, anyway ! "

The skylark smiled. " Well," he said, " I believe it 's simply a mistake, and that the powers above have forgotten all about you. I will do the best I can to advertise the fact, and it may reach their ears. You just wait here a minute."

Thereupon he spread his wings and soared aloft. As he arose toward the clouds he sang, in clear, far-reaching notes, —

" Not a woman in the world ! "

Higher and higher he went, until, to the anxious bachelor, he became a tiny speck in the sky, the note growing fainter all the while. At last the blue ether closed in about him and shut the messenger from sight.

That First Affair

A long time he was gone, but he finally returned, and out of breath.

"Well, I have spread it through the heavens," he said; "and if there is justice anywhere, you ought to get it."

The very next day, rather early in the afternoon, our hero, yielding to a heavier drowsiness than usual, reclined in the cool shade of a fern, — an antediluvian fern about a hundred feet in height, — and fell straightway into a deep slumber. When he awoke the surprise was there! She was close beside him, leaning over and gazing down into his face, and he, in unspeakable rapture, looked up into another pair of human eyes. Fearing it a dream, he blinked and looked again. It surely was the prayed-for girl! Her eyes, surprised and timid; the delicate contour of her face and neck; the luxuriant locks that grazed his cheek as she bent forward, — all filled him with a gentle ecstasy.

He smiled; she returned the smile,

14

and, either from embarrassment or alarm,
edged further away. Still sitting among
the flowers, she watched him intently,
as if trying to comprehend the situation.
As for him, so great was his joy that
he found no words to express it. He
continued, however, to manifest his
intense delight by a series of welcom-
ing smiles, but these at last were dis-
concerting to the maiden, compelling
her to turn away in some confusion.
For it must be remembered that this
was not only her first appearance in
any society, but it had come with un-
precedented suddenness. Her ward-
robe, being a thing of the future, might
also have troubled her under different
circumstances, but at this informal period
no fashions had been set in clothing;
in fact, no standards of any kind were
as yet established for the guidance of
beginners.

She seemed even more amazed than
he, and stared at everything about her
in a charming bewilderment.

That First Affair

" Where did you come from ? " he finally asked.

"I am sure I don't know!" she answered; " I just found myself here."

Her voice was gentler, more melodious than his own He put his hand to his side as if something were missing, but his face expressed no regret.

" You are very beautiful ! far more interesting than anything in this garden."

"Thank you," she replied, with a blush; " I have never seen myself, but it is very kind of you to think so."

" I am glad enough you have come," he continued. " I have lived here some days, and it's dull being alone."

" Where are the others ? " she asked.

" The other animals ? "

" The other people."

" There are no others."

She seemed disappointed. But this brief conversation had given her more confidence in herself, and she replied, with a suspicious look, " So you are the only man ! "

"Yes."

Now this was an unacceptable truth to a belle who was making a brilliant *début*.

"How do you know that?"

"Because I have n't seen any, or heard of any; and I have inquired far and near."

"Have you been everywhere yourself?" and then, as her eyes swept the distant hills she added, "It seems quite a place! There must be *some* variety in the way of men."

"Well, it 's what all the animals tell me, and the birds too: and some of them are tremendous travellers."

As he gazed in admiration upon this new companion, he could not conceal his contentment in being able to make such a reply. But she was evidently far from satisfied. After a pause, during which she caused him to feel that he was taking an ignoble advantage of a trusting girl, she inquired, without looking toward him, "Then what on earth do you do with yourself?"

" Oh, nothing much : generally as
the others do."

" Then there *are* others ? "

" I mean the other animals."

" And how do they pass the time ? "

" Oh, stroll about and eat things,
mostly fruit and berries ; and take
naps."

" What a life ! "

" It *is* dull."

" Dull ! I should die ! "

" There are some fine views."

But she made no reply, and there was
another silence in which he felt her
contempt. At last, in a consoling manner he remarked, " But then *you* will
have *me !* "

" Really ! "

He blushed and tried to assert himself against a foolish diffidence that was
constantly possessing him ever since he
had met this person.

" What I mean is that you will have
one companion, such as it is, while I
have been all alone by myself."

She put her hand to her mouth as if to conceal a yawn, then sighed as she asked, —

"And the neighbors? Are they pleasant people?"

"But there *are* none, I say."

"Not hereabouts, perhaps, but further away. Off there, or there," she exclaimed nervously, pointing in different directions.

"There is nobody anywhere. I have inquired and hunted, and we are the only ones."

"Impossible!" and she arose to her feet with a look of alarm. "I can't believe it. It is terribly inconsiderate; and I am sure it's unusual."

"Unusual!" he repeated; "why, what is the usual custom?"

"I don't know, but it seems queer. Are you sure it's all right? I was never in such a position before."

"But you never were in any position before," he answered with a smile.

She made no reply, simply expressing

by her manner an increased distrust, and strolled slowly away.

He hastened after and did his best to make her cheerful: he told her how delicious was the fruit; how refreshing to lie down when tired; of the delightful heat of the sun when the wind blew cold, and how welcome the cooling wind and the shadowy places when the sun was over-hot. But she paid little attention, and appeared thoroughly depressed, turning away as if mankind had ceased to interest. She gazed about at the sky, the trees, the birds and butterflies, fixing her eyes, at last, with an absent look, upon a towering megatherium nibbling tree-tops in the distance.

She plucked a flower and held it to her nostrils, then studied it in admiration.

"I can show you some that are much prettier than that," he remarked in the tone of a man of the world who has travelled extensively and seen much.

" Did you make this one ? " she asked.

" No ! "

" Did you make all the rest ? "

" All what ? "

" Everything," and with a little wave
of her hand she indicated the trees and
the distant hills.

" No, that was all finished when I
came."

And pointing upward to the great
white clouds floating majestically across
the heavens, " And did n't you arrange
those, either ? "

" No ! " And he saw in her face
that the awe which he at first inspired
was gone forever.

Passing her hands through the long
tresses that hung about her shoulders,
at first in an idle way, she at last
began to gather them into a definite
shape. " Your hair is very beautiful,"
he remarked. " How fast it must
have grown ; and you so young ! "

She looked up at his own head
and asked, after hesitating a moment,

" What happened to yours ?   Did something bite it off ? "

" No ; it was never any longer."

" That 's too bad ! "

" Oh, I don't care ; I supposed it was the regular thing until you turned up."

" I wish I could see my own face. I have no idea how I look."

" You look like me in a general way ; but you are far more beautiful of course, as I was only an experiment."

" How do you know how you look ? "

" I have seen my reflection in water."

This was quite exciting ; and she showed a livelier interest than in any subject they had yet approached. So together they started off to find the mirror.

Beneath a certain apple-tree he paused a moment, and told her this was the forbidden fruit ; that of all else in the garden they could take what they wished, but if they tasted this there would be a serious punishment. Then, continuing their walk, he brought her to a quiet nook by a river's bank, and there, surprised and delighted, she gazed upon a fresh young face smiling back at her from the water.

"Why, how lovely! I am not at all like you, and my hair is beautiful — simply beautiful!"

Then she began to arrange this hair in different fashions, trying new effects, he watching her like a creature beneath a spell. At last, turning toward him, a little color in her cheeks, she inquired with a smile of various meanings, "How many men did you say there are in the world?"

"One."

"That's a great many, is n't it?"

"You think one is a great many!"

"It seems so just now."

He laughed and strolled away. She called after him, "And I will let you know when you are needed."

That First Affair

After a while, when tired of her own face and of rearranging her hair, she looked about for other pleasures. The world was young, and so was she, and there were fresh surprises on every side, — in the colors and perfumes of the flowers, in the clouds, the birds, and the whispering trees. For a happy period, no one knows how long, she played about, until at last, throwing herself upon a shady bank to rest a little, she recognized in the branches above her head the apples of the forbidden tree. But she was a good girl — so far — and resisted a temptation — quite a strong temptation, just to know how it tasted. As thus she lay, a languor came stealing through her brain; her eyelids shut out the light; her senses seemed to float away, and then — all was as nothing.

From this sleep she was gently awakened by the pressure of a diminutive hand upon her heart, and warm lips against her own. Opening her eyes,

at first slowly, and then wider in alarm,
she looked upon a curious little being
who leaned over her with a mischievous
smile upon his cherubic face. He was
short, very plump, and quite a handsome boy. She sat up and pushed
him back, a look both of
fear and indignation in her
face. But he continued to
smile, and said, —

"Oh, don't be angry.
You will understand it
later. You don't know
me yet."

"No, I do not."

"I am the serpent."

"The serpent?"

"Yes. Do I look it?"

She did not answer, as she felt he
was not serious, and she had begun to
fear him. In his face and manner
there was a recklessness and audacity
that augmented her distrust; moreover,
his lips were amorous and his eyes were
bold. The impression given was of

27

an impulsive, happy person, warm and open-hearted perhaps, but who loved the Devil and was full thereof. Had he worn a halo, it would not have been straight upon his head, but cocked to one side, and he would have doffed it to every girl he met.

"Yes," he went on, his hands upon his hips; "I am the tempter, the thing that is to bring disgrace upon you,— upon you, the mother of the human race."

His speech was meaningless, at least to her, and she began to regard him as some evil spirit.

"Are you a man?" she whispered.

"A man? No; I am the essence of all men,— of the millions yet unborn. I am the sap and soul of human life, the realization of lovers' dreams. I am the absorbing and resistless passion; the one undying thing; the everlasting joy and torture. That's what I am!"

He smiled as he spoke, yet there

was enough of earnestness to convince his listener that he was something of importance. The more she studied him the more she yielded to an indefinable bewitchment. He seemed to exercise a dangerous spell, and she looked uneasily about. Her thoughts flew to the man, whose absence she now regretted, and she remembered him with a warmer interest and a deeper longing than she had yet experienced.

"You kind of half know what love is, don't you?" exclaimed her new acquaintance. "Whenever you think of that fellow you feel this way." And, reaching out his arms, he moved them slowly up and down, wiggling every finger; "and it goes tingling all through you, up your spine, along your drunken nerves, and into your nice little heart. It brings the color to your cheeks and the light of Heaven to your

eyes. Oh, it is the big thing of creation!" and then, as she tried to hide
her embarrassment by a careless smile,
finally putting her hands before her face,
he laughed aloud, a triumphant, mocking laugh, threw himself upon the grass,
and repeated, as he rolled over and over
among the flowers, "What fun this is!"

Then he sat up and said with a
smile, — an exasperating smile of superior wisdom, —

"Tell me honestly what you think
of him?"

In spite of herself, the color came
into her cheeks.

"Who?"

"Who?" he repeated in a jeering
tone. "Who, indeed? There are so
many."

"You are an impudent little thing."

"Worse than that," he replied. "I
am the wicked thing that tempted
Eve;" and he hunched up his shoulders
and rubbed his hands in a kind of reckless glee.

That First Affair

" That tempted whom ? "

" You. But tell me honestly if the world is not pleasanter since you took that nap. Is n't the sky bluer, the air softer? Are n't the flowers more fragrant? and is n't your heart a heap sight fuller since I had the honor of awakening you ? "

Again the color came to her cheeks as she replied, with a frown, " I don't know why I should talk about it to every stranger who comes along."

" True; but you are not likely to encounter many strangers, and, besides, I am an exceptional person. I am an institution by myself, — a whole principle, in fact, — and a huge one, too."

" You are here for mischief, I am sure of that."

He laughed again. " For love and trouble, that 's what I am here for."

" Must they go together ? "

" Well, yes ; I suppose they must.

31

You see love requires that two shall be in it."

She nodded.

Then, with a solemn shake of his head, " There 's trouble right away."

She reflected a moment, then replied, " I don't see why."

" Because one at least is in love. If the man, for instance, could pine away for love of himself, for what is already his; if he could be satisfied with holding his own hand, sitting in his own lap, breathing love into his own ear, and after all, perhaps, changing his mind and throwing himself over at the end, — you can see how much suffering would be avoided. And the same with a woman. No; it 's having two that will lead to complications."

" But how do you know all this when nothing has happened, — before anything is tried ? "

" By eating that fruit," he answered pointing to the branches above her head.

32

" By the way, have an apple," and he proffered one.

But she pushed it away. " That is the tree of knowledge, the forbidden fruit."

" Oh, come now ! what do apples grow for ? You will never have any fun, unless you know enough to take it. It 's the best fruit in the garden. Do you want to be a brainless old goody, and never know what life is — to say nothing of blighting the hopes of the only lover in the world ? Eat it, and trust me. I can furnish you more fun and tragedy, more poetry and life, than the deepest ignorance can ever offer. Besides, you won't get another such chance for a finished education with so little trouble."

She was puzzled. There were too many new ideas in this, and they came rapidly for a brain not three hours old.

" What do you mean ? "

" This being the tree of knowledge, it follows that the more you eat the more you will know; and you will know things

3   33

you ought n't to know, which is considerable sport, as you can imagine."

Although she smiled and nodded in approval she could not avoid a suspicion that, for inexperienced maidens, he was not the safest guide.

"But we are commanded not to eat it, and to disobey would be wrong."

"Look here," he said, cocking his head to one side and half closing his eyes. "You are inclined to be too superior. Now, beware of an excess of virtue. It is a good thing, like water, purifying while you are in it, but too much of it becomes the chill of death. Take my advice and eat that apple. It will bring a scrap of wisdom, and that man will like you all the better for being a little cleverer than himself."

"Are you sure?"

"Sure."

That First Affair

She still hesitated, but finally bit into it cautiously, and made a little face.

"Why, it is n't as good as it looks! It is bitter, and yet," after another bite, — "it has a sweet taste."

Then she finished the whole apple and, as she tossed aside the core, inquired, —

"If I eat another shall I be wiser still?"

"Yes."

"Then give me another."

But he squatted upon the grass in front of her and said, —

"Just wait a minute, and hear a word before you go on. In the first place, wisdom and fun are two different things. Now, if you eat too many apples you will be too wise to fall in love with that man."

"I don't see why!" she exclaimed. "I should love him all the same. He is not a fool."

"Yes, he is, or he would be with you now."

" But I sent him off."

" What did you say to him ? "

She remembered her clever little speech, and smiled. " I told him one man was too many."

" One man too many for a woman ! Well, that would make a holoptychius laugh."

Seeing that she failed to comprehend, he edged a little nearer and laid a hand on her knee.

" Excuse me ; but you are still very simple in certain directions. However, if you eat any more of these apples you will be too far ahead of the man."

" But he can eat the apples too."

The fatling shook his head.

" What you want from that man is an absorbing love, is it not ? "

" Oh, yes ! "

" And if that love were so tempest-uous and all-conquering as to blind his reason you would not complain."

" No, never ! "

" Well, it hurts me to say it, but

excessive wisdom is not a safe companion for that kind of love."

"Then he shall never taste an apple!"

"You had better let him have one, — just one, — or it may all end in a kind of toleration on your part, which is also dangerous. You don't want him *too* dull."

"Well, he shall eat one; but only *one*."

"You are a sensible girl. And there is one thing more I ought to tell you; that is, that you will have to leave this garden, now that you have eaten the apple."

This alarmed her, and she exclaimed reproachfully, "And you made me do it!"

"Yes; but you never could have lived without it. You see this garden is laid out exclusively for frigid old maids, — hard-headed, apathetic old maids, — who abominate men. Now, I would n't live in it if I could, and I know that

man would n't either. And you are
not the girl to be happy in here all by
yourself, with us fellows outside."

"No, I certainly am not!"

"Good for you! I knew you were
not. So there is no damage done.
The fun begins earlier, that's all. Now
good-by, for I must leave you;
but I shall be within call if
you ever need me;" and
with a knowing smile he
added, "Don't be cruel to
him."

And he skipped away,
half running, half fly-
ing, singing as he went;
and she noticed that
birds and animals pricked up their ears
as if his song was interesting, certain
of them following the singer, and always
in pairs. She wondered who and what
he was, and had little doubt of his being a person of importance.

And she was right. He was a person of considerable importance. And

38

ever since that day — which was so
long ago that no human being pretends to reckon it — he has led mankind the liveliest jig, upsetting the
natural course of history, dispensing
joy and agony with reckless waste,
and making hopeless fools of men
and women of every class and sta-
tion, and of all ages, colors and condi-
tions. And he is at it still.

He was hardly out of sight before
she began upon a second apple. That
clever little stranger might be correct
in theory but her instinct told her, that
in any relations between the sexes,
there could be no possible disadvantage
to the woman if she were a trifle
wiser than the man. After the second
apple she realized a mental change — a
quicker insight, a clearer comprehension, and, not least, a splendid confidence in herself that alone was worth
the price of all. She felt able to cope
with any masculine adversary. And
that second apple easily explains — at

least in this writer's opinion — certain
mental differences between men and
women that have flourished ever since
that day.

When the man returned, uncertain
of his reception, for he had heard no
call, he found the belle of the garden
reclining beneath the apple-tree, weaving
a sash of vine-leaves. For, among the
various ideas that had come to her since
partaking of the fruit, was a yearning
for personal decoration, — that desire to
wear something which has since developed into such unreasoning dimen-
sions. Throwing himself upon the grass
at her feet, he began with his old argument, that they marry at once, like the
rest of the world, and go to housekeeping. For a time she made no
answer, fearing he might suspect, either
by her language or by her manner, that
she was not the simple maid he had
known but an hour ago.

At last she moved her lips, raised her
eyebrows, and held her head a trifle to

one side, as if trying to think well of a poor suggestion.

"Come," he urged, "what do you say? It is a splendid idea."

"There is no hurry."

"As well do it now as later."

"As later? You speak as if it were sure to happen sometime; but I don't know why!"

"Because everybody else is married, birds, beasts and fishes, everything, from the elephant to the ant. It's a law of nature, an example we certainly ought to follow; and a fine one, too!"

"But there is not the least hurry, and you must remember that I never met you before to-day. However, I will think about it and tell you later."

"Oh, don't say that. It is mournful to be alone. Why, the world is a different thing since you came into it."

"Thank you; but I would like to look about a little before I settle down. I have seen nothing yet."

41

That First Affair

"We'll see it all on our wedding journey. I will take you everywhere. Come, please say yes."

She shook her head. "This is all dreadfully sudden; and how do I know that your love for me is serious."

"Indeed it is!"

"Am I worth a sacrifice?"

"Try me."

"Would you rather live alone in this beautiful garden, or with me outside?"

"With you outside, a thousand times over!" and he sat up with uplifted hand, as if taking an oath.

"Then eat this," and she took an apple from the ground beside her and held it toward him.

It was rather sudden, and he had a wholesome reverence for the garden authorities.

"No," he said with a shake of his head; "I will not do that, for we can both live here by letting the apples alone."

42

" But I have already eaten one."

" You have ! " and he looked seriously alarmed.

" I have," she answered calmly, and in her voice there was a shade of contempt. " I hardly supposed your devotion would stand a very serious test."

" You did n't ? Then you made a mistake. I will eat a dozen ! " and he took half the apple at a single bite.

" No ! you must eat but one ! "

" Why ? How many did you eat ? "

She hesitated, then compromised with truth, and answered, as she looked calmly into his eyes, " One."

He finished the apple, then looked up with a smile. " Now are you satisfied ? "

" Yes, partly. You have given a proof of your sincerity, but you cannot expect me to fall in love at such very short notice and with the first man I meet."

" Why not ? You can't do better, no matter how long you wait ; " and he added with a smile, "I am your only chance."

"A tempting assortment to pick from, but I must have time to consider. We never met before, and I know nothing whatever about you. Who are your parents? Where do they live, and what sort of people are they?"

For a moment he was disconcerted. Then he smiled as he answered, "My parents, I fancy, are much like your own."

"My own! Why, have I parents?"

"Have you never seen them?"

"No."

"Then probably you have n't any."

"Is it customary?" she inquired.

"Is what customary?"

"To have parents?"

"Not that I know of, but there would be no harm in them, I think. Young animals, I notice, depend entirely on their parents; but you and I were never young, so we did n't need them."

44

That First Affair

"I must say it seems more respectable in a way. A man without parents is a terrible mystery. You may be some awful animal in disguise; how do I know? Is n't there some one to refer me to? Have you no relations, no antecedents whatever?"

"No more than you have yourself."

This style of conversation was evidently beginning to annoy the suitor; but she could not resist having a little more fun with him, and replied, with exasperating sweetness, —

"But I don't ask you to marry me. I should certainly be rather hasty, to say the least, if I presented myself to the first person I encountered, when others are surely coming later."

"Other women may come too," he retorted.

"Then you can have one;" with which reply she arose and walked away. He remained seated upon the grass, also pretending to be more

45

offended than he was, and thus came
the first lovers' quarrel, similar in motive, execution, and result to the un-
numbered millions that have followed
since.

The cruel maiden disappeared among
the antediluvian plants, not halting until
well out of sight, and then she turned
and peered through the leaves, and
watched him. And when, a moment
later, he started after her, she ran further
into the forest seeking out-of-the-way
places, that his search might be in
vain. There was a sense of triumph
in this, and a pleasant excitement, as
the apples had taught her the importance of not yielding too easily. Of
time she took no thought, until in
sudden terror she realized what was
going on about her. It had all been
so gradual as to escape her notice;
but now the trees, the sky, and all the
flowers began to lose their color, and
those at a distance disappeared entirely.
They had vanished and ceased to exist.

That First Affair

At least, so it seemed to one of her
brief experience, and there was no one
to explain.

The big luminary had disappeared
behind a line of purple mountains that
seemed, in that direction, to mark the
edges of the world. She saw with
alarm that a peculiar change was creep-
ing over the earth. The air was
damper; the resplendent, many-colored
world she had known so short a time
ago had died away. In place of the
bright blue sky with its shining clouds,
there came, enveloping all things, a
solid mass of threatening black, through
which myriads of little eyes were glittering with a cold, unearthly light. She
trod on unfamiliar things, and they
tickled the soles of her tender, inexperienced feet. Twigs and branches
and mysterious things seemed to reach
out and touch her, like wicked fingers,
and she shrunk and grew weaker with
every step. She dared not call aloud,
for he might be far away, and these

other things would hear her voice and might eat her up.

At last, sinking to the ground, she wept from fear, for whatever existed was surely coming to an end. Crouching at the mercy of unknown things, with hope and courage gone, the approaching footsteps of some invisible creature brought a climax to her terror. But this terror changed suddenly to an overwhelming happiness as she recognized the outline of a human form.

With a joyful cry she ran toward him. The trembling figure found a welcome refuge in the encircling arms, and the encircling arms were exceeding glad to hold her.

The next morning, as they were finishing a simple but beatific breakfast, a dignified messenger, with wings and snowy draperies, appeared before them and gave official notice that they must quit the garden. But the apples had opened two pairs of eyes, and the youth

That First Affair

marched out with head erect and a smiling face, for he knew he carried with him the flower of the universe, the only one of her kind.

As for that loveless garden, nobody knows where it is.

And nobody cares.

THE QUEEN OF CALIFORNIA

Edward Everett Hale

THE QUEEN OF CALIFORNIA.

[IN the winter of 1862, I read for the first time the Spanish romance of the " Sergas of Esplandian." It is sometimes cited as the fifth book of Amadis of Gaul, but is by Garcia Ordoñez de Montalvo, the translator of Amadis, — a workman very inferior to Lobeira, who must be rated, I think, very highly among the writers of narrative. Coming to the allusion, in this forgotten romance, to " the island of California, very near to the Terrestrial Paradise," I saw at once that here was the origin of the name of the State of California, long sought for by the antiquarians of that State, but long forgotten. For the romance seems to have been published in 1510, — the edition of 1521 is now in existence, — while our California, even the peninsula of that name, was not discovered by the Spaniards till 1526, and was not named California till 1535.

At the next meeting of the American Antiquarian Society, I called their attention to this derivation of the name; and it has since been universally recognized as the origin of the name now so familiar to us. The romance of " Esplandian " is now so rare that I translated for the Atlantic Monthly all the parts which relate to the Queen of California, and I now republish them. The reader may be interested in examining first the history of the discussion of the subject, and then of the romance.]

THE name of California was given by Cortez, who discovered the peninsula in the year 1535. For the statement that he named it, we have the authority of Herrera.* It is proved, I think, that the expedition of Mendoza, in 1532, did not see California: it is certain that they gave it no name. Humboldt saw, in the archives of Mexico, a statement in manuscript that it was discovered in 1526 ; † but for this there is no other authority. It is certain that the name does not appear till 1535.

No etymology of this name has been presented satisfactory to the historians. Venegas,‡ the Jesuit historian of California, writing in 1758, sums up the matter in these words: "The most ancient name is California, used by Bernal Diaz, limited to a single bay. I could wish to gratify the reader by the etymology and true origin of this name ; but in none of the various dialects of the natives could the missionaries find the least traces of such a name being given by them to the country, or even to any harbor, bay, or small part of it. Nor can I subscribe to the etymology of some writers, who suppose the name to be given to it by the Spaniards, on their feeling an unusual heat at their first landing here ; that they thence called the country *California*, compounding the two Latin words *calida* and *fornax*, 'a hot furnace.' I

---

* Decade VIII. Book VI.

† It would be very desirable to have a new examination of the manuscript alluded to.

‡ The work of Venegas is chiefly due to the labors of Father Andres Marcos Buniel, according to Greenhow.

believe few will think the adventurers could boast of
so much literature."

I believe the Californian authors of our own time
agree with Venegas in rejecting this forced etymology.
The word to be made from it should be " Calidafor-
nacia." Dr. Bushnell, who says the heat of the interior valleys is that of a baker's furnace, speaks of a
region which Cortez never saw. It must be recollected, that, though Bernal Diaz only uses the name
for the bay, we have Herrera's better authority for
saying that Cortez gave it to the peninsula. But
neither peninsula nor bay is the oven described by Dr.
Bushnell.

Clavigero, in his " History of California," after giving this etymology, offers as an alternative the following, as the opinion " of the learned Jesuit, D. Giuseppe
Compoi ": " He believes that the name is composed of
the Spanish word *cala*, which means 'a little cove of
the sea'; and the Latin *fornix*, which means 'the
vault of a building.'" He thinks these words are thus
applied, " because, within Cape St. Lucas there is a
little cove of the sea, towards the western part of
which rises a rock, so worn out that on the upper part
of the hollow is seen a vault, as perfect as if made by
art. Cortez, therefore, observing this *cala*, or cove, and
this vault, probably called this port *California*, or *cala*
and *fornix*, — speaking half in Spanish, half in Latin."

Clavigero suggests, as an improvement on this somewhat wild etymology, that Cortez may have said *Cala*

fornax, " Cove furnace," — speaking, as in the Jesuit's suggestion, in two languages.

I am told that the Rev. Dean Trench, in one of his etymological works, suggests the Greek καλὴ πορνεία, — implying that the province seemed to the early settlers to have the attractions of a " beautiful adultery." I have not myself found this passage ; but I remember that Mr. Powers, the sculptor, represents California as a naked woman, seductive in front, but concealing a thorn-bush in her hands behind ; and he describes his statue as intended to represent her false seductions. Of this etymology, it is enough to say that Cortez and his men knew nothing of the seductions, — never finding gold or anything else tempting there ; and that the theory requires more, yet worse, scholarship at their hands than that of *calida fornax.*

Of all such speculations, Mr. Greenhow says very fitly, " None of them are satisfactory, or even ingenious."

It is in the worthless romance of the " Sergas of Esplandian," the son of Amadis of Gaul, — a book long since deservedly forgotten, — that there is to be found the source from which the adventurers transferred the name " California " to the new region of their discovery.

Towards the close of this romance, the various Christian knights assemble to defend the Emperor of the Greeks and the city of Constantinople against the attacks of the Turks and Infidels. On this occasion, in a romance published first in 1510, — twenty-five years before Cortez discovered the American California, — the name appears with precisely our spelling, in the following passage : —

Sergas, ch. 157. — " Know that, on the right hand of the Indies, there is an island called California, very near to the Terrestrial Paradise, which was peopled with black women, without any men among them, because they were accustomed to live after the fashion of Amazons. They were of strong and hardened bodies, of ardent courage, and of great force. The island was the strongest in the world, from its steep rocks and great cliffs. Their arms were all of gold ; and so were the caparisons of the wild beasts which they rode, after having tamed them ; for in all the island there is no other metal. They lived in caves very well worked out ; they had many ships, in which they sailed to other parts to carry on their forays." . . . .

In the paper to which these paragraphs are an introduction, I have translated every passage in the " Esplandian " which relates to the Queen of California, — the name appearing, as will be seen, in several distinct passages in the history.

This romance, as I have said, is believed to have been printed first in 1510. No copies of this edition, however, are extant. But of the edition of 1519 a copy is preserved ; and there are copies of successive editions of 1521, 1525, and 1526 ; in which last year two editions were published, — one at Seville, and the other at Burgos. All of these are Spanish.

It follows, almost certainly, that Cortez and his followers, in 1535, must have been acquainted with the romance ; and, as they sailed up the west side of Mexico, they supposed they were precisely at the place indicated, — " in the right hand of the Indies." It will be remembered also, that, by sailing in the same direction, Columbus, in his letter to the sovereigns, says, " he shall be sailing towards the Terrestrial Paradise." * We need not suppose that Cortez believed the romance, more than we do ; though we assert that he borrowed a name from it to indicate the peninsula he found " on the right side of the Indies, near to the Terrestrial Paradise." If it is necessary to analyze very carefully his motive for borrowing a name from a romance then so generally known, it will be enough to say that this romance credited the " Island of California " with great treasures of gold, and that it placed it very near the East Indies, in quest of which all the adventurers of that time were sailing. There is, however, no more reason for giving a serious motive for such a nomenclature than there is for the motive with which La Salle or his companions gave the name of La Chine to the point in Canada from which they hoped to reach China.

It is not strange that ecclesiastical historians, like

* See Appendix to this paper.

Venegas, should, in the eighteenth century, have lost sight of this origin of the name. It was not until 1683 that the Jesuit fraternity succeeded in planting an establishment there. Even then, their establishment was not permanent. For a century and a half, therefore, after Cortez's discovery, the province was of no value to any one, and its name was of as little interest. Long before the Jesuits planted it, the romance which gave it name was forgotten.

After 1542 no edition of the "Sergas of Esplandian" was printed in Spain, so far as we know, till 1575; and, after that of 1587, none for two hundred and seventy years more. The reaction had come. When the curate burned the books of Don Quixote, he burned this among the rest: he saved "Amadis of Gaul," but he burned "Esplandian." "We will not spare the son," said he, "for the virtues of his father." These words show Cervantes's estimate of it as early as 1605. It is not surprising, then, that an ecclesiastic like Venegas should not know, in 1758, the wild geography of the romance two centuries and more after it was written. D'Herbelay, the early French paraphraser of this romance, retains the whole story of the queen, but transfers the situation of California to the source of the River Borysthenes, near the descent of the Riphean Mountains.

The only effort to introduce it to modern readers, in any European country, until the recent Spanish reprint of 1857, is in the wretched paraphrase by Tressan, published in France in the last century. This author, as if to add to the probability of the tale, omits the name " California" in each of the passages relating to it ; so that, even in his forgotten work, we do not get hold of the lost clew.

The original work is now so rare that the copies in the valuable collection of Mr. Ticknor (now in the Boston Public Library) were till lately the only ones in Massachusetts. To that kind courtesy which opened his invaluable stores to every student, and illustrated it from the treasures of his own studies, am I indebted for all the authorities of value which I am able to cite here. In the large public libraries of the city of New York, I found in 1862 no copy of any of these romances, which made the lay literature of the first century after printing was invented ; but in the small yet well-selected library of the Free Academy of New York, and in that of Congress, are the " Amadis " and " Esplandian," in the recent Spanish edition edited by D. Pascal de Gayangos ; and the same edition is now, in 1872, in the Boston Library.

In ascribing to the " Esplandian " the origin of the name " California," I know that I furnish no etymology for that word. I have not found the word in any earlier romances. I will only suggest that the root *Calif*, the Spanish spelling for the sovereign of the Mussulman power of the time, was in the mind of the author as he invented these Amazon allies of the Infidel power.

The following is the account above referred to, with everything from the "Esplandian" which relates to the "Queen of California."

I can see the excitement which this title arouses as it is flashed across the sierras, down the valleys, and into the various reading-rooms and parlors of the Golden City of the Golden State. As the San Francisco "Bulletin" announces some day, that in the "Atlantic Monthly," issued in Boston the day before, one of the articles is on "The Queen of California," what contest, in every favored circle of the most favored of lands, who the Queen may be! Is it the blond maiden who took a string of hearts with her in a leash, when she left us one sad morning? is it the hardy, brown adventuress, who, in her bark-roofed lodge, serves us out our boiled dog daily, as we come home from our water-gullies, and sews on for us weekly the few buttons which we still find indispensable in that toil? is it some Jessie of the lion-heart, heroine of a hundred days or of a thousand? is it that witch with gray eyes, cunningly hidden, — were they puzzled last night, or were they all wisdom crowded? — as she welcomed me, and as she bade me good by? Good Heavens! how many Queens of California are regnant this day! and of any one of them this article might be written.

No, *Señores!* No, *Caballeros!* Throng down to the wharves to see the Golden Era or the Cornelius's Coffin, or whatever other mail-steamer may bring these words to your longing eyes. Open to the right and

left as Adams's express messenger carries the earliest
copy of the "Atlantic Monthly," sealed with the reddest wax, tied with the reddest tape, from the Corner
Store direct to him who was once the light and life of
the Corner Store, who now studies eschscholtzias
through a telescope thirty-eight miles away on Monte
Diablo!* Rush upon the newsboy who then brings
forth the bale of this Journal for the Multitude, to
find that the Queen of California of whom we write
is no modern queen, but that she reigned some five
hundred and fifty-five years ago. Her precise contem-
poraries were Amadis of Gaul, the Emperor Esplandian, and the Sultan Radiaro. And she *flourished*, as
the books say, at the time when this sultan made his
unsuccessful attack on the city of Constantinople, —
all of which she saw, part of which she was.

She was not *petite*, nor blond, nor golden-haired.
She was large, and black as the ace of clubs. But the
prejudice of color did not then exist even among the
most brazen-faced or the most copper-headed. For, as
you shall learn, she was reputed the most beautiful of
women; and it was she, O Californians! who wedded
the gallant Prince Talanque, — your first-known king.
The supporters of the arms of the beautiful shield of
the State of California should be, on the right, a knight
armed *cap-à-pie*, and, on the left, an Amazon sable,
clothed in skins, as you shall now see.

* In a letter from Starr King, written not long before I wrote these
words, he spoke of seeing the color of Monte Diablo change when the
eschscholtzias were in bloom.

Mr. E. E. Hale, of Boston, sent to the Antiquarian Society last year a paper which shows that the name of California was known to literature before it was given to our peninsula by Cortez. Cortez discovered the peninsula in 1535, and seems to have called it California then. But Mr. Hale shows that, twenty-five years before that time, in a romance called the "Deeds of Esplandian," the name of California was given to an island "on the right hand of the Indies." This romance was a sequel, or fifth book, to the celebrated romance of "Amadis of Gaul." Such books made the principal reading of the young blades of that day who could read at all. It seems clear enough that Cortez and his friends, coming to the point farthest to the west then known, — which all of them, from Columbus down, supposed to be the East Indies, — gave to their discovery the name, familiar to romantic adventurers, of *California*, to indicate their belief that it was on the "right hand of the Indies." Just so Columbus called his discoveries "the Indies"; just so was the name "El Dorado" given to regions which it was hoped would prove to be golden. The romance had said, that, in the whole of the romance-island of California, there was no metal but gold. Cortez, who did not find a pennyweight of dust in the real California, still had no objection to giving so golden a name to his discovery.

Mr. Hale, with that brevity which becomes antiquarians, does not go into any of the details of the life and adventures of the Queen of California as the romance describes them. We propose, in this paper, to supply from it this reticency of his essay.

The reader must understand, then, that, in this romance, printed in 1510, sixty years or less after Constantinople really fell into the hands of the Turks, the author describes a pretended assault made upon it by the Infidel powers, and the rallying for its rescue of Amadis and Perion and Lisuarte, and all the princes of chivalry with whom the novel of " Amadis of Gaul" has dealt. They succeed in driving away the Pagans, " as you shall hear." In the midst of this great crusade, every word of which, of course, is the most fictitious of fiction, appear the episodes which describe California and its Queen.

First, of California itself here is the description : —

" Now you are to hear the most extraordinary thing that ever was heard of in any chronicles, or in the memory of man, by which the city would have been lost on the next day, but that where the danger came, there the safety came also. Know, then, that, on the right hand of the Indies, there is an island called California, very close to the side of the Terrestrial Paradise,* and it was peopled by black women, without

* This was according to the cosmogony of the days when Columbus sailed on his fourth voyage, in which he hoped to pass through what we now know as the Isthmus of Panama, and sail northwestward. He wrote to his king and queen that thus he should come as near as men could come to "the Terrestrial Paradise." On this curious subject I venture to add to this article a paper which I submitted to the American Antiquarian Society, at its meeting in April, 1872.

any man among them, for they lived in the fashion of Amazons. They were of strong and hardy bodies, of ardent courage and great force. Their island was the strongest in all the world, with its steep cliffs and rocky shores. Their arms were all of gold, and so was the harness of the wild beasts which they tamed and rode. For, in the whole island, there was no metal but gold. They lived in caves wrought out of the rock with much labor. They had many ships with which they sailed out to other countries to obtain booty.

"In this island, called California, there were many griffins, on account of the great ruggedness of the country, and its infinite host of wild beasts, such as never were seen in any other part of the world. And when these griffins were yet small, the women went out with traps to take them. They covered themselves over with very thick hides, and when they had caught the little griffins, they took them to their caves, and brought them up there. And being themselves quite a match for the griffins, they fed them with the men whom they took prisoners, and with the boys to whom they gave birth, and brought them up with such arts that they got much good from them, and no harm. Every man who landed on the island was immediately devoured by these griffins; and although they had had enough, none the less would they seize them, and carry them high up in the air in their flight; and when they were tired of carrying them, would let them fall anywhere as soon as they died."

These griffins are the Monitors of the story, or, if the reader pleases, the Merrimacs. After this description, the author goes on to introduce us to our Queen. Observe, O reader, that, although very black and very large, she is very beautiful. Why did not Powers carve his statue of California out of the blackest of Egyptian marbles ? Try once more, Mr. Powers ! We have found her now. Εὑρήκαμεν.

"Now, at the time when those great men of the Pagans sailed with their great fleets, as the history has told you, there reigned in this island of California a Queen, very large in person, the most beautiful of all of them, of blooming years, and in her thoughts desirous of achieving great things, strong of limb, and of great courage, more than any of those who had filled her throne before her. She heard tell that all the greater part of the world was moving in this onslaught against the Christians. She did not know what Christians were ; for she had no knowledge of any parts of the world excepting those which were close to her. But she desired to see the world and its various people ; and thinking, that, with the great strength of herself and of her women, she should have the greater part of their plunder, either from her rank or from her prowess, she began to talk with all of those who were most skilled in war, and told them that it would be well, if, sailing in their great fleets, they also entered on this expedition, in which all these great princes and lords were embarking. She animated and excited

them, showing them the great profits and honors which
they would gain in this enterprise, — above all, the
great fame which would be theirs in all the world;
while, if they stayed in their island, doing nothing but
what their grandmothers did, they were really buried
alive, — they were dead while they lived, passing their
days without fame and without glory, as did the very
brutes."

Now, the people of California were as willing then
to embark in distant expeditions of honor as they are
now. And the first battalion that ever sailed from the
ports of that country was thus provided.

"So much did this mighty Queen, Calafia, say to
her people, that she not only moved them to consent
to this enterprise, but they were so eager to extend
their fame through other lands that they begged her to
hasten to sea, so that they might earn all these honors,
in alliance with such great men. The Queen, seeing
the readiness of her subjects, without any delay gave
order that her great fleet should be provided with food,
and with arms all of gold, — more of everything than
was needed. Then she commanded that her largest
vessel should be prepared with gratings of the stoutest
timber; and she bade place in it as many as five hundred of these griffins, of which I tell you that, from
the time they were born, they were trained to feed on
men. And she ordered that the beasts on which she
and her people rode should be embarked, and all the
best-armed women and those most skilled in war whom

she had in her island. And then, leaving such force in the island that it should be secure, with the others she went to sea. And they made such haste that they arrived at the fleets of the Pagans the night after the battle of which I have told you; so that they were received with great joy, and the fleet was visited at once by many great lords, and they were welcomed with great acceptance. She wished to know at once in what condition affairs were, asking many questions, which they answered fully. Then she said, —

" ' You have fought this city with your great forces, and you cannot take it; now, if you are willing, I wish to try what my forces are worth to-morrow, if you will give orders accordingly.'

" All these great lords said that they would give such commands as she should bid them.

" ' Then send word to all your other captains that they shall to-morrow on no account leave their camps, they nor their people, until I command them; and you shall see a combat more remarkable than you have ever seen or heard of.'

" Word was sent at once to the great Sultan of Liquia, and the Sultan of Halapa, who had command of all the men who were there; and they gave these orders to all their people, wondering much what was the thought of this Queen."

Up to this moment, it may be remarked, these Monitors, as we have called the griffins, had never been fairly tried in any attack on fortified towns. The Dupont of the fleet, whatever her name may have been, may well have looked with some curiosity on the issue. The experiment was not wholly successful, as will be seen.

"When the night had passed and the morning came, the Queen Calafia sallied on shore, she and her women, armed with that armor of gold, all adorned with the most precious stones, — which are to be found in the island of California like stones of the field for their abundance. And they mounted on their fierce beasts, caparisoned as I have told you; and then she ordered that a door should be opened in the vessel where the griffins were. They, when they saw the field, rushed forward with great haste, showing great pleasure in flying through the air, and at once caught sight of the host of men who were close at hand. As they were famished, and knew no fear, each griffin pounced upon his man, seized him in his claws, carried him high into the air, and began to devour him. They shot many arrows at them, and gave them many great blows with lances and with swords. But their feathers were so tight joined and so stout, that no one could strike through to their flesh." (This is Armstrong *versus* Monitor.) "For their own party, this was the most lovely chase and the most agreeable that they had ever seen till then; and as the Turks saw them flying on high with their enemies, they gave such loud and clear shouts of joy as pierced the heavens. And it was the most sad and bitter thing for those in the city, when the father saw the son lifted in the air, and the son his father, and the brother his brother; so that they all wept and raved, as was sad indeed to see.

"When the griffins had flown through the air for a while, and had dropped their prizes, some on the earth and some on the sea, they turned, as at first, and, without any fear, seized up as many more; at which their masters had so much the more joy, and the Christians so much the more misery. What shall I tell you? The terror was so great among them all that, while some hid themselves away under the vaults of the towers for safety, all the others disappeared from the ramparts, so that there were none left for the defence. Queen Calafia saw this, and, with a loud voice, she bade the two Sultans, who commanded the troops, send for the ladders, for the city was taken. At once they all rushed forward, placed the ladders, and mounted upon the wall. But the griffins, who had already dropped those whom they had seized before, as soon as they saw the Turks, having no knowledge of them, seized upon them just as they had seized upon the Christians, and, flying through the air, carried them up also, when, letting them fall, no one of them escaped death. Thus were exchanged the pleasure and the pain. For those on the outside now were those who mourned in great sorrow for those who were so handled; and those who were within, who, seeing their enemies advance on every side, had thought they were beaten, now took great comfort. So, at this moment, as those on the ramparts stopped, panic-struck, fearing that they should die as their comrades did, the Christians leaped forth from the vaults where they were hiding, and quickly slew many of the Turks who were gathered on the walls, and compelled the rest to leap down, and then sprang back to their hiding-places, as they saw the griffins return.

"When Queen Calafia saw this she was very sad ; and she said, 'O ye idols in whom I believe and whom I worship, what is this which has happened as favorably to my enemies as to my friends? I believed that with your aid and with my strong forces and great munition I should be able to destroy them. But it has not so proved.' And she gave orders to her women that they should mount the ladders and struggle to gain the towers and put to the sword all those who took refuge in them to be secure from the griffins. They obeyed their Queen's commands, dismounted at once, placing before their breasts such breastplates as no weapon could pierce, and, as I told you, with the armor all of gold which covered their legs and their arms. Quickly they crossed the plain, and mounted the ladders lightly, and possessed themselves of the whole circuit of the walls, and began to fight fiercely with those who had taken refuge in the vaults of the towers. But they defended themselves bravely, being indeed in quarters well protected, with but narrow doors. And those of the city, who were in the streets below, shot at the women with arrows and darts, which pierced them through the sides, so that they received many wounds, because their golden armor was so weak." (This is Keokuk *versus* Armstrong.) * " And the griffins returned, flying above them, and would not leave them.

" When Queen Calafia saw this, she cried to the Sultans, ' Make your troops mount, that they may defend mine against these fowls of mine who have dared attack them.' At once the Sultans commanded their people to ascend the ladders and gain the circle and the towers, in order that by night the whole host might join them, and they might gain the city. The soldiers rushed from their camps, and mounted on the wall where the women were fighting; but when the griffins saw them, at once they seized on them as ravenously as if all that day they had not caught anybody. And when the women threatened them with their knives, they were only the more enraged, so that, although they took shelter for themselves, the griffins dragged them out by main strength, lifted them up into the air, and then let them fall, — so that they all died. The fear and panic of the Pagans were so great that, much more quickly than they had mounted, did they descend, and take refuge in their camp. The Queen, seeing this rout without remedy, sent at once to command those who held watch and guard on the griffins,

---

* It is perhaps already forgotten that the plated ship Keokuk did not withstand the Armstrong bolts as well as the turrets of the Monitors.

that they should recall them, and shut them up in the
vessel. They, then, hearing the Queen's command,
mounted on top of the mast, and called them with
loud voices in their language ; and they, as if they had
been human beings, all obeyed, and obediently returned
into their cages."

The first day's attack of these flying Monitors on
the beleaguered city was not, therefore, a distinguished
success. The author derives a lesson from it, which
we do not translate, but recommend to the students of
present history. It fills a whole chapter, of which the
title is, "Exhortation addressed by the author to the
Christians, setting before their eyes the great obedience
which these griffins, brute animals, rendered to those
who had instructed them."

The Sultans may have well doubted whether their
new ally was quite what she had claimed to be. She
felt this herself, and said to them, —

" ' Since my coming has caused you so much injury,
I wish that it may cause you equal pleasure. Command your people that they shall sally out, and we will
go to the city against those knights who dare to appear
before us, and we will let them press on the most severe
combat that they can, and I, with my people, will take
the front of the battle.'

" The Sultans gave command at once to all of their
soldiers who had armor, that they should rush forth
immediately, and should join in mounting upon the
rampart, now that these birds were encaged again.

And they, with the horsemen, followed close upon Queen Calafia, and immediately the army rushed forth, and pressed upon the wall; but not so prosperously as they had expected, because the people of the town were already there in their harness; and, as the Pagans mounted upon their ladders, the Christians threw them back, whence very many of them were killed and wounded. Others pressed forward with their iron picks and other tools, and dug fiercely in the circuit of the wall. These were very much distressed and put in danger by the oil and other things which were thrown upon them, but not so much but that they succeeded in making many breaches and openings. But when this came to the ears of the Emperor, who always kept command of ten thousand horsemen, he commanded all of them to defend these places as well as they could. So that, to the grief of the Pagans, the people repaired the breaches with many timbers and stones and piles of earth.

"When the Queen saw this repulse, she rushed with her own attendants with great speed to the gate Aquileña, which was guarded by Norandel.* She herself went in advance of the others, wholly covered with one of those shields which we have told you they wore, and with her lance held strongly in her hand. Norandel, when he saw her coming, went forth to meet her, and they met so vehemently that their lances were

* Norandel was the half-brother of Amadis, both of them being sons of Lisuarte, King of England.

broken in pieces, and yet neither of them fell. Norandel at once put hand upon his sword, and the Queen
upon her great knife, of which the blade was more
than a palm broad, and they gave each other great
blows. At once they all joined in a *mêlée*, one against
another, all so confused and with such terrible blows
that it was a great marvel to see it; and if some of the
women fell upon the ground, so did some of the cavaliers. And if this history does not tell in extent which
of them fell, and by what blow of each, showing the
great force and courage of the combatants, it is because
their number was so great, and they fell so thick, one
upon another, that that great master, Helisabat, who
saw and described the scene, could not determine what
in particular passed in these exploits, except in a few
very rare affairs, like this of the Queen and Norandel,
who both joined fight as you have heard."

It is to the great master Helisabat that a grateful
posterity owes all these narratives and the uncounted
host of romances which grew from them. For, in the
first place, he was the skilful leech who cured all the
wounds of all the parties of distinction who were not
intended to die; and, in the second place, his notes
furnish the *mémoires pour servir*, of which all the
writers say they availed themselves. The originals,
alas! are lost.

"The tumult was so great that at once the battle
between these two was ended, those on each side coming to the aid of their chief. Then, I tell you that

the things that this Queen did in arms, like slaying knights, or throwing them wounded from their horses, as she pressed audaciously forward among her enemies, were such, that it cannot be told nor believed that any woman has ever shown such prowess.

"And as she dealt with so many noble knights, and no one of them left her without giving her many and heavy blows, yet she received them all upon her very strong and hard shield.

"When Talanque and Maneli* saw what this woman was doing, and the great loss which those of their own party were receiving from her, they rushed out upon her, and struck her with such blows as if they considered her possessed. And her sister, who was named Liota, who saw this, rushed in, like a mad lioness, to her succor, and pressed the knights so mortally that, to the loss of their honor, she drew Calafia from their power, and placed her among her own troops again. And at this time you would have said that the people of the fleets had the advantage, so that, if it had not been for the mercy of God and the great force of the Count Frandalo and his companions, the city would have been wholly lost. Many fell dead on both sides, but many more of the Pagans, because they had the weaker armor.

"Thus," continues the romance, " as you have heard, went on this attack and cruel battle till nearly night. At this time there was no one of the gates open, ex-

* Maneli was son of Cildadan, King of Ireland.

cepting that which Norandel guarded. As to the others, the knights, having been withdrawn from them, ought, of course, to have bolted them; yet it was very different, as I will tell you. For, as the two Sultans greatly desired to see these women fight, they had bidden their own people not to enter into the lists. But when they saw how the day was going, they pressed upon the Christians so fiercely that gradually they might all enter into the city; and, as it was, more than a hundred men and women did enter. And God, who guided the Emperor, having directed him to keep the other gates shut, knowing in what way the battle fared, he pressed them so hardly with his knights that, killing some, he drove the others out. Then the Pagans lost many of their people, as they slew them from the towers, — more than two hundred of the women being slain. And those within also were not without great loss, since ten of the *cruzados* were killed, which gave great grief to their companions. These were Ledaderin de Fajarque, Trion and Imosil de Borgona, and the two sons of Isanjo. All the people of the city having returned, as I tell you, the Pagans also retired to their camps, and the Queen Calafia to her fleet, since she had not yet taken quarters on shore. And the other people entered into their ships; so that there was no more fighting that day."

I have translated this passage at length, because it gives the reader an idea of the romantic literature of that day, — literally its only literature, excepting books

of theology or of devotion. Over acres of such reading, served out in large folios, — the yellow-covered
novels of their time, — did the Pizarros and Balboas
and Cortezes and other young blades while away the
weary hours of their camp life. Glad enough was
Cortez out of such a tale to get the noble name of his
great discovery.

The romance now proceeds to bring the different
princes of chivalry from the West, as it has brought
Calafia from the East. As soon as Amadis arrives at
Constantinople, he sends for his son Esplandian, who
was already in alliance with the Emperor of Greece.
The Pagan Sultan of Liquia, and the Queen Calafia,
hearing of their arrival, send them the following challenge : —

"Radiaro, Sultan of Liquia, shield and rampart of
the Pagan Law, destroyer of Christians, cruel enemy
of the enemies of the Gods, and the very Mighty Queen
Calafia, Lady of the great island of California, famous
for its great abundance of gold and precious stones:
we have to announce to you, Amadis of Gaul, King of
Great Britain, and you his son, Knight of the Great
Serpent, that we are come into these parts with the
intention of destroying this city of Constantinople, on
account of the injury and loss which the much hon-
ored King Amato of Persia, our cousin and friend, has
received from this bad Emperor, giving him favor and
aid because a part of his territory has been taken away
from him by fraud. And as our desire in this thing is

also to gain glory and fame in it, so also has fortune treated us favorably in that regard, for we know the great news, which has gone through all the world, of your great chivalry. We have agreed, therefore, if it is agreeable to you, or if your might is sufficient for it, to attempt a battle of our persons against yours in presence of this great company of the nations, the conquered to submit to the will of the conquerors, or to go to any place where they may order. And if you refuse this, we shall be able, with much cause, to join all your past glories to our own, counting them as being gained by us, whence it will clearly be seen in the future how the victory will be on our side."

This challenge was taken to the Christian camp by a black and beautiful damsel, richly attired, and was discussed there in council. Amadis put an end to the discussion by saying, —

" ' My good lords, as the affairs of men, like those of nations, are in the hands and will of God, whence no one can escape but as He wills, if we should in any way withdraw from this demand, it would give great courage to our enemies, and, more than this, great injury to our honor; especially so in this country, where we are strangers, and no one has seen what our power is, which in our own land is notorious, so that, while there we may be esteemed for courage, here we should be judged the greatest of cowards. Thus, placing confidence in the mercy of the Lord, I determine that the battle shall take place without delay.'

" ' If this is your wish,' said King Lisuarte and King Perion, ' so may it be, and may God help you with His grace !'

" Then the King Amadis said to the damsel, —

" ' Friend, tell your lord and the Queen Calafia that we desire the battle with those arms that are most agreeable to them ; that the field shall be this field, divided in the middle, — I giving my word that for nothing which may happen will we be succored by our own. And let them give the same order to their own ; and if they wish the battle now, now it shall be.'

" The damsel departed with this reply, which she repeated to those two princes. And the Queen Calafia asked her how the Christians appeared.

" ' Very nobly,' replied she ; ' for they are all handsome and well armed. Yet I tell you, Queen, that, among them, this Knight of the Serpent [Esplandian, son of Amadis] is such as neither the past nor the present, nor, I believe, any who are to come, have ever seen one so handsome and so elegant, nor will see in the days which are to be. O Queen, what shall I say to you, but that, if he were of our faith, we might believe that our Gods had made him with their own hands, with all their power and wisdom, so that he lacks in nothing ?'

" The Queen, who heard her, said, —

" ' Damsel, my friend, your words are too great.'

" ' It is not so,' said she ; ' for, excepting the sight of him, there is nothing else which can give account of his great excellence.'

"'Then I say to you,' said the Queen, 'that I will not fight with such a man until I have first seen and talked with him; and I make this request to the Sultan, that he will gratify me in this thing, and arrange that I may see him.'

"The Sultan said, —

"'I will do everything, O Queen, agreeably to your wish.'

"'Then,' said the damsel, 'I will go and obtain that which you ask for, according to your desire.'

"And, turning her horse, she approached the camp again, so that all thought that she brought the agreement for the battle. But as she approached, she called the Kings to the door of the tent, and said, —

"'King Amadis, the Queen Calafia demands of you that you give order for her safe conduct, that she may come to-morrow morning and see your son.'

"Amadis began to laugh, and said to the Kings, —

"'How does this demand seem to you?'

"'I say, let her come,' said King Lisuarte: 'it is a very good thing to see the most distinguished woman in the world.'

"'Take this for your reply,' said Amadis to the damsel; 'and say that she shall be treated with all truth and honor.'

"The damsel, having received this message, returned with great pleasure to the Queen, and told her what it was. The Queen said to the Sultan, —

"'Wait and prosper, then, till I have seen him; and

charge your people that in the mean time there may be no outbreak.'

" ' Of that,' he said, ' you may be secure.'

" At once she returned to her ships ; and she spent the whole night thinking whether she would go with arms or without them. But at last she determined that it would be more dignified to go in the dress of a woman. And when the morning came she rose, and directed them to bring one of her dresses, all of gold, with many precious stones, and a turban wrought with great art. It had a volume of many folds, in the manner of a *toca*, and she placed it upon her head as if it had been a hood [*capellina*] ; it was all of gold, embroidered with stones of great value. They brought out an animal which she rode, the strangest that ever was seen. It had ears as large as two shields ; a broad forehead which had but one eye, like a mirror ; the openings of its nostrils were very large, but its nose was short and blunt. From its mouth turned up two tusks, each of them two palms long. Its color was yellow, and it had many violet spots upon its skin, like an ounce. It was larger than a dromedary, had its feet cleft like those of an ox, and ran as swiftly as the wind, and skipped over the rocks as lightly, and held itself erect on any part of them, as do the mountain-goats. Its food was dates and figs and peas, and nothing else. Its flank and haunches and breast were very beautiful. On this animal, of which you have thus heard, mounted this beautiful Queen, and there rode behind her two thousand women of her train, dressed in the very richest clothes. There brought up the rear twenty damsels clothed in uniform, the trains of whose dresses extended so far that, falling from each beast, they dragged four fathoms on the ground.

"With this equipment and ornament the Queen proceeded to the Emperor's camp, where she saw all the Kings, who had come out upon the plain. They had seated themselves on very rich chairs, upon cloth of gold, and they themselves were armed, because they had not much confidence in the promises of the Pagans. So they sallied out to receive her at the door of the tent, where she was dismounted into the arms of Don Quadragante;* and the two Kings, Lisuarte and Perion, took her by the hands, and placed her between them in a chair. When she was seated, looking from one side to the other, she saw Esplandian next to King Lisuarte, who held him by the hand; and from the superiority of his beauty to that of all the others, she knew at once who he was, and said to herself, ' O, my Gods! what is this? I declare to you, I have never seen any one who can be compared to him, nor shall I ever see any one.' And he turning his beautiful eyes upon her beautiful face, she perceived that the rays which leaped out from his resplendent beauty, entering in at her eyes, penetrated to her heart in such a way, that, if she were not conquered yet by the great

* Quadragante was a distinguished giant, who had been conquered by Amadis, and was now his sure friend.

force of arms, or by the great attacks of her enemies, she was softened and broken by that sight and by her amorous passion, as if she had passed between mallets of iron. And as she saw this, she reflected that, if she stayed longer, the great fame which she had acquired as a manly cavalier, by so many dangers and labors, would be greatly hazarded. She saw that by any delay she should expose herself to the risk of dishonor, by being turned to that native softness which women of nature consider to be an ornament; and therefore resisting, with great pain, the feelings which she had subjected to her will, she rose from her seat, and said, —

"'Knight of the Great Serpent, for two excellences which distinguish you above all mortals I have made inquiry. The first, that of your great beauty, which, if one has not seen, no relation is enough to tell the greatness of; the other, the valor and force of your brave heart. The one of these I have seen, which is such as I have never seen nor could hope to see, though many years of searching should be granted me. The other shall be made manifest on the field, against this valiant Radiaro, Sultan of Liquia. Mine shall be shown against this mighty king your father; and if fortune grant that we come alive from this battle, as we hope to come from other battles, then I will talk with you, before I return to my home, of some things of my own affairs.'

"Then, turning towards the Kings, she said to them,

"'Kings, rest in good health. I go hence to that place where you shall see me with very different dress from this which I now wear, hoping that in that field the King Amadis, who trusts in fickle fortune that he may never be conquered by any knight, however valiant, nor by any beast, however terrible, may there be conquered by a woman.'

"Then taking the two older Kings by the hand, she permitted them to help her mount upon her strange steed."

At this point the novel assumes a tone of high virtue (*virtus*, mannishness, prejudice of the more brutal sex) on the subject of woman's rights, in especial of woman's right to fight in the field with gold armor, lance in rest, and casque closed. We will show the reader, as she follows us, how careful she must be, if, in any island of the sea which has been slipped by, unknown, by the last five centuries, she ever happen to meet a cavalier of the true school of chivalry.

Esplandian himself would not in any way salute the Queen Calafia, as she left him. Nor was this a copperhead prejudice of color; for that prejudice was not yet known.

"He made no reply to her, both because he looked at her as something strange, however beautiful she appeared to him, and because he saw her come thus in arms, so different from the style in which a woman should have come. For he considered it as very dishonorable that she should attempt anything so differ-

ent from what the word of God commanded her, that
the woman should be in subjection to the man, but
rather should prefer to be the ruler of all men, not by
her courtesy, but by force of arms, and, above all, because he hated to place himself in relations with her,
because she was one of the infidels whom he mortally
despised and had taken a vow to destroy."

The romance then goes into an account of the preparations for the contest on both sides.

After all the preliminaries were arranged, " they separated for a little, and rode together furiously in full
career. The Sultan struck Esplandian in the shield
with so hard a blow that a part of the lance passed
through it for as much as an ell, so that all who saw it
thought that it had passed through the body. But it
was not so, but the lance passed under the arm next
the body, and went out on the other side without
touching him. But Esplandian, who knew that his
much-loved lady was looking on [Leonorina, the
daughter of the Emperor of Constantinople], so struck
the Sultan's shield that the iron passed through it and
struck him on some of the strongest plates of his
armor, upon which the spear turned. But, with the
force of the encounter, it shook him so roughly from
the saddle that it rolled him upon the ground, and so
shook the helmet as to tear it off from his head; and
thus Esplandian passed by him very handsomely, without receiving any stroke himself. The Queen rushed
upon Amadis, and he upon her, and, before they met,

each pointed lance at the other, and they received the blows upon their shields in such guise that her spear flew in pieces, while that of Amadis slipped off and was thrown on one side. Then they both met, shield to shield, with such force that the Queen was thrown upon the ground, and the horse of Amadis was so wounded that he fell with his head cut in two, and held Amadis with one leg under him. When Esplandian saw this, he leaped from his horse and saved him from that peril. Meanwhile, the Queen, being put to her defence, put hand to her sword, and joined herself to the Sultan, who had raised himself with great difficulty, because his fall was very heavy, and stood there with his sword and helmet in his hand. They came on to fight very bravely; but Esplandian, standing, as I told you, in presence of the Infanta whom he prized so much, gave the Sultan such hard pressure with such heavy blows, that, although he was one of the bravest knights of the Pagans, and by his own prowess had won many dangerous battles, and was very dexterous in that art, yet all this served him for nothing; he could neither give nor parry blows, and constantly lost ground. The Queen, who had joined fight with Amadis, began giving him many fierce blows, some of which he received upon his shield, while he let others be lost; yet he would not put his hand upon his sword, but, instead of that, took a fragment of the lance which she had driven through his shield, and struck her on the top of the helmet with it, so that in a little while he had knocked the crest away."

We warned those of our fair readers who may have occasion to defend their rights at the point of the lance, that the days of chivalry or the cavaliers of chivalry would be very unhandsome in applying to them the rules of the tourney. Amadis, it will be observed here, does not condescend to use his sword against a woman. And this is not from tenderness, but from contempt. For when the Queen saw that he only took the broken truncheon of his lance to her, she fairly asked him why.

"'How is this, Amadis?' she said. 'Do you consider my force so slight that you think to conquer me with sticks?'

"And he said to her, —

"'Queen, I have always been in the habit of serving women and aiding them; and as you are a woman, if I should use any weapon against you, I should deserve to lose all the honors I have ever gained.'

"'What, then!' said the Queen, 'do you rank me among them? You shall see!'

"And taking her sword in both her hands, she struck him with great rage. Amadis raised his shield and received the blow upon it, which was so brave and strong that the shield was cut in two. Then, seeing her joined to him so closely, he passed his stick into his left hand, seized her by the rim of the shield, and pulled her so forcibly that, breaking the great thongs by which she held upon it, he took it from her, lifting it up in one hand, and forced her to kneel with one knee on the ground; and when she lightly sprang up, Amadis threw away his own shield, and, seizing the other, took the stick, and sprang to her, saying, —

" 'Queen, yield yourself my prisoner, now that your Sultan is conquered.'

" She turned her head, and saw that Esplandian had the Sultan already surrendered as his prize. But she said, ' Let me try fortune yet one more turn'; and then, raising her sword with both her hands, she struck upon the crest of his helmet, thinking she could cut it and his head in two. But Amadis warded the blow very lightly and turned it off, and struck her so heavy a stroke with that fragment of the lance upon the crest of her helmet that he stunned her, and made her sword fall from her hands. Amadis seized the sword, and, when she was thus disarmed, caught at her helmet so strongly that he dragged it from her head, and said, —

" ' Now are you my prisoner ? '

" ' Yes,' replied she; ' for there is nothing left for me to do.'

" At this moment Esplandian came to them with the Sultan, who had surrendered himself; and, in sight of all the army, they repaired to the royal encampment, where they were received with great pleasure, not only on account of the great victory in battle, which, after the great deeds in arms which they had wrought before, as this history has shown, they did not regard as very remarkable, but because they took this success as a good omen for the future. The King Amadis asked the Count Gandalin to lead their prisoners to the Infanta Leonorina, in his behalf and that of his son Esplandian, and to say to her that he begged her to do honor to the Sultan, because he was so great a prince and so strong a knight, and, withal, very noble ; and to do honor to the Queen, *because she was a woman ;* and to say that he trusted in God that thus they should send to her all those whom they took captive alive in the battles which awaited them.

"The Count took them in charge, and, as the city was very near, they soon arrived at the palace. Then, coming into the presence of the Infanta, he delivered to her the prisoners, and gave the message with which he was intrusted. The Infanta replied to him, —

"'Tell King Amadis that I thank him greatly for this present which he sends me ; that I am sure that the good fortune and great courage which appear in this adventure will appear in those which await us ; and that we are very desirous to see him here, that, when we discharge our obligation to his son, we may have him as a judge between us.'

"The Count kissed her hand, and returned to the royal camp. Then the Infanta sent to the Empress, her mother, for a rich robe and head-dress, and, having disarmed the Queen, made her array herself in them ; and she did the same for the Sultan, having sent for other robes from the Emperor, her father, and having dressed their wounds with certain preparations made by Master Helisabat. Then the Queen, though of so great fortune, was much astonished to see the great beauty of Leonorina, and said, —

"'I tell you, Infanta, that in the same measure in which I was astonished to see the beauty of your cavalier, Esplandian, am I now overwhelmed, beholding yours. If your deeds correspond to your appearance, I hold it no dishonor to be your prisoner.'

"'Queen,' said the Infanta, 'I hope the God in whom I trust will so direct events that I shall be able to fulfil every obligation which conquerors acknowledge toward those who submit to them.'"

With this chivalrous little conversation the Queen of California disappears from the romance, and consequently from all written history, till the very *dénouement* of the whole story, where, when the rest is "wound up," she is wound up also, to be set a-going again in her own land of California. And if the chroniclers of California find no records of her in any of the griffin caves of the Black Cañon, it is not our fault, but theirs. Or, possibly, did she and her party suffer shipwreck on the return passage from Constantinople to the Golden Gate? Their probable route must have been through the Ægean, over Lebanon and Anti-Lebanon to the Euphrates ("I will sail a fleet over the Alps," said Cromwell), down Chesney's route to the Persian Gulf, and so home.

After the Sultan and the Queen are taken prisoners, there are reams of terrific fighting, in which King

Lisuarte and King Perion and a great many other people are killed ; but finally the " Pagans" are all routed, and the Emperor of Greece retires into a monastery, having united Esplandian with his daughter Leonorina, and abdicated the throne in their favor. Among the first acts of their new administration is the disposal of Calafia.

"As soon as the Queen Calafia saw these nuptials, having no more hope of him whom she so much loved [Esplandian], for a moment her courage left her ; and coming before the new Emperor and these great lords, she thus spoke to them : —

" ' I am a queen of a great kingdom, in which there is the greatest abundance of all that is most valued in the world, such as gold and precious stones. My lineage is very old, — for it comes from royal blood so far back that there is no memory of the beginnings of it, — and my honor is as perfect as it was at my birth. My fortune has brought me into these countries, whence I hoped to bring away many captives, but where I am myself a captive. I do not say of this captivity in which you see me, that, after all the great experiences of my life, favorable and adverse, I had believed that I was strong enough to parry the thrusts of fortune ; but I have found that my heart was tried and afflicted in my imprisonment, because the great beauty of this new Emperor overwhelmed me in the moment that my eyes looked upon him. I trusted in my greatness, and that immense wealth which excites and unites so many, that, if I would turn to your religion, I might gain him for a husband; but when I came into the presence of this lovely Empress, I regarded it as certain that they belonged to each other by their equal rank; and that argument, which showed the vanity of my thoughts, brought me to the determination in which I now stand. And since Eternal Fortune has taken the direction of my passion, I, throwing all my own strength into oblivion, as the wise do in those affairs which have no remedy, seek, if it please you, to take for my husband some other man, who may be the son of a king, to be of such power as a good knight ought to have; and I will become a Christian. For, as I have seen the ordered order of your religion, and the great disorder of all others, I have seen that it is clear that the law which you follow must be the truth while that which we follow is lying and falsehood.'

"When the Emperor had heard all this, embracing her, with a smile he said, 'Queen Calafia, my good friend, till now you have had from me neither word nor argument; for my condition is such that I cannot permit my eyes to look, without terrible hatred, upon any but those who are in the holy law of truth, nor wish well to such as are out of it. But now that the Omnipotent Lord has had such mercy on you as to give you such knowledge that you become his servant, you excite in me at once the same love as if the King, my father, had begotten us both. And as for this you ask, I will give you, by my troth, a knight

who is even more complete in valor and in lineage
than you have demanded.'

" Then, taking by the hand Talanque, his cousin,
the son of the King of Sobradisa, — very large he was
of person, and very handsome withal, — he said, —

" ' Queen, here you see one of my cousins, son of the
King whom you here see, — the brother of the King
my father: take him to yourself, that I may secure
to you the good fortune which you will bring to him.'

" The Queen looked at him, and, finding his appearance good, said, —

" ' I am content with his presence, and well satisfied
with his lineage and person, since you assure me of
them. Be pleased to summon for me Liota, my sister,
who is with my fleet in the harbor, that I may send
orders to her that there shall be no movement among
my people.'

" The Emperor sent the Admiral Tartarie for her
immediately, and he, having found her, brought her
with him, and placed her before the Emperor. The
Queen Calafia told her all her wish, commanding her
and entreating her to confirm it. Her sister, Liota,
kneeling upon the ground, kissed her hands, and said
that there was no reason why she should make any
explanation of her will to those who were in her service. The Queen raised her and embraced her, with
the tears in her eyes, and led her by the hand to Talanque, saying, —

" ' Thou shalt be my lord, and the lord of my land,

which is a very great kingdom ; and, for thy sake, this island shall change the custom which for a very long time it has preserved, so that the natural generations of men and women shall succeed henceforth, in place of the order in which the men have been separated so long. And if you have here any friend whom you greatly love, who is of the same rank with you, let him be betrothed to my sister here ; and no long time shall pass, before, with thy help, she shall be queen of a great land.'

" Talanque greatly loved Maneli the Prudent, both because they were brothers by birth and because they held the same faith. He led him forth, and said to her, —

" ' My Queen, since the Emperor, my lord, loves this knight as much as he loves me, and as much as I love thee, take him, and do with him as you would do by me.'

" ' Then, I ask,' said she, ' that we, accepting your religion, may become your wives.'

" Then the Emperor Esplandian and the several Kings, seeing their wishes thus confirmed, took the Queen and her sister to the chapel, turned them into Christians, and espoused them to those two so famous knights ; and thus they converted all who were in the fleet. And immediately they gave order, so that Talanque, taking the fleet of Don Galaor, his father, and Maneli that of King Cildadan, with all their people, garnished and furnished with all things necessary, set sail with their wives, plighting their faith to the Emperor that, if he should need any help from them, they would give it as to their own brother.

"What happened to them afterwards, I must be excused from telling; for they passed through many very strange achievements of the greatest valor; they fought many battles, and gained many kingdoms, of which, if we should give the story, there would be danger that we should never have done."

With this tantalizing statement, California and the Queen of California pass from romance and from history. But, some twenty-five years after these words were written and published by Garcia Ordoñez de Montalvo, Cortez and his braves happened upon the peninsula, which they thought an island, which stretches down between the Gulf of California and the sea. This romance of Esplandian was the yellow-covered novel of their day; Talanque and Maneli were their Aramis and Athos. " Come," said some one, " let us name the new island California : perhaps some one will find gold here yet, and precious stones." And so, from the romance, the peninsula, and the gulf, and afterwards the State, got their name. And they have rewarded the romance by giving to it in these later days the fame of being godmother of a great republic.

The antiquarians of California have universally, we believe, recognized this as the origin of her name, since Mr. Hale called attention to this rare romance.

As, even now, there are not perhaps half a dozen copies of it in America, we have transferred to our pages every word which belongs to that primeval history of California and her Queen.

NOTE.

[From the Proceedings of the American Antiquarian Society, October, 1872.]

THE COSMOGONY OF DANTE AND COLUMBUS.

When Columbus sailed on his fourth voyage, he wrote to Ferdinand and Isabella a letter which contains the following statement with regard to the South Sea, then undiscovered, known to us as the Pacific Ocean : —

"I believe that if I should pass under the equator, in arriving at this higher region of which I speak, I should find there a milder temperature and a diversity in the stars and in the waters. Not that I believe that the highest point is navigable whence these currents flow, nor that we can mount there, because I am convinced that there is the terrestrial paradise, whence no one can enter but by the will of God."

This curious passage, of which the language seems so mystical, represents none the less the impression which Columbus had of the physical cosmogony of the undiscovered half of the world. It is curious to observe that the most elaborate account of this cosmogony, and that by which alone it has been handed down to the memory of modern times, is that presented in Dante's "Divina Commedia," where he represents the mountain of Purgatory, at the antipodes of Jerusalem, crowned by the Terrestrial Paradise. It is this paradise of which Columbus says, "No one can enter it but by the will of God."

Of Dante's Cosmogony a very accurate account is given by

Miss Rossetti in her essay on Dante, recently published, to which she gives the name of " The Shadow of Dante." Her statement is in these words : —

"Dante divides our globe into two elemental hemispheres, — the Eastern, chiefly of land; the Western, almost wholly of water. In the midst of the inhabited land-hemisphere he places Jerusalem, within the same hemisphere, so that its central and Hell's lowest point is exactly under Jerusalem; he places Hell in the midst of the uninhabited sea-hemisphere; he places Purgatory, as the antipodes to Jerusalem, distant from it by the whole diameter of the globe. Thus, on and within the earth, are situated the temporal and the eternal prison-house of sin. Neither, in Dante's view, formed part of God's original creation, wherein sin was not; but the fall of Lucifer at once produced the one and prepared the other, convulsing and inverting the world which God had made. The rebel Seraph fell headlong from Heaven directly above the Western hemisphere, till then a continent, in whose midst was Eden; and Earth, in the twofold horror of his sight and presence, underwent a twofold change. First, to veil her face, she brought in upon herself the vast floods of the Eastern sea-hemisphere, transferring to their place all her dry land, save Eden, which thus was left insulated in mid-ocean. And secondly, to escape his contact as he sank and sank through her surface, through her bowels, till the middle of his colossal frame, having reached the centre of gravity, remained there fixed from the sheer physical impossibility of sinking any lower, she caused a vast mass of her internal substance to flee before his face, and, leaving eternally void the space it once had occupied to form the inverted pit-cone of Hell, she heaved it up directly under Eden, amid the new waste of waters, to form the towering mountain-cone on whose peak the Terrestrial Paradise should thenceforth, to the end of time, sit by, above all elemental strife, and whose sides should, after the Redemption of Man, furnish the Purgatorial stair whereby his foot might aspire once more to tread, his eye to contemplate, his regained inheritance."

The allusion thus made by Columbus to the mystical cosmogony on which Dante wrought, is, I suppose, the last serious allusion made to it, as to a matter of fact, by any geographer. On the other hand, I am not aware that any of the distinguished critics of Dante have called attention to the fact, that, so late as the year 1503, a navigator so illustrious as Columbus was still conducting his voyages on the supposition that Dante's cosmogony was true in fact. All readers of later voyages will remember how often, without any reference to this cosmogony, the islands of the Southern Pacific have been spoken of as a terrestrial paradise. It may be worthy, therefore, of remark, that the precise antipodes of Jerusalem, which, according to the cosmogony of Dante, would be the place of the summit of the terrestrial paradise, is just south of Tahiti and southwest of Pitcairn's Island, the two points where different enthusiasts among modern navigators have fancied that their terrestrial paradise was found. These islands are, in fact, the nearest land to the spot which Columbus, in the half mystical and half geographical letter which I have cited, indicates as the terrestrial paradise.

It is to be remembered, also, that it has been proved that the Pacific islands have grown up on the crests of extinct volcanoes.

Mr. Longfellow's note to the " Purgatorio " thus describes the mountain which Columbus expected to find there : —

" The mountain of Purgatory is a vast conical mountain, rising steep and high from the waters of the Southern Ocean, at a point antipodal to Mount Sion, in Jerusalem. Around it run seven terraces, on which are punished severally the Seven Deadly Sins. Rough stairways, cut in the rock, lead up from terrace to terrace, and on the summit is the garden of the Terrestrial Paradise." — *Longfellow's first Note to the Purgatorio, Vol. II, Div. Com., p.* 159.

E. E. H.

RUTHERFORD THE TWICE-BORN

Edwin Lester Arnold

RUTHERFORD THE TWICE-BORN

AT the twentieth outset of this story, when I have made up my mind many times to tell it, and have as often shrunk back from the paper and pen unwilling, I still hesitate and doubt, weighing with the wretched sensitiveness of my nature your certain ridicule against the hunger of confession that is within me. Yet I must speak, and I will! Here on the twentieth venturing I feel the crowded incidents of that one marvellous evening of my life well up strongly before me; the giddy, fantastic thrall of the strangest hour that ever a mortal man lived through possesses me again; my cold pen slips eagerly forward to the betrayal, and this is the narrative of my shame and my penance, just as it came unasked upon me out of the invisible past.

I was the younger son of an ancient family boasting an untarnished reputation, and one of the best rent-rolls in the northern country. When I was

very young I gloried in the splendid sweep of
territory that spread out in purple vistas round
Wanleigh Court, weaving golden fancies of the
sweet share I would play in the rule of my mimic
kingdom, and when I was a little older I quickly
learned with a sigh that I had no more part in
that fertile realm than the meanest peasant on it.
Briefly, I was the younger son of three, and before I was come to manhood, I had had a fiery
word or two with those above me, and taken the
younger son's portion, and went out into the world,
and ate husks with the social swine, and, too proud
to ask and too poor to beg, kept that sensitive,
self-searching soul my ancestors had bequeathed
me, and my frail, fine body together on the scanty
wages of two unable hands.   Lord! how I suffered
during those years, how nicely I measured each
black abyss of humiliation, and probed each raw
wound that my sensitive nature took in the rough
and tumble of that grim, ugly strife for bare main-
tenance,—and then—even now I cannot write it
without a lump of genuine sorrow in my throat—
my father died, and Wanleigh passed to my elder
brother in the summer, and before the next spring
it had gone again from that brother's dead hands

into those of Guy who came between us, and here, in a trice Guy's horse had tripped and tumbled at a fence and Guy was gone in turn!—and I, ragged John Rutherford, who had feasted for years on poor men's leavings, and kennelled with his peers in leaky attics, was Lord of Lutterworth, and Worsborough, of Warkworth and Torsonce, of Thenford House and Sudley Park, with a new world of delights opening at my feet.

It was as sweet a flying sip from the full cup of pleasure as ever a man tasted, and my starving body and my hungry soul, I remember, burst into new young life with the bare conception of it. And that brief glimpse of delight lasted one day. Before I had scarcely ventured from my lair or shaken off those cruel rags which weighed like lead on my proud spirit, some rolls were handed to me as eldest now and heir, the most secret archives of our race, and therefrom I learned in a few numb minutes what had been to me before only a vague, whispered hearsay—that we held our splendid holdings by fraud, and that many generations back, but well within the discovery of research and the possibility of restitution, should a Rutherford arise so minded, was a foul deed of treachery and usurpation whereby the lawful line had been ousted from their right and ours substituted.   That was all!

For six long black hours I—ragged, hungry John Rutherford—lay white and silent and speechless in my garret, my head on my arm on the table, that dreadful thing crushed in my unfeeling fingers, my corporal body inert and lifeless, while the good and the bad within me fought desperate and long for the mastery,—and then, when the sodden dusk of a December evening had fallen across my cheerless window, the fight was finished and won, and I rose to my feet pale and faint and grateful.   I went out and ordered that search which I felt would condemn me for ever to my kennel and the blank drudgery of living from which my soul revolted, then, I remember, I came back in the dark and took down my crust and my pitcher, and could not eat or drink, but sat like that all the night, cold and alone, fighting again all the incidents of the fight, and so fell asleep at last in my chair in the twilight strangely, incredibly contented.

And now begins the strangest part of the story! The search begun at my orders prospered so well that soon the long sequence of the wrong had been followed down until at last it seemed there was only a step or two needed to snatch the splendid pageantry of Lutterworth and Worsborough, Warkworth and gay Torsonce, from me for all time. I bore those endless days of torture in dull resignation, and then, on the very morrow of the final discovery, a fierce yearning took possession of me to see the old house once more, a fierce hunger which overlapped even the physical hunger in which I lived, an insatiable longing to touch even though it were but the humblest thing that friendly hands had touched, to hide my heavy loneliness even for a moment in the kind mother shadows of my home; and so I went.

'It was a wet, rough evening, when I turned off the high-road I had been trudging, and picking my way in the stillness of the dark along broad avenues and through lonely fir plantations, every turn and bend of which were redolent to me of bygone memories, presently found myself amongst the tangled, neglected lawns and effaced flower-beds of Wanleigh Hall itself. And as I stood there in the sullen drip of the trees while the white moon shone between the chinks of the storm upon the desolate face of that splendid sorrow in front, and the black feet of the clouds trod in gloomy procession across the sodden, unkempt lawns, the measure of the price of my victory, the depth of my loneliness was forced upon me, and I wrung my hands and hid my face and prayed to the night-time, prayed to the great unforgiving, inscrutable powers,—prayed as I had never prayed before in shame or in sickness, cursing in my blindness and folly that black debt, and him who had bequeathed me to pay it,—and leant me against a tree and wept like the weak fool that I was,— wept, but did not waver.

Presently the gust was over, and walking out into the light I hardened my heart and approached the house, from whose many windows only one small streak of brightness shone into the dark air, from where an old servitor and her husband lodged. The hall had been left in charge of these, and it was they who gave me admittance and had prepared in some measure for my coming. I will not say what a flood of memories rushed upon me as I stood again in the old wainscotted hall, or later on ascended the broad staircase and passed down a long ranked avenue of my ances-

tors' portraits to my bedroom; those crowding
recollections of dead days were infinitely painful,
my senses were all on the alert for laughing
voices the memory of which filled every echo in
these gloomy corridors with ghostly meaning, and
my heart hungered for some sign of life or love
to break the speechless loneliness of the desolate
place. I washed and dressed in moody abstrac-
tion, and then made my way down to the great
banquet-room, where a solitary stately supper was
laid for me in grim parody of my condition.

There I supped under the wide vaulted roof
at the table that had sat a hundred, the pale
shine of my two tall candles making a bright
island of my supper napkin and my plate and
tankard in the ocean of the gloom around,—
touching the white tips of the antlers my
kinsmen had brought home from long-forgotten
hunts, 'and gilding with their faint yellow beams
buckler and breastplate of that ranked armour
they had worn in long-forgotten fights. On the
one hand—far down the hall—the lonely fire burnt
away back in the great cavernous grate-place,
singing low, sad songs, it seemed, to itself as the
grey smoke twined in wreaths up the wide chim-

ney; and on the other hand the long, uncurtained
sequence of the mullioned windows and the wet
raven night outside,—the plaintive rustle of the
dead unseen summer things that for ever drew
their withered strands to and fro against the
streaked diamond panes, and the sad sob of the
evening wind wandering like a restless spirit on
the broken terrace outside, lifting with the invisible hem of its sable skirt the rustling dead leaves,
and gently trying in turn with wet soft fingers
each casement catch and latchet! Not a being
in that full-haunted house, not a sound broke the
dead stillness; my head dropped upon my hand,
and I grieved with a stony, emotionless grief like
the grief of the stones around me.

Then—all on a sudden—some one was coming, and upon my empty ear fell the sound of
fine small footsteps in the dim corridors at the
distant end of the hall! Those steps were like
the dripping of water in the silence of a cavern,
and somehow every awakening fibre in me
thrilled instinctively to the measured approach
of my invisible visitor. I held my breath and
gripped the carved lions on my chair and stared,
and then very gently, inch by inch, and foot

by foot, the heavy tapestries down beyond the bottom of the long table were parted, and from between them came an immaterial something, a smoothly stepping shadow that dropped the draperies behind it and came meditatively forward into the radiance of the low-burning fire; and there in the glow stood a black-velvet clad Elizabethan gentleman, as like to myself somehow and yet not quite alike, as one bird is to another of kindred feather! For some minutes that strange figure stood there gazing into the blaze, while I strove to steady my beating heart and wondering fancies, and then it looked up! My whole nature was fascinated by that glance; I felt a secret unknown association between my essence and that thin essence in front of me, which was like the eager attraction of the two parted elements of one common whole in a chemist's crucible; I did not fear or tremble; but a quick, strong, expressionless apprehension of my visitor — of every turn and motion of him, of every touch and play the firelight made on his soft velvet garments, the hilt of his silver rapier, or the lines of his strong passionful features enthralled me. And when he spoke my heart was in my throat. "John Ruther-

ford!" he said in a low cadenced way,—and I
thought even the wind outside and the raindrops
had stopped to listen to him, "I have come to-
night to explain, to help you to explain, some
things which you find inexplicable. You have
been wondering, and fuming, and fretting; cursing
the unknown origin of your sorrow, and even
blaming with bitter rashness the stable equity of
chance! Your grief in this is my grief, and both
might end," he said with a gentle courtierly in-
flexion suiting him strangely, "if you will but lend
yourself to me. Now!" he said, gliding gently up
until I felt the thrill of the cold smooth presence
that hung about him; "now!—think—remember!
back son of a hundred fathers—back into the dim,
—back up the long path you have come—think!
remember, I conjure you!" and he laid a light thin
hand upon my wrist, and at the touch of it every
fibre in me began fiercely pulsing, my breath came
thick and short, my head grew light and giddy,
and all the real about became dissolved into a
vague immaterial shadow; I, me, the hard, material, passion-aching me and the solid life around
was wiped out, and down I went out of my own
control, down the plane of the immaterial, into a

fantastic world remembering at that magic touch
all, everything I had done; step by step, backwards into the past my wondering wide-eyed
consciousness receded, watching that immortal ego
which was myself shrink from manhood down to
babiness, and then materialise again into another
life in another age, and heave and push and
struggle, and shout and laugh and cry, and ever
acting as though that life it lived upon the minute
were the only one, the while it floundered slowly
through ambiguous sloughs, towards the pale deathless glimmer of that distant godly Hope which was
its life and being,—back reeled my consciousness,
back by deathbeds and altars and cradles, and
cradles and deathbeds and altars;—at one minute
of that compressed understanding I saw myself
loathsome for base design and deed, and then the
rhythm of that ceaseless struggle for the better
which my ego waged, mended as the baseness
mended,—at one minute my staggering, startled
consciousness saw itself grey and lean and wrinkled
stretched in courtly obsequies upon a bed of silk
and minever,—and then as a soldier hot and young,
waving a broken hilt in the thick red tangles of
charging squadrons—at one minute of those lives

that flashed in endless sequence before their liver, that liver sunk in shameful hopelessness scarcely lived, and then anon, at a hair's-breadth interval, it rose to heroic heights. I could not stand the stress of that wild vision, and presently ceased remembering, all on a sudden, the material materialised again, and with a gasp I was myself; the opaque curtain of corporeal living clouded my mind, leaving only a vague consciousness behind that I had forgotten something I had lately remembered!

"Back again, sweet kinsman," cried the shadow, standing right in front of me, "back again, sweet comrade, back into the black sea of the forgotten, for that great pearl of fact you have not found," and he touched me once more upon the wrist.

I struggled, I would not go, I gasped; and in a minute I had gone again and was spinning down the long dim vistas of the by and done-with, until I came at last, by episode of love and fear and hate and redeeming sadness, to where two half-brothers jointly owned our land. This was the kernel of it all. The elder of those two close comrades was learned and gentle, serene in his confidence of the brother whose loyal friendship

I

made half the sweetness of the wide dominion that they shared. Another breathing space, and I saw mad envy growing in the younger till it ripened into malice and savagery, and pictured against the dark background of my fancy in his every pose and gesture; and lastly, in one minute of shame and sorrow incredible I saw him decoy the other to a pleasant tryst and stab him most foully in the back, stab him twice and thrice, till he lay bloody and dead in the screen of the woods, and all for the sake of a few more acres; then sneaking home, traitor no less than coward, I saw him by lies and forgery brand with infamy the true wife and children of that brother, and as he rose, wicked and flushed and triumphant on their ruin, undivided master of Wanleigh and Worsborough, of Torsonce and Lutterworth, I saw his face,—and it was my own.

With a scream and a start I awoke, all the terror and shame and confusion of that dread discovery working in my features; I threw myself out upon the table in an agony of contrition, and locking my clasped hands above my head, shut out for a minute the long, dim length of the hall half seen in the golden gloom of the candles and the deathless eyes of that grey inquisitor who stood watching the tempest of emotions that racked my soul.   So it was I, was it ?   I who had done that black, foul deed in another life, and sown the miserable seed of which the harvesting also was mine; it was myself then, on whose head I had heaped an hundred thousand curses; it was I, gentle John Rutherford, that was the best butcher of them all.   In my wild incoherent grief and astonishment I lay moaning like that for a minute, thinking over in my living mind each step of the motley pageantry which had carried me back into the past and given me that strange knowledge, that one chance insight, into what seemed the great methods of the inscrutable powers.   I forgot the grey shadow by me until in a minute he touched me again and said, more gently this time, " The wrong was great, and great has had to be the repentance, but the methods of the law which governs your life and mine, there where you are, and here where I am, are as just, and as generous, as they are unalterable.   You have offended and made restitution, good ! this single circle of the hundred thousand which compose your life is completed, now see how nicely the ways of 'chance' (forsooth!) fit to the needs of justice—think again, kinsman."

But I dared not. I staggered back, back from the glamour of that shrouding presence about him, —back from those inflexible grey eyes standing out keen and bright as two pale planets in the dusky soliditude of my hall; I wrung my hands in my stress like a woman, and wailed as the fear and the doubt and the wonder played like hot metal in my veins. In a frenzy of terror, with the courage of a rat in a corner, I remember swearing I would not remember again, and for answer, in a thought, he had touched me with that smooth, cold, velvet touch and I was away, nerveless, dreaming anew, right back into that age where my earlier self had done the baseness, and thence, this time descending through the years, I followed on the heels of the outlawed ones I wronged. I saw those dear, flitting phantoms stream across the stage of my comprehension, dropping as they went from their gentle condition down into lesser ranks, son succeeding to father, and brother to brother, a long line of yeomanry living in forgetfulness on the outskirts of the land that was theirs but for my treachery;

marrying and working and dying, writing their names in churches and chapels and Bibles, until so many of them had slipped by that presently all knowledge of the wrong that had been suffered and the right unrestored was gone from amongst them! But could *I* overlook it? Step by step, and life by life I saw the right in the cottage come down step by step and life by life with the wrong in the hall; I saw that right inviolate, slip from name to name and hand to hand; twice it was nearly extinguished, and then, when I some-how knew in my sleep I had followed it down all but to the actual present day, all the right and heirship of our wide acres and many halls was concentrated by true descent and existed only in one fair, unwotting, yeoman girl. I saw her bud in the swift, bright sequence of my involuntary recollection from a tender cottage maid into a comely woman with averted face, I saw one in dress of better kind ride down and woo her by cottage door and hazel copse, and win,—and lead her to the altar,—and all my straining soul and aching heart and stretching nerves were breaking to look upon their faces, for here were they who had bred him who was to-day true Lord of

Lutterworth and Worsborough—he to whom I must give place, and light and life, the embodied heir of that deathless wrong I had done. I half dragged the white linen from the table and the clattering plates and cups in the bitterness of my expectation, I half rose from my chair with starting, straining eyes still body-senseless as I was, and waited for those two to turn. And turn they did in a minute, and with a stagger and a start and a cry out of the lowermost depths of my soul, I tottered out of my vision into the material world again, and tossed my arms aloft, and laughed and wept, and reeled, and then fell fainting right across the floor, right at the feet of the grave, calm, gently smiling shadow who was watching me, for I had seen them,—all in one blinding, dazzling moment of swift compre-hension I had perceived that in myself was the focus of wrong and of right, in me was both the debt and the credit,—for those two were my father and mother!

.   .   .   .   .   .

There is nothing more to say. I was ill after that, and when I was well a bulky blue letter was handed to me saying those who had undertaken my search had, to their marvel, come to conclusions the same as my own, but it need hardly be added by methods much more prosaic. And Wanleigh and Worsborough, and Torsonce and Lutterworth have a new master, a humble open-handed master who goes about thinking he sees better men than himself in every wastrel that he meets, and purpose in the purposeless, and justice in injustice, and the clear heart of eternal equity beating inviolate, imperturbable, and perpetual under all the noisy pulses of casual life.

THE JOURNEY OF THE KING

Lord Dunsany

PART II

The Journey of the King

I

ONE day the King turned to the women that
danced and said to them : " Dance no more," and
those that bore the wine in jewelled cups he sent
away. The palace of King Ebalon was emptied of
sound of song and there rose the voices of heralds
crying in the streets to find the prophets of the
land.

Then went the dancers, the cupbearer and the
singers down into the hard streets among the
houses, Pattering Leaves, Silvern Fountain and
Summer Lightning, the dancers whose feet the gods
had not devised for stony ways, which had only
danced for princes. And with them went the
singer, Soul of the South, and the sweet singer,
Dream of the Sea, whose voices the gods had
attuned to the ears of kings, and old Istahn the
cupbearer left his life's work in the palace to tread

123

the common ways, he that had stood at the elbows
of three kings of Zarkandhu and had watched his
ancient vintage feeding their valour and mirth as
the waters of Tondaris feed the green plains to the
south.   Ever he had stood grave among their jests,
but his heart warmed itself solely by the fire of the
mirth of Kings.   He too, with the singers and
dancers, went out into the dark.

And throughout the land the heralds sought out
the prophets thereof.   Then one evening as King
Ebalon sat alone within his palace there were
brought before him all who had repute for
wisdom and who wrote the histories of the times
to be.   Then the King spake, saying : "The
King goeth upon a journey with many horses,
yet riding upon none, when the pomp of travelling
shall be heard in the streets and the sound of the
lute and the drum and the name of the King.   And
I would know what princes and what people shall
greet me on the other shore in the land to which
I travel."

Then fell a hush upon the prophets for they
murmured : " All knowledge is with the King."

Then said the King : " Thou first, Samahn, High
Prophet of the Temple of gold in Azinorn, answer
or thou shalt write no more the history of the times
to be, but shalt toil with thy hand to make record of
the little happenings of the days that were, as do
the common men."

Then said Samahn : " All knowledge is with

the King," and when the pomp of travelling shall
be heard in the streets and the slow horses whereon
the King rideth not go behind lute and drum,
then, as the King well knoweth, thou shalt go
down to the great white house of Kings and,
entering the portals where none are worthy to
follow, shalt make obeisance alone to all the elder
Kings of Zarkandhu, whose bones are seated upon
golden thrones grasping their sceptres still. Therein thou shalt go with robes and sceptre through
the marble porch, but thou shalt leave behind thee
thy gleaming crown that others may wear it, and
as the times go by come in to swell the number of
the thirty Kings that sit in the great white house
on golden thrones. There is one doorway in the
great white house, and it stands wide with marble
portals yawning for kings, but when it shall
receive thee, and thine obeisance hath been
made because of thine obligation to the thirty
Kings, thou shalt find at the back of the house an
unknown door through which the soul of a
King may just pass, and leaving thy bones upon
a golden throne thou shalt go unseen out of
the great white house to tread the velvet spaces
that lie among the worlds. Then, O King, it
were well to travel fast and not to tarry about the
houses of men as do the souls of some who still
bewail the sudden murder that sent them upon the
journey before their time, and who, being yet loth
to go, linger in dark chambers all the night.

125

These, setting forth to travel in the dawn and travelling all the day, see earth behind them gleaming when evening falls, and again are loth to leave its pleasant haunts, and come back again through dark woods and up into some old loved chamber, and ever tarry between home and flight and find no rest.

Thou wilt set forth at once because the journey is far and lasts for many hours ; but the hours on the velvet spaces are the hours of the gods, and we may not say what time such an hour may be if reckoned in mortal years.

At last thou shalt come to a grey place filled with mist, with grey shapes standing before it which are altars, and on the altars rise small red flames from dying fires that scarce illumine the mist. And in the mist it is dark and cold because the fires are low. These are the altars of the people's faiths, and the flames are the worship of men, and through the mist the gods of Old go groping in the dark and in the cold. There thou shalt hear a voice cry feebly : " Inyāni, Inyāni, lord of the thunder, where art thou, for I cannot see ? " And a voice shall answer faintly in the cold: " O maker of many worlds, I am here." And in that place the gods of Old are nearly deaf for the prayers of men grow few, they are nigh blind because the fires burn low upon the altars of men's faiths and they are very cold. And all about the place of mist there lies a moaning sea which is called the

Sea of Souls. And behind the place of mist are the dim shapes of mountains, and on the peak of one there glows a silvern light that shines in the moaning sea; and ever as the flames on the altars die before the gods of Old the light on the mountain increases, and the light shines over the mist and never through it as the gods of Old grow blind. It is said that the light on the mountain shall one day become a new god who is not of the gods of Old.

There, O King, thou shalt enter the Sea of Souls by the shore where the altars stand which are covered in mist. In that sea are the souls of all that ever lived on the worlds and all that ever shall live, all freed from earth and flesh. And all the souls in that sea are aware of one another but more than with hearing or sight or by taste or touch or smell, and they all speak to each other yet not with lips, with voices which need no sound. And over the sea lies music as winds o'er an ocean on earth, and there unfettered by language great thoughts set outward through the souls as on earth the currents go.

Once did I dream that in a mist-built ship I sailed upon that sea and heard the music that is not of instruments, and voices not from lips, and woke and found that I was upon the earth and that the gods had lied to me in the night. Into this sea from fields of battle and cities come down the rivers of lives, and ever the gods have taken onyx cups and far and wide into the worlds again have flung the souls out of the sea, that each soul may find a prison in the body of a man with five small windows closely barred, and each one shackled with forgetfulness.

But all the while the light on the mountain grows, and none may say what work the god that shall be born of the silvern light shall work on the Sea of Souls, when the gods of Old are dead and the Sea is living still.

And answer made the King:

"Thou that art a prophet of the gods of Old, go back and see that those red flames burn more brightly on the altars in the mist, for the gods of Old are easy and pleasant gods, and thou canst not say what toil shall vex our souls when the god of the light on the mountain shall stride along the shore where bleach the huge bones of 'the gods of Old."

And Samahn answered : " All knowledge is with the King."

II

THEN the King called to Ynath bidding him speak concerning the journey of the King. Ynath was the prophet that sat at the Eastern gate of the Temple of Gorandhu. There Ynath prayed his prayers to all the passers by lest ever the gods should go abroad, and one should pass him dressed in a mortal guise. And men are pleased as they walk by that Eastern gate that Ynath should pray to them for fear that they be gods, so men bring gifts to Ynath in the Eastern gate.

And Ynath said: "All knowledge is with the King. When a strange ship comes to anchor in the air outside thy chamber window, thou shalt leave thy well-kept garden and it shall become a prey to the nights and days and be covered again with grass. But going aboard thou shalt set sail over the Sea of Time and well shall the ship steer through the many worlds and still sail on. If other ships shall pass thee on the way and hail thee saying: 'From what port?' thou shalt answer them: 'From Earth.' And if they ask thee 'whither bound?' then thou shalt answer: 'The End.' Or thou shalt hail them saying:

TIME AND THE GODS

'From what port?' And they shall answer. 'From The End called also The Beginning, and bound to Earth.' And thou shalt sail away till like an old sorrow dimly felt by happy men the worlds shall gleam in the distance like one star, and as the star pales thou shalt come to the shore of space where æons rolling shorewards from Time's sea shall lash up centuries to foam away in years. There lies the Centre Garden of the gods, facing full seawards. All around lie songs that on earth were never sung, fair thoughts not heard among the worlds, dream pictures never seen that drifted over Time without a home till at last the æons swept them on to the shore of space. And in the Centre Garden of the gods bloom many fancies. Therein once some souls were playing where the gods walked up and down and to and fro. And a dream came in more beauteous than the rest on the crest of a wave of Time, and one soul going downward to the shore clutched at the dream and caught it. Then over the dreams and stories and old songs that lay on the shore of space the hours came sweeping back, and the centuries caught that soul and swirled him with his dream far out to the Sea of Time, and the æons swept him earthwards and cast him into a palace with all the might of the sea and left him there with his dream. The child grew to a King and still clutched at his dream till the people wondered and laughed. Then, O king, Thou didst

130

cast thy dream back into the Sea, and Time
drowned it and men laughed no more, but thou
didst forget that a certain sea beat on a distant
shore and that there was a garden and therein souls.
But at the end of the journey that thou shalt take,
when thou comest to the shore of space again
thou shalt go up the beach, and coming to a
garden gate that stands in a garden wall shalt
remember these things again, for it stands where
the hours assail not above the beating of Time,
far up the shore, and nothing altereth there.
So thou shalt go through the garden gate and hear
again the whispering of the souls when they talk
low where sing the voices of the gods. There
with kindred souls thou shalt speak as thou didst
of yore and tell them what befell thee beyond the
tides of time and how they took thee and made of
thee a King so that thy soul found no rest. There
in the Centre Garden thou shalt sit at ease and
watch the gods all rainbow-clad go up and down
and to and fro on the paths of dreams and songs,
and shalt not venture down to the cheerless sea.
For that which a man loves most is not on this
side of Time, and all which drifts on its æons is a
lure.

" All knowledge is with the King."

Then said the King: " Ay, there was a dream
once but Time hath swept it away."

III

THEN spake Monith, Prophet of the Temple of Azure that stands on the snow-peak of Ahmoon and said : " All knowledge is with the King. Once thou didst set out upon a one day's journey riding upon thy horse and before thee had gone a beggar down the road, and his name was Yeb. Him thou didst overtake and when he heeded not thy coming thou didst ride over him.

" Upon the journey that thou shalt one day take riding upon no horse, this beggar has set out before thee and is labouring up the crystal steps towards the moon as a man goeth up the steps of a high tower in the dark. On the moon's edge beneath the shadow of Mount Angises he shall rest awhile and then shall climb the crystal steps again. Then a great journey lies before him before he may rest again till he come to that star that is called the left eye of Gundo. Then a journey of many crystal steps lieth before him again with nought to guide him but the light of Omrazu. On the edge of Omrazu shall Yeb tarry long, for the most dreadful part of his journey lieth before him. Up the crystal steps that lie beyond Omrazu he

132

must go, and any that follow, through the howling
of all the meteors that ride the sky ; for in that part
of the crystal space go many meteors up and down all
squealing in the dark, which greatly perplex all
travellers.   And, if he may see through the gleaming of the meteors and in spite of their uproar
come safely through, he shall come to the star
Omrund at the edge of the Track of Stars.   And
from star to star along the Track of Stars the soul
of a man may travel with more ease, and there the
journey lies no more straight forward, but curves
to the right. ''

Then said King Ebalon :

'' Of this beggar whom my horse smote down
thou hast spoken much, but I sought to know by
what road a King should go when he taketh his
last royal journey, and what princes and what
people should meet him upon another shore. ''

Then answered Monith :

'' All knowledge is with the King.   It hath been
doomed by the gods, who speak not in jest, that
thou shalt follow the soul that thou didst send alone
upon its journey, that that soul go not unattended
up the crystal steps.

'' Moreover, as this beggar went upon his lonely
journey he dared to curse the King, and his curses
lie like a red mist along the valleys and hollows
wherever he uttered them.   By these red mists, O
King, thou shalt track him as a man follows a river
by night until thou shalt fare at last to the land

wherein he hath blessed thee (repenting of anger at last), and thou shalt see his blessing lie over the land like a blaze of golden sunshine illumining fields and gardens."

Then said the King :

" The gods have spoken hard above the snowy peak of this mountain Ahmoon."

And Monith said :

" How a man may come to the shore of space beyond the tides of time I know not, but it is doomed that thou shalt certainly first follow the beggar past the moon, Omrund and Omrazu till thou comest to the Track of Stars, and up the Track of Stars coming towards the right along the edge of it till thou comest to Ingazi. There the soul of the beggar Yeb sat long, then, breathing deep, set off on his great journey earthward adown the crystal steps. Straight through the spaces where no stars are found to rest at, following the dull gleam of earth and her fields till he come at last where journeys end and start."

Then said King Ebalon :

" If this hard tale be true, how shall I find the beggar that I must follow when I come again to the earth ? "

And the Prophet answered :

" Thou shalt know him by his name and find him in this place, for that beggar shall be called King Ebalon and he shall be sitting upon the throne of the Kings of Zarkandhu."

And the King answered :

"If one sit upon this throne whom men call King Ebalon, who then shall I be ?"

And the Prophet answered :

"Thou shalt be a beggar and thy name shall be Yeb, and thou shalt ever tread the road before the palace waiting for alms from the King whom men shall call Ebalon."

Then said the King :

"Hard gods indeed are those that tramp the snows of Ahmoon about the temple of Azure, for if I sinned against this beggar called Yeb, they too have sinned against him when they doomed him to travel on this weary journey though he hath not offended."

And Monith said :

"He too hath offended, for he was angry as thy horse struck him, and the gods smite anger. And his anger and his curses doom him to journey without rest as also they doom thee."

Then said the King :

"Thou that sittest upon Ahmoon in the Temple of Azure, dreaming thy dreams and making prophecies, foresee the ending of this weary quest and tell me where it shall be ?"

And Monith answered :

"As a man looks across great lakes I have gazed into the days to be, and as the great flies come upon four wings of gauze to skim over blue waters, so have my dreams come sailing two by two out of the

135

days to be.   And I dreamed that that King Ebalon, whose soul was not thy soul, stood in his palace in a time far hence, and beggars thronged the street outside, and among them was Yeb, a beggar, having thy soul.   And it was on the morning of a festival and the King came robed in white, with all his prophets and his seers and magicians, all down the marble steps to bless the land and all that stood therein as far as the purple hills, because it was the morning of festival.   And as the King raised up his hand over the beggars' heads to bless the fields and rivers and all that stood therein, I dreamed that the quest was ended.

"All knowledge is with the King."

IV

Evening darkened and above the palace domes gleamed out the stars whereon haply others missed the secret too.

And outside the palace in the dark they that had borne the wine in jewelled cups mocked in low voices at the King and at the wisdom of his prophets.

Then spake Ynar, called the prophet of the Crystal Peak ; for there rises Amanath above all that land, a mountain whose peak is crystal, and Ynar beneath its summit hath his Temple, and when day shines no longer on the world Amanath takes the sunlight and gleams afar as a beacon in a bleak land lit at night.   And at the hour when all faces are turned on Amanath, Ynar comes forth beneath the Crystal Peak to weave strange spells and to make signs that people say are surely for the gods. Therefore it is said in all those lands that Ynar speaks at evening to the gods when all the world is still.

And Ynar said :

" All knowledge is with the King, and without doubt it hath come to the King's ears how certain speech is held at evening on the Peak of Amanath.

137

TIME AND THE GODS

The
Journey
of the
King

"They that speak to me at evening on the Peak are They that live in a city through whose streets Death walketh not, and I have heard it from Their Elders that the King shall take no journey ; only from thee the hills shall slip away, the dark woods, the sky and all the gleaming worlds that fill the night, and the green fields shall go on untrodden by thy feet and the blue sky ungazed at by thine eyes, and still the rivers shall all run seaward but making no music in thine ears. And all the old laments shall still be spoken, troubling thee not, and to the earth shall fall the tears of the children of earth and never grieving thee. Pestilence, heat and cold, ignorance, famine and anger, these things shall grip their claws upon all men as heretofore in fields and roads and cities but shall not hold thee. But from thy soul, sitting in the old worn track of the worlds when all is gone away, shall fall off the shackles of circumstance and thou shalt dream thy dreams alone.

"And thou shalt find that dreams are real where there is nought as far as the Rim but only thy dreams and thee.

"With them thou shalt build palaces and cities resting upon nothing and having no place in time, not to be assailed by the hours or harmed by ivy or rust, not to be taken by conquerors, but destroyed by thy fancy if thou dost wish it so or by thy fancy rebuilded. And nought shall ever disturb these dreams of thine which here are troubled and

138

lost by all the happenings of earth, as the dreams of one who sleeps in a tumultuous city. For these thy dreams shall sweep outward like a strong river over a great waste plain wherein are neither rocks nor hills to turn it, only in that place there shall be no boundaries nor sea, neither hindrance nor end. And it were well for thee that thou shouldst take few regrets into thy waste dominions from the world wherein thou livest, for such regrets or any memory of deeds ill done must sit beside thy soul for ever in that waste, singing one song always of forlorn remorse ; and they too shall be only dreams but very real.

"There nought shall hinder thee among thy dreams, for even the gods may harass thee no more when flesh and earth and events with which They bound thee shall have slipped away."

Then said the King :

" I like not this grey doom, for dreams are empty. I would see action roaring through the world, and men and deeds."

Then answered the prophet :

"Victory, jewels and dancing but please thy fancy. What is the sparkle of the gem to thee without thy fancy which it allures, and thy fancy is all a dream. Action and deeds and men are nought without dreams and do but fetter them, and only dreams are real, and where thou stayest when the worlds shall drift away there shall be only dreams.

And the King answered :

" A mad prophet."

And Ynar said :

" A mad prophet, but believing that his soul possesseth all things of which his soul may become aware and that he is master of that soul, and thou a high-minded King believing only that thy soul possesseth such few countries as are leaguered by thine armies and the sea, and that thy soul is possessed by certain strange gods of whom thou knowest not, who shall deal with it in a way whereof thou knowest not. Until a knowledge come to us that either is wrong I have wider realms, O King, than thee and hold them beneath no overlords."

Then said the King :

" Thou hast said no overlords ! To whom then dost thou speak by strange signs at evening above the world ? "

And Ynar went forward a few paces and whispered to the King. And the King shouted :

" Seize ye this prophet for he is a hypocrite and speaks to no gods at evening above the world, but has deceived us with his signs."

And Ynar said :

" Come not near me or I shall point towards you when I speak at evening upon the mountain with Those that ye know of."

Then Ynar went away and the guards touched him not.

V

THEN spake the prophet Thun, who was clad in seaweed and had no Temple, but lived apart from men. All his life he had lived on a lonely beach and had heard for ever the wailing of the sea and the crying of the wind in hollows among the cliffs. Some said that having lived so long by the full beating of the sea, and where always the wind cries loudest, he could not feel the joys of other men, but only felt the sorrow of the sea crying in his soul for ever.

" Long ago on the path of stars, midmost between the worlds, there strode the gods of Old. In the bleak middle of the worlds They sat and the worlds went round and round, like dead leaves in the wind at Autumn's end, with never a life on one, while the gods went sighing for the things that might not be. And the centuries went over the gods to go where the centuries go, toward the End of Things, and with Them went the sighs of all the gods as They longed for what might not be.

" One by one in the midst of the worlds, fell dead the gods of Old, still sighing for the things that might not be, all slain by Their own regrets. Only Shimono Káni, the youngest of the gods, made him a harp out of the heart strings of all the elder gods, and, sitting upon the Path of Stars all in the Midst of Things, played upon the harp a dirge for the gods of Old. And the song told of all vain regrets and of unhappy loves of the gods in the olden time, and of Their great deeds that were to adorn the future years. But into the dirge of Shimono Kani came voices crying out of the heart strings of the gods, all sighing still for the things that might not be. And the dirge and the voices crying, go drifting away from the Path of Stars, away from the Midst of Things, till they come twittering among the Worlds, like a great host of birds that are lost by night. And every note is a life, and many notes become caught up among the worlds to be entangled with flesh for a little while before they pass again on their journey to the great Anthem that roars at the End of Time. Shimono Káni hath given a voice to the wind and added a sorrow to the sea. But when in lighted chambers after feasting there arises the voice of the singer to please the King, then is the soul of that singer crying aloud to his fellows from where he stands chained to earth. And when at the sound of the singing the heart of the King grows sad and his princes lament then they remember, though knowing not that, they remember it, the sad face of Shimono Káni sitting by his dead brethren, the elder gods, playing on

that harp of crying heart strings whereby he sent their souls among the worlds.

"And when the music of one lute is lonely on the hills at night, then one soul calleth to his brother souls—the notes of Shimono Káni's dirge which have not been caught among the worlds—and he knoweth not to whom he calls or why, but knoweth only that minstrelsy is his only cry and sendeth it out into the dark.

"But although in the prison houses of earth all memories must die, yet as there sometimes clings to a prisoner's feet some dust of the fields wherein he was captured, so sometimes fragments of re-membrance cling to a man's soul after it hath been taken to earth. Then a great minstrel arises, and, weaving together the shreds of his memories, maketh some melody such as the hand of Shimono Káni smites out of his harp; and they that pass by say: 'Hath there not been some such melody before?' and pass on sad at heart for memories which are not.

"Therefore, O King, one day the great gates of thy palace shall lie open for a procession wherein the King comes down to pass through a people, lamenting with lute and drum; and on the same day a prison door shall be opened by relenting hands, and one more lost note of Shimono Káni's dirge shall go back to swell his melody again.

"The dirge of Shimono Kani shall roll on till one day it shall come with all its notes complete to

143

TIME AND THE GODS

The Journey of the King

overwhelm the Silence that sits at the End of Things. Then shall Shimono Káni say to his brethren's bones : 'The things that might not be have at last become.'

" But very quiet shall be the bones of the gods of Old, and only Their voices shall live which cried from the harp of heart strings, for the things which might not be."

VI

WHEN the caravans, saying farewell to Zandara, set out across the waste northwards towards Einandhu, they follow the desert track for seven days before they come to water where Shubah Onath rises black out of the waste, with a well at its foot and herbage on its summit. On this rock a prophet hath his Temple and is called the Prophet of Journeys, and hath carven in a southern window smiling along the camel track all gods that are benignant to caravans.

There a traveller may learn by prophecy whether he shall accomplish the ten days' journey thence across the desert and so come to the white city of Einandhu, or whether his bones shall lie with the bones of old along the desert track.

No name hath the Prophet of Journeys, for none is needed in that desert where no man calls nor ever a man answers.

Thus spake the Prophet of Journeys standing before the King:

" The journey of the King shall be an old journey pushed on apace.

" Many a year before the making of the moon

145   L

thou camest down with dream camels from the City without a name that stands beyond all the stars. And then began thy journey over the Waste of Nought, and thy dream camel bore thee well when those of certain of thy fellow travellers fell down in the Waste and were covered over by the silence and were turned again to nought ; and those travellers when their dream camels fell, having nothing to carry them further over the Waste, were lost beyond and never found the earth. These are those men that might have been but were not. And all about thee fluttered the myriad hours travelling in great swarms across the Waste of Nought.

" How many centuries passed across the cities while thou wast making thy journey none may reckon, for there is no time in the Waste of Nought, but only the hours fluttering earthwards from beyond to do the work of Time. At last the dream-borne travellers saw far off a green place gleaming and made haste towards it and so came to Earth. And there, O King, ye rest for a little while, thou and those that came with thee, making an encampment upon earth before journeying on. There the swarming hours alight, settling on every blade of grass and tree, and spreading over your tents and devouring all things, and at last bending your very tent poles with their weight and wearying you.

" Behind the encampment in the shadow of the

tents lurks a dark figure with a nimble sword, having the name of Time. This is he that hath called the hours from beyond and he it is that is their master, and it is his work that the hours do as they devour all green things upon the earth and tatter the tents and weary all the travellers. As each of the hours does the work of Time, Time smites him with his nimble sword as soon as his work is done, and the hour falls severed to the dust with his bright wings scattered, as a locust cut asunder by the scimitar of a skilful swordsman.

" One by one, O King, with a stir in the camp, and the folding up of the tents one by one, the travellers shall push on again on the journey begun so long before out of the City without a name to the place where dream camels go, striding free through the Waste. So into the Waste, O King, thou shalt set forth ere long, perhaps to renew friendships begun during thy short encampment upon earth.

" Other green places thou shalt meet in the Waste and thereon shalt encamp again until driven thence by the hours. What prophet shall relate how many journeys thou shalt make or how many encampments ? But at last thou shalt come to the place of The Resting of Camels, and there shall gleaming cliffs that are named The Ending of Journeys lift up out of the Waste of Nought, Nought at their feet, Nought laying wide before them, with only the glint of worlds far off to illumine the Waste. One by one, on tired dream camels, the travellers shall come in, and going up the pathway through the cliff in that land of The Resting of Camels shall come on The City of Ceasing. There, the dream-wrought pinnacles and the spires that are builded of men's hopes shall rise up real before thee, seen only hitherto as a mirage in the Waste.

" So far the swarming hours may not come, and far away among the tents shall stand the dark figure with the nimble sword. But in the scintillant streets, under the song-built abodes of the last of cities, thy journey, O King, shall end."

VII

In the valley beyond Sidono there lies a garden
of poppies, and where the poppies' heads are all
a-swing with summer breezes that go up the valley
there lies a path well strewn with ocean shells.
Over Sidono's summit the birds come streaming
to the lake that lies in the valley of the garden, and
behind them rises the sun sending Sidono's shadow
as far as the edge of the lake. And down the
path of many ocean shells when they begin to
gleam in the sun, every morning walks an aged
man clad in a silken robe with strange devices
woven. A little temple where the old man lives
stands at the edge of the path. None worship
there, for Zornadhu, the old prophet, hath for-
saken men to walk among his poppies.

For Zornadhu hath failed to understand the purport of Kings and cities and the moving up and
down of many people to the tune of the clinking
of gold. Therefore hath Zornadhu gone far away
from the sound of cities and from those that are
ensnared thereby, and beyond Sidono's mountain
hath come to rest where there are neither kings
nor armies nor bartering for gold, but only the

149

heads of the poppies that sway in the wind together and the birds that fly from Sidono to the lake, and then the sunrise over Sidono's summit ; and afterwards the flight of birds out of the lake and over Sidono again, and sunset behind the valley, and high over lake and garden the stars that know not cities. There Zornadhu lives in his garden of poppies with Sidono standing between him and the whole world of men ; and when the wind blowing athwart the valley sways the heads of the tall poppies against the Temple wall, the old prophet says : " The flowers are all praying, and lo! they be nearer to the gods than men."

But the heralds of the King coming after many days of travel to the crest of Sidono perceived the garden valley. By the lake they saw the poppy garden gleaming round and small like a sunrise over water on a misty morning seen by some shepherd from the hills. And descending the bare mountain for three days they came to the gaunt pines, and ever between the tall trunks came the glare of the poppies that shone from the garden valley. For a whole day they travelled through the pines. That night a cold wind came up the garden valley crying against poppies. Low in his Temple, with a song of exceeding grief, Zornadhu in the morning made a dirge for the passing of poppies, because in the night time there had fallen petals that might not return or ever come again into the garden valley. Outside the Temple

TIME AND THE GODS

on the path of ocean shells the heralds halted, and read the names and honours of the King; and from the Temple came the voice of Zornadhu still singing his lament. But they took him from his garden because of the King's command, and down his gleaming path of ocean shells and away up Sidono, and left the Temple empty with none to lament when silken poppies died. And the will of the wind of the autumn was wrought upon the poppies, and the heads of the poppies that rose from the earth went down to the earth again, as the plume of a warrior smitten in a heathen fight far away, where there are none to lament him. Thus out of his land of flowers went Zornadhu and came perforce into the lands of men, and saw cities, and in the city's midst stood up before the King.

And the King said:

"Zornadhu, what of the journey of the King and of the princes and the people that shall meet me?"

Zornadhu answered:

"I know nought of Kings, but in the night time the poppy made his journey a little before dawn. Thereafter the wildfowl came as is their wont over Sidono's summit, and the sun rising behind them gleamed upon Sidono, and all the flowers of the lake awoke. And the bee passing up and down the garden went droning to other poppies, and the flowers of the lake, they that had known the poppy, knew him no more. And the sun's rays slanting from Sidono's crest lit still a garden valley where one poppy waved his petals to the dawn no more. And I, O King, that down a path of gleaming ocean shells walk in the morning, found not, nor have since found, that poppy again, that hath gone on the journey whence there is not returning, out of my garden valley. And I, O King, made a dirge to cry beyond that valley and the poppies bowed their heads ; but there is no cry nor no lament that may adjure the life to return again to a flower that grew in a garden once and hereafter is not.

" Unto what place the lives of poppies have gone no man shall truly say. Sure it is that to that place are only outward tracks. Only it may be that when a man dreams at evening in a garden where heavily the scent of poppies hangs in the air, when the winds have sunk, and far away the sound of a lute is heard on lonely hills, as he dreams of silken-scarlet poppies that once were a-swing together in the gardens of his youth, the lives of those old lost poppies shall return, living again in his dream. *So there may dream the gods.* And through the dreams of some divinity reclining in tinted fields above the morning we may haply pass again, although our bodies have long swirled up and down the world with other dust. In these strange dreams our lives may be again, all in the centre of our hopes, rejoicings and laments, until above the morning the gods wake to go about their work, haply to remember still Their idle dreams, haply to dream them all again in the stillness when shines the starlight of the gods."

VIII

THEN said the King : " I like not these strange
journeys nor this faint wandering through the
dreams of gods like the shadow of a weary camel that
may not rest when the sun is low. The gods that
have made me to love the earth's cool woods and
dancing streams do ill to send me into the starry
spaces that I love not, with my soul still peering
earthward through the eternal years, as a beggar
who once was noble staring from the street at
lighted halls. For wherever the gods may send
me I shall be as the gods have made me, a creature
loving the green fields of earth.

" Now if there stand one prophet here that hath
the ear of those too splendid gods that stride
above the glories of the orient sky, tell them
that there is on earth one King in the land called
Zarkandhu to the south of the opal mountains,
who would fain tarry among the many gardens
of earth, and would leave to other men the splendours that the gods shall give the dead above the
twilight that surrounds the stars."

Then spake Yamen, prophet of the Temple of
Obin that stands on the shores of a great lake,

facing east. Yamen said : " I pray oft to the gods
who sit above the twilight behind the east. When
the clouds are heavy and red at sunset, or when
there is boding of thunder or eclipse, then I pray
not, lest my prayers be scattered and beaten earthward. But when the sun sets in a tranquil sky,
pale green or azure, and the light of his farewells
stays long upon lonely hills, then I send forth my
prayers to flutter upward to gods that are surely
smiling, and the gods hear my prayers. But, O
King, boons sought out of due time from the gods
are never wholly to be desired, and, if They should
grant to thee to tarry on the earth, old age would
trouble thee with burdens more and more till thou
wouldst become the driven slave of the hours in
fetters that none may break."

The King said : " They that have devised this
burden of age may surely stay it, pray therefore on
the calmest evening of the year to the gods above
the twilight that I may tarry always on the earth
and always young, while over my head the scourges
of the gods pass and alight not.

Then answered Yamen : " The King hath commanded, yet among the blessings of the gods there
always cries a curse. The great princes that make
merry with the King, who tell of the great deeds
that the King wrought in the former time, shall one
by one grow old. And thou, O King, seated at
the feast crying, ' make merry ' and extolling the
former time shall find about thee white heads

nodding in sleep, and men that are forgetting the The
former time. Then one by one the names of *Journey*
those that sported with thee once called by the *of the*
gods, one by one the names of the singers that *King*
sing the songs thou lovest called by the gods,
lastly of those that chased the grey boar by night
and took him in Orghoom river—only the
King. Then a new people that have not known
the old deeds of the King nor fought and chased
with him, who dare not make merry with the
King as did his long dead princes. And all the
while those princes that are dead growing dearer
and greater in thy memory, and all the while
the men that served thee then growing more
small to thee. And all the old things fading and
new things arising which are not as the old things
were, the world changing yearly before thine eyes
and the gardens of thy childhood overgrown.
Because thy childhood was in the olden years thou
shalt love the olden years, but ever the new years
shall overthrow them and their customs, and not
the will of a King may stay the changes that the
gods have planned for all of the customs of old.
Ever thou shalt say " This was not so," and ever the
new custom shall prevail even against a King.
When thou hast made merry a thousand times thou
shalt grow tired of making merry. At last thou
shalt become weary of the chase, and still old age
shall not come near to thee to stifle desires that
have been too oft fulfilled ; then, O King, thou

shalt be a hunter yearning for the chase but with nought to pursue that hath not been oft overcome. Old age shall come not to bury thine ambitions in a time when there is nought for thee to aspire to any more. Experience of many centuries shall make thee wise but hard and very sad, and thou shalt be a mind apart from thy fellows and curse them all for fools, and they shall not perceive thy wisdom because thy thoughts are not their thoughts and the gods that they have made are not the gods of the olden time. No solace shall thy wisdom bring thee but only an increasing knowledge that thou knowest nought, and thou shalt feel as a wise man in a world of fools, or else as a fool in a world of wise men, when all men feel so sure and ever thy doubts increase. When all that spake with thee of thine old deeds are dead, those that saw them not shall speak of them again to thee ; till one speaking to thee of thy deeds of valour add more than even a man should when speaking to a King, and thou shalt suddenly doubt whether these great deeds were ; and there shall be none to tell thee, only the echoes of the voices of the gods still singing in thine ears when long ago They called the princes that were thy friends. And thou shalt hear the knowledge of the olden time most wrongly told and afterwards forgotten. Then many prophets shall arise claiming discovery of that old knowledge. Then thou shalt find that seeking knowledge is vain, as the chase is vain, as making

merry is vain, as all things are vain.   One day
thou shalt find that it is vain to be a King.   Greatly
then will the acclamations of the people weary
thee, till the time when people grow aweary of
Kings.   Then thou shalt know that thou hast been
uprooted from thine olden time and set to live in
uncongenial years, and jests all new to royal ears
shall smite thee on the head like hailstones, when
thou hast lost thy crown, when those to whose
grandsires thou hadst granted to bring them as
children to kiss the feet of the King shall mock at
thee because thou hast not learnt to barter with
gold.

"Not all the marvels of the future time shall atone
to thee for those old memories that glow warmer
and brighter every year as they recede into the ages
that the gods have gathered.   And always dreaming of thy long dead princes and of the great Kings
of other kingdoms in the olden time thou shalt fail to
see the grandeur to which a hurrying jesting people
shall attain in that kingless age.   Lastly, O King, thou
shalt perceive men changing in a way thou shalt
not comprehend, knowing what thou canst not
know, till thou shalt discover that these are men
no more and a new race holds dominion over the
earth whose forefathers were men.   These shall
speak to thee no more as they hurry upon a quest
that thou shalt never understand, and thou shalt
know that thou canst no longer take thy part in
shaping destinies, but in a world of cities shall only

pine for air and the waving grass again and the sound of a wind in trees. Then even this shall end with the shapes of the gods in the darkness gathering all lives but thine, when the hills shall fling up earth's long stored heat back to the heavens again, when earth shall be old and cold, with nothing alive upon it but one King."

Then said the King:

"Pray to those hard gods still, for those that have loved the earth with all its gardens and woods and singing streams will love earth still when it is old and cold with all its gardens gone and all the purport of its being failed and nought but memories."

IX

THEN spake Paharn, a prophet of the land of Hurn.

And Paharn said :

" There was one man that knew, but he stands not here."

And the King said :

" Is he further than my heralds might travel in the night if they went upon fleet horses ? "

And the prophet answered :

" He is no further than thy heralds may well travel in the night, but further than they may return from in all the years. Out of this city there goes a valley wandering through all the world and opens out at last on the green land of Hurn. On the one side in the distance gleams the sea, and on the other side a forest, black and ancient, darkens the fields of Hurn ; beyond the forest and the sea there is no more, saving the twilight and beyond that the gods. In the mouth of the valley sleeps the village of Rhistaun.

" Here I was born, and heard the murmur of the flocks and herds, and saw the tall smoke standing between the sky and the still roofs of Rhistaun, and

TIME AND THE GODS

The Journey of the King

learned that men might not go into the dark forest, and that beyond the forest and the sea was nought saving the twilight, and beyond that the gods. Often there came travellers from the world all down the winding valley, and spake with strange speech in Rhistaun and returned again up the valley going back to the world. Sometimes with bells and camels and men running on foot, Kings came down the valley from the world, but always the travellers returned by the valley again and none went further than the land of Hurn.

"And Kithneb also was born in the land of Hurn and tended the flocks with me, but Kithneb would not care to listen to the murmur of the flocks and herds and see the tall smoke standing between the roofs and the sky, but needed to know how far from Hurn it was that the world met the twilight, and how far across the twilight sat the gods.

"And often Kithneb dreamed as he tended the flocks and herds, and when others slept he would wander near to the edge of the forest wherein men might not go. And the elders of the land of Hurn reproved Kithneb when he dreamed ; yet Kithneb was still as other men and mingled with his fellows until the day of which I will tell thee, O King. For Kithneb was aged about a score of years, and he and I were sitting near the flocks, and he gazed long at the point where the dark forest met the sea at the end of the land of Hurn. But when night drove the twilight down under the forest we

160

brought the flocks together to Rhistaun, and I went up the street between the houses to see four princes that had come down the valley from the world, and they were clad in blue and scarlet and wore plumes upon their heads, and they gave us in exchange for our sheep some gleaming stones which they told us were of great value on the word of princes. And I sold them three sheep, and Darniag sold them eight.

"But Kithneb came not with the others to the market place where the four princes stood, but went alone across the fields to the edge of the forest.

"And it was upon the next morning that the strange thing befell Kithneb; for I saw him in the morning coming from the fields, and I hailed him with the shepherd's cry wherewith we shepherds call to one another, and he answered not. Then I stopped and spake to him, and Kithneb said not a word till I became angry and left him.

"Then we spake together concerning Kithneb, and others had hailed him, and he had not answered them, but to one he had said that he had heard the voices of the gods speaking beyond the forest and so would never listen more to the voices of men.

"Then we said : 'Kithneb is mad,' and none hindered him.

"Another took his place among the flocks, and Kithneb sat in the evenings by the edge of the forest on the plain, alone.

"So Kithneb spake to none for many days, but when any forced him to speak he said that every evening he heard the gods when they came to sit in the forest from over the twilight and sea, and that he would speak no more with men.

"But as the months went by, men in Rhistaun came to look on Kithneb as a prophet, and we were wont to point to him when strangers came down the valley from the world, saying :

"'Here in the land of Hurn we have a prophet such as you have not among your cities, for he speaks at evening with the gods.'

"A year had passed over the silence of Kithneb when he came to me and spake. And I bowed before him because we believed that he spake among the gods. And Kithneb said :

"'I will speak to thee before the end because I am most lonely. For how may I speak again with men and women in the little streets of Rhistaun among the houses, when I have heard the voices of the gods singing above the twilight ? But I am more lonely than ever Rhistaun wots of, for this I tell thee, *when I hear the gods I know not what They say.* Well indeed I know the voice of each, for ever calling me away from contentment ; well I know Their voices as they call to my soul and trouble it ; I know by Their tone when They rejoice, and I know when They are sad, for even the gods feel sadness. I know when over fallen cities of the past, and the curved white bones of heroes They

162

sing the dirges of the gods' lament. But alas !
Their words I know not, and the wonderful strains
of the melody of Their speech beat on my soul and
pass away unknown.

" ' Therefore I travelled from the land of Hurn till
I came to the house of the prophet Arnin-Yo, and
told him that I sought to find the meaning of the
gods ; and Arnin-Yo told me to ask the shepherds
concerning all the gods, for what the shepherds
knew it was meet for a man to know, and, beyond
that, knowledge turned into trouble.

" ' But I told Arnin-Yo that I had heard myself
the voices of the gods and knew that They were
there beyond the twilight and so could never more
bow down to the gods that the shepherds made
from the red clay which they scooped with their
hands out of the hillside.

" ' Then said Arnin-Yo to me :

" ' Natheless forget that thou hast heard the gods
and bow down again to the gods of the red clay
that the shepherds make, and find thereby the ease
that the shepherds find, and at last die, remembering devoutly the gods of the red clay that the
shepherds scooped with their hands out of the hill.
For the gifts of the gods that sit beyond the twilight and smile at the gods of clay, are neither ease
nor contentment."

" ' And I said :

" ' The god that my mother made out of the red
clay that she had got from the hill, fashioning it

with many arms and eyes as she sang me songs of its power, and told me stories of its mystic birth, this god is lost and broken ; and ever in my ears is ringing the melody of the gods."

" ' And Arnin-Yo said :

" ' If thou wouldst still seek knowledge know that only those that come behind the gods may clearly know their meaning. And this thou canst only do by taking ship and putting out to sea from the land of Hurn and sailing up the coast towards the forest. There the sea cliffs turn to the left or southward, and full upon them beats the twilight from over the sea, and there thou mayest come round behind the forest. Here where the world's edge mingles with the twilight the gods come in the evening, and if thou canst come behind Them thou shalt hear Their voices clear, beating full seaward and filling all the twilight with sound of song, and thou shalt know the meaning of the gods. But where the cliffs turn southward there sits behind the gods Brimdono, the oldest whirlpool in the sea, roaring to guard his masters. Him the gods have chained for ever to the floor of the twilit sea to guard the door of the forest that lieth above the cliffs. Here, then, if thou canst hear the voices of the gods as thou hast said, thou wilt know their meaning clear, but this will profit thee little when Brimdono drags thee down and all thy ship.' "

" Thus spake Kithneb to me.

" But I said :

"'O Kithneb, forget those whirlpool-guarded gods
beyond the forest, and if thy small god be lost thou
shalt worship with me the small god that my mother
made. Thousands of years ago he conquered cities
but is not any longer an angry god. Pray to him,
Kithneb, and he shall bring thee comfort and increase
to thy flocks and a mild spring, and at the last a
quiet ending for thy days.'

" But Kithneb heeded not, and only bade me find
a fisher ship and men to row it. So on the next day
we put forth from the land of Hurn in a boat that
the fisher folk use. And with us came four of the
fisher folk who rowed the boat while I held the
rudder, but Kithneb sat and spake not in the prow.
And we rowed westward up the coast till we came
at evening where the cliffs turned southward and
the twilight gleamed upon them and the sea.

" There we turned southwards and saw at once
Brimdono. And as a man tears the purple cloak of
a king slain in battle to divide it with other
warriors,—Brimdono tore the sea. And ever
around and around him with a gnarled hand Brimdono whirled the sail of some adventurous ship,
the trophy of some calamity wrought in his greed
for shipwreck long ago where he sat to guard his
masters from all who fare on the sea. And ever
one far-reaching empty hand swung up and down
so that we durst go no nearer.

" Only Kithneb neither saw Brimdono nor heard
his roar, and when we would go no further bade

us lower a small boat with oars out of the ship. Into this boat Kithneb descended, not heeding words from us, and onward rowed alone. A cry of triumph over ships and men Brimdono uttered before him, but Kithneb's eyes were turned toward the forest as he came behind the gods. Upon his face the twilight beat full from the haunts of evening to illumine the smiles that grew about his eyes as he came behind the gods. Him that had found the gods above Their twilit cliffs, him that had heard Their voices close at last and knew Their meaning clear, him, from the cheerless world with its doubtings and prophets that lie, from all hidden meanings, where the truth rang clear at last, Brimdono took."

But when Paharn ceased to speak, in the King's ears the roar of Brimdono exulting over ancient triumphs and the whelming of ships seemed still to ring.

X

Then Mohontis spake, the hermit prophet, who lived in the deep untravelled woods that seclude Lake Ilāna.

"I dreamed that to the west of all the seas I saw by vision the mouth of Munra-O, guarded by golden gates, and through the bars of the gates that guard the mysterious river of Munra-O I saw the flashes of golden barques, wherein the gods went up and down, and to and fro through the evening dusk. And I saw that Munra-O was a river of dreams such as came through remembered gardens in the night, to charm our infancy as we slept beneath the sloping gables of the houses of long ago. And Munra-O rolled down her dreams from the unknown inner land and slid them under the golden gates and out into the waste, unheeding sea, till they beat far off upon low-lying shores and murmured songs of long ago to the islands of the south, or shouted tumultuous pæans to the Northern crags ; or cried forlornly against rocks where no one came, dreams that might not be dreamed.

TIME AND THE GODS

" Many gods there be, that through the dusk of an evening in the summer go up and down this river. There I saw, in a high barque all of gold, gods of the pomp of cities ; there I saw gods of splendour, in boats bejewelled to the keels ; gods of magnificence and gods of power. I saw the dark ships and the glint of steel of the gods whose trade was war, and I heard the melody of the bells of silver arow in the rigging of harpstrings as the gods of melody went sailing through the dusk on the river of Munra-O. Wonderful river of Munra-O! I saw a grey ship with sails of the spider's web all lit with dewdrop lanterns, and on its prow was a scarlet cock with its wings spread far and wide when the gods of the dawn sailed also on Munra-O.

" Down this river it is the wont of the gods to carry the souls of men eastward to where the world in the distance faces on Munra-O. Then I knew that when the gods of the Pride of Power and gods of the Pomp of Cities went down the river in their tall gold ships to take earthward other souls, swiftly adown the river and between the ships had gone in his boat of birch bark the god Tarn, the hunter, bearing my soul to the world. And I know now that he came down the stream in the dusk keeping well to the middle, and that he moved silently and swiftly among the ships, wielding a twin-bladed oar. I remember, now, the yellow gleaming of the great boats of the gods

of the Pomp of Cities, and the huge prow above
me of the gods of the Pride of Power, when Tarn,
dipping his right blade into the river, lifted his
left blade high, and the drops gleamed and fell.
Thus Tarn the hunter took me to the world that
faces across the sea of the west on the gate of
Munra-O.   And so it was that there grew upon
me the glamour of the hunt, though I had forgotten Tarn, and took me into mossy places and into
dark woods, and I became the cousin of the wolf
and looked in the lynx's eyes and knew the bear ;
and the birds called to me with half-remembered
notes, and there grew in me a deep love of great
rivers and of all western seas, and a distrust
of cities, and all the while I had forgotten
Tarn.

"I know not what high galleon shall come for
thee, O King, nor what rowers, clad with purple,
shall row at the bidding of gods when thou goest
back with pomp to the river of Munra-O.   But
for me Tarn waits where the Seas of the West
break over the edge of the world, and, as the years
pass over me and the love of the chase sinks low,
and as the glamour of the dark woods and mossy
places dies down in my soul, ever louder and
louder lap the ripples against the canoe of birch
bark where, holding his twin-bladed oar, Tarn
waits.

"But when my soul hath no more knowledge
of the woods nor kindred any longer with the

169

creatures of the dark, and when all that Tarn hath given it shall be lost, then Tarn shall take me back over the western seas, where all the remembered years lie floating idly aswing with the ebb and flow, to bring me again to the river of Munra-O. Far up that river we shall haply chase those creatures whose eyes are peering in the night as they prowl around the world, for Tarn was ever a hunter."

XI

THEN Ulf spake, the prophet who in Sistrame-
ides lives in a temple anciently dedicated to the
gods. Rumour hath guessed that there the gods
walked once some time towards evening. But
Time whose hand is against the temples of the
gods hath dealt harshly with it and overturned its
pillars and set upon its ruins his sign and seal : now
Ulf dwells there alone. And Ulf said, " There
sets, O King, a river outward from earth which
meets with a mighty sea whose waters roll through
space and fling their billows on the shores of
every star. These are the river and the sea of
the Tears of Men."

And the King said :

" Men have not written of this sea."

And the prophet answered :

" Have not tears enough burst in the night
time out of sleeping cities ? Have not the
sorrows of 10,000 homes sent streams into this
river when twilight fell and it was still and there
was none to hear ? Have there not been hopes,
and were they all fulfilled ? Have there not been
conquests and bitter defeats ? And have not

171

flowers when spring was over died in the gardens
of many children ? Tears enough, O King, tears
enough have gone down out of earth to make such
a sea ; and deep it is and wide and the gods know
it and it flings its spray on the shores of all the
stars. Down this river and across this sea thou
shalt fare in a ship of sighs and all around thee
over the sea shall fly the prayers of men which
rise on white wings higher than their sorrows.
Sometimes perched in the rigging, sometimes crying around thee, shall go the prayers that availed
not to stay thee in Zarkandhu. Far over the
waters, and on the wings of the prayers beats the
light of an inaccessible star. No hand hath
touched it, none hath journeyed to it, it hath no
substance, it is only a light, it is the star of Hope,
and it shines far over the sea and brightens the
world. It is nought but a light, but the gods gave
it.

" Led only by the light of this star the myriad
prayers that thou shalt see all around thee fly to
the Hall of the gods.

" Sighs shall waft thy ship of sighs over the sea of
Tears. Thou shalt pass by islands of laughter and
lands of song lying low in the sea, and all of them
drenched with tears flung over their rocks by the
waves of the sea all driven by the sighs.

" But at last thou shalt come with the prayers of
men to the great Hall of the gods where the chairs
of the gods are carved of onyx grouped round the

TIME AND THE GODS

golden throne of the eldest of the gods.   And
there, O King, hope not to find the gods, but reclining upon the golden throne wearing a cloak of
his master's thou shalt see the figure of Time
with blood upon his hands, and loosely dangling
from his fingers a dripping sword, and spattered
with blood but empty shall stand the onyx
chairs.

" There he sits on his master's throne dangling
idly his sword, or with it flicking cruelly at the
prayers of men that lie in a great heap bleeding at
his feet.

" For a while, O King, the gods had sought to
solve the riddles of Time, for a while They made
him Their slave, and Time smiled and obeyed his
masters, for a while, O King, for a while.   He that
hath spared nothing hath not spared the gods, nor
yet shall he spare thee."

Then the King spake dolefully in the Hall of
Kings, and said :

" May I not find at last the gods, and must it be
that I may not look in Their faces at the last to see
whether They be kindly ?   They that have sent me
on my earthward journey I would greet on my
returning, if not as a King coming again to his
own city, yet as one who having been ordered had
obeyed, and obeying had merited something of
those for whom he toiled.   I would look Them in
Their faces, O prophet, and ask Them concerning
many things and would know the wherefore of

173

much. I had hoped, O prophet, that those gods that had smiled upon my childhood, Whose voices stirred at evening in gardens when I was young, would hold dominion still when at last I came to seek Them. O prophet, if this is not to be, make you a great dirge for my childhood's gods and fashion silver bells and, setting them mostly a-swing amidst such trees as grew in the garden of my childhood, sing you this dirge in the dusk : and sing it when the low moth flies up and down and the bat first comes peering from her home, sing it when white mists come rising from the river, when smoke is pale and grey, while flowers are yet closing, ere voices are yet hushed, sing it while all things yet lament the day, or ever the great lights of heaven come blazing forth and night with her splendours takes the place of day. For, if the old gods die, let us lament Them or ever new knowledge comes, while all the world still shudders at Their loss.

"For at the last, O prophet, what is left ? Only the gods of my childhood dead, and only Time striding large and lonely through the spaces, chilling the moon and paling the light of stars and scattering earthward out of both his hands the dust of forgetfulness over the fields of heroes and smitten Temples of the older gods."

But when the other prophets heard with what doleful words the King spake in the Hall they all cried out :

"It is not as Ulf has said but as I have said —and I."

Then the King pondered long, not speaking. But down in the city in a street between the houses stood grouped together they that were wont to dance before the King, and they that had borne his wine in jewelled cups. Long they had tarried in the city hoping that the King might relent, and once again regard them with kindly face calling for wine and song. The next morning they were all to set out in search of some new Kingdom, and they were peering between the houses and up the long grey street to see for the last time the palace of King Ebalon ; and Pattering Leaves, the dancer, cried :

"Not any more, not any more at all shall we drift up the carven hall to dance before the King. He that now watches the magic of his prophets will behold no more the wonder of the dance, and among ancient parchments, strange and wise, he shall forget the swirl of drapery when we swing together through the Dance of the Myriad Steps."

And with her were Silvern Fountain and Summer Lightning and Dream of the Sea, each lamenting that they should dance no more to please the eyes of the King.

And Intahn who had carried at the banquet for fifty years the goblet of the King set with its four sapphires each as large as an eye, said as he spread

175

his hands towards the palace making the sign of farewell :

" Not all the magic of prophecy nor yet foreseeing nor perceiving may equal the power of wine. Through the small door in the King's Hall one goes by one hundred steps and many sloping corridors into the cool of the earth where lies a cavern vaster than the Hall. Therein, curtained by the spider, repose the casks of wine that are wont to gladden the hearts of the Kings of Zarkandhu. In islands far to the eastward the vine, from whose heart this wine was long since wrung, hath climbed aloft with many a clutching finger and beheld the sea and ships of the olden time and men since dead, and gone down into the earth again and been covered over with weeds. And green with the damp of years there lie three casks that a city gave not up until all her defenders were slain and her houses fired ; and ever to the soul of that wine is added a more ardent fire as ever the years go by. Thither it was my pride to go before a banquet in the olden years, and coming up to bear in the sapphire goblet the fire of the elder Kings and to watch the King's eye flash and his face grow nobler and more like his sires as he drank the gleaming wine.

"And now the King seeks wisdom from his prophets while all the glory of the past and all the clattering splendour of to-day grows old, far down, forgotten beneath his feet."

And when he ceased the cupbearers and the

women that danced looked long in silence at the
palace. Then one by one all made the farewell
sign before they turned to go, and as they did this
a herald unseen in the dark was speeding towards
them.

After a long silence the King spake :

" Prophets of my Kingdom," he said, " you
have not prophesied alike, and the words of each
prophet condemn his fellows' words so that wisdom
may not be discovered among prophets. But I
command that none in my Kingdom shall doubt
that the earliest King of Zarkandhu stored wine
beneath this palace before the building of the city
or ever the palace arose, and I shall cause commands to be uttered for the making of a banquet
at once within this Hall, so that ye shall perceive that the power of my wine is greater than
all your spells, and dancing more wondrous than
prophecy."

The dancers and the winebearers were summoned
back, and as the night wore on a banquet was
spread and all the prophets bidden to be seated,
Samahn, Ynath, Monith, Ynar Thun, the prophet of
Journeys, Zornadhu, Yamen, Paharn, Ilāna, Ulf, and
one that had not spoken nor yet revealed his name,
and who wore his prophet's cloak across his face.

And the prophets feasted as they were commanded and spake as other men spake, save he
whose face was hidden, who neither ate nor spake.
Once he put out his hand from under his cloak and

touched a blossom among the flowers upon the table and the blossom fell.

And Pattering Leaves came in and danced again, and the King smiled, and Pattering Leaves was happy though she had not the wisdom of the prophets. And in and out, in and out, in and out among the columns of the Hall went Summer Lightning in the maze of the dance. And Silvern Fountain bowed before the King and danced and danced and bowed again, and old Intahn went to and fro from the cavern to the King gravely through the midst of the dancers but with kindly eyes, and when the King had often drunk of the old wine of the elder Kings he called for Dream of the Sea and bade her sing. And Dream of the Sea came through the arches and sang of an island builded by magic out of pearls, that lay set in a ruby sea, and how it lay far off and under the south, guarded by jagged reefs whereon the sorrows of the world were wrecked and never came to the island. And how a low sunset always reddened the sea and lit the magic isle and never turned to night, and how someone sang always and endlessly to lure the soul of a King who might by enchantment pass the guarding reefs to find rest on the pearl island and not be troubled more, but only see sorrows on the outer reef battered and broken. Then Soul of the South rose up and sang a song of a fountain that ever sought to reach the sky and was ever doomed to fall to the earth again until at last . . .

TIME AND THE GODS

Then whether it was the art of Pattering Leaves or the song of Dream of the Sea, or whether it was the fire of the wine of the elder Kings, Ebalon bade farewell kindly to the prophets when morning paled the stars. Then along the torchlit corridors the King went to his chamber, and having shut the door in the empty room, beheld suddenly a figure wearing the cloak of a prophet; and the King perceived that it was he whose face was hidden at the banquet, who had not revealed his name.

And the King said:

" Art thou, too, a prophet ? "

And the figure answered:

" I am a prophet."

And the King said: " Knowest *thou* aught concerning the journey of the King ? " And the figure answered: " I know, but have never said."

And the King said: " Who art thou that knowest so much and hast not told it ? "

And he answered:

" I am THE END."

Then the cloaked figure strode away from the palace; and the King, unseen by the guards, followed upon his journey.

THE END

THE
SEEKERS

THE SEEKERS

by

H. E. BATES

* *
*

LONDON
JOHN AND EDWARD BUMPUS
1926

PRINTED IN GREAT BRITAIN
BY R. & R. CLARK, LIMITED, EDINBURGH

I

ON A CERTAIN NIGHT when the sky was as black as if the moon had gone into mourning for some lost star, a little swallow, with a sudden, despairing burst of wings flew to the top of a great hill and settled there with a sigh. Then, after looking over the dark masses of land ahead it rose upward again, twittered brightly and called down the hill: "Here is a land which I never remember seeing before! Oh! come quickly!"

This it called several times before receiving an answer, which when it came was as faint as if its speaker were dying and no more than a brief "In a little while, swallow, in a little while."

To which the swallow replied insistently: "But, Prince, this is a discovery most wonderful! Oh! come quickly!"

But it was a long time before there crawled over the edge of the cliff a young man, shabbily dressed and looking as if he had not slept for many nights, and whose eyes shone with tiredness as he searched the sky for the restless swallow.

Unable to find it he called it feebly, at

which it settled on his breast as he lay staring up at the sky.

"Prince, oh, Happy Prince!" it whispered to him. "Cannot you see that this is a new land, a land we have never seen before? Let us make haste and go down to it."

The prince smiled.

"I have no strength," he said. "I could no more go down this hill than I could fly as you do."

"But, oh, master! it may be a rich land, or a beautiful one!" The swallow touched the face of the prince. "We must go," it said earnestly, "we must go. Something tells me that there we should never be tired again."

"But I am tired now," replied the man— "so tired it seems to me that I am going to be tired for ever."

"Do you mean you are tired of wandering?"

"Yes, of wandering. Since they cast me out of my own town I have been a little wearier every day."

The swallow pressed its breast against the prince's throat, and in the deep silence whispered: "But already the air is sweeter and fresher. Come down!"

The prince, however, shook his head.

"I must sleep," he muttered, closing his eyes.

Suddenly, however, he opened them again, very bright, as if he had dreamed happily, and taking the swallow into his hands, said: "But you can go. In a little while you could find out everything."

The swallow struggled with joy.

"I will go," it told him, "and you may sleep!"

And, breaking from the Prince's hold it cut with its white bosom into the dark air and flew madly away, calling "Adieu! Adieu!"

The prince, however, neither heard nor spoke, for he was already asleep.

II

THE SWALLOW flew swiftly and with a
new vigour. For some time he travelled
far above the land as if afraid of some danger
lurking in its darkness, but by and by found
that the hills were so near to him as almost to
touch his breast. Then he found they were
smooth, and not only smooth but warm; but
he did not descend, and flying quickly he
passed over lakes where people were singing
and weeping on the white shores. Beyond
these the hills grew more gigantic, stretching
out into terrible darkness, so that the swallow
became afraid and flew faster and faster,
searching for the faintest spot of light in the
land beneath.

At last he saw what looked to him like two
little lamps set in the hills to guide him, and
descending, settled on a sharp ridge between
them, wondering who had set them there.

But as he sat there they went out, then as
suddenly shone again, brighter than ever. He
trembled. The next moment, as if to show
him that he was not alone in his trembling,
the whole mountain shook beneath his feet.
Somewhere afar off a dark shape explored the

air and disappeared again, while beneath his feet was set up a great growl that shot him fearfully into the sky.

From there he looked down on what he had thought were hills, but which he now knew was some sleeping giant.

Then the swallow knew that he must have alighted on the nose of a giant in the Valley of Giants (of which his mother had told him) and had mistaken his eyes for lamps.

As he continued his journey it grew colder—though it may have been fear which chilled him—and he began to wish for the warm hand of the prince he had left on the hill behind. Yet he dare not fly low, because of the giant he had disturbed and the wolves which he now heard barking across the valleys. So he turned his course slightly towards his left leg.

Almost at once the air grew warmer. The swallow flew on in comfort. The wind no longer dug its cold nails into his feathers. But suddenly, with a burst of heat like that when an oven is opened, he found himself over a land of great fires which cast their orange reflections up into his face, the heat from whose flames scorched his feet and singed his precious wings.

Then the swallow knew that he must be passing over the Valley of Fire (about which his mother had warned him), and, with his feet tucked as close to him as possible, flew on and on, scarcely aware of pain and still less aware of time, so that he did not know how long had passed since he had said "Adieu" to the prince on the mountain.

III

So THE SWALLOW came to where he
could hear the sea complaining as its
own waves tangled themselves up with each
other, and could see the great Beacons reflected in its water.

And that night (though he could not of
course know it) he must have passed over the
mouth of the Dream River, near the Castle
of Seven Towers, and across the wood of
witches, by Castle Warlock and the Valley
of Dragons, where the air became hot again,
and over the strange places where the Rocs
build their dark enormous nests—for only
by passing that way could he have come to
where the cliffs of Diamond glisten in the hard
morning sun.

It was actually a little farther on from there
that he at last alighted—for the first time since
he had perched between the giant's eyes—and
looked about him.

The place he had chosen was a grassy cliff,
cut with little holes like caves. From some
of these, before long, one or two little men
appeared, scratching their long, untidy beards
with wakefulness and stretching their sleepy

arms to the sun. Never had the swallow seen men so small; and he was puzzled—indeed puzzled enough to ask:

"Can you tell me who you are—and where I am?"

In answer, and at the same time tossing his beard as if to keep all intruders at a distance, the little man cried:

"Don't you know by this time that you are in fairyland?" He laughed. "Why!—you must know—I can see through your wings. Your wings have the fairy look about them and are like gossamer!"

At which the swallow looked at his wings and felt a new joy, for he could certainly see the green earth through them. But all he could say was:

"So this is Fairyland!"

"Yes!" replied the dwarf, "and if you doubt me fly on, over the Great Wall and the forests until you come to the sea again." And with what was for him a majestic gesture he waved his hand to west of where the moon lay invisible and disappeared.

Surprised, but joyful too, the swallow flew on over the Great Wall of which the dwarf had spoken; and in a moment or two he was able to see it, glinting like a great curved shell in the morning sun. And he flew on more swiftly than ever as the sun climbed the sky.

That day he saw many strange things and (though he could not of course know it) must have passed over the whole of Elfland, by Cock Robin's grave, by Deidre's house, and by the homes of a hundred people of which his mother had told him (just as your mother has told you)—past the great gate of Ivory, over the River of White Nymphs and the Pool of the Nereids which lies at the feet of the great forests, and on and on (just as the little whiskered dwarf had told him) until he came to the sea again.

There the sun was already setting, throwing gold on his wings and the waves he could see through his wings; and, on the sails of the ships he saw in the harbour there, bright colours that grew richer and deeper as the sun fell nearer the water. On those sails he saw the imprint of strange things—quaint birds and shields and the heads of animals he had never seen before. They waved their sleepy folds; they whispered to him:

"This is the Harbour of Dreamland and we are its ships."

He felt sleepy there. The ships seemed to beckon him to ride out over the shadowy sea; and it was only the thought of the prince on the mountain that made him pass on.

Once out of the Harbour of Dreamland the way grew bright again, as if the harbour had been nothing but a dream itself, and the sun shone again, burning his dark back. And this time he passed over the Field of Centaurs, and the shores where the sirens lie on the warm rocks, over the beach where thousands of pearls lay as carelessly as if children had scattered them there, and finally across the Garden of Proserpine, where the scent of flowers made him faint and drop to earth. And as he lay there in the dark silence of his swoon, a voice asked :

"Who are you? Why do you lie there looking as if you are dead?"

The swallow fluttered and, opening his eyes, saw before him a quaint little boy, who laughed:

"The flowers have been too much for you."

He bent and kissed the swallow.

"My name is Puck," he said. "Fly on again. I have given you the Kiss of Youth!"

And thanking him, though not quite understanding, and still with a drowsy wonder in his eyes, the swallow flew up and away. And in this flight he must have passed over the great forest of Lyonnesse and the Holy Mountain of Monsalvat, for only by going this way could he have come to Honeymouth Cove, and through the Never Never Land into the open sea, over which the moon was already beginning to chase the first timid stars into the darkening sky.

Passing over here he looked down with

amazement, for it seemed to him that many of the ships he saw there floating like curled leaves across the path of the moon were those he had seen waving their sails in the Harbour of Dreamland.

He knew then that the end of his journey must be near.

But a strange thing happened. The air grew suddenly cold, great rainbows appeared mysteriously in the sky, looking like the perfect reflections of each other, twilight descended, mighty winds blew his body hither and thither, and the sky itself thundered and thundered. Below him only a solitary ship slid across the lonely water as if frightened.

And the swallow too was frightened, imagining he might never see the prince again, but almost before he was aware of it he found that the wind had blown him out of reach of the thunder and that where the rainbows had been were only quiet untroubled stars. The hills lay pale and friendly beneath him, and in the distance a lake shone up at him like a clear blue stone with a light in its breast.

He grew giddy with joy at having crossed that strange sea, and began to fall as he had fallen in the Garden of Proserpine. For what seemed an age he fell through the air. Below him were confused shouts and in the direction of the lake a sound as of someone singing.

But all this ceased when his fall ceased, and he lay for a moment bewildered.

In the silence he opened his eyes. . . . Then he saw he had fallen again into the arms of the Happy Prince.

IV

FTER HE HAD LAIN there for some
minutes he became aware of many voices
chattering and looked up at the prince as if
to say:

"Who are these people?"

(And he wrinkled up his feathers just as
you wrinkle up your brows.)

The prince laughed.

"Oh!" he said, "all these have come since
you flew away; and each of them is like me—
a wanderer and tired of wandering. Each is
looking for a happy land in which to rest and
abide."

Then the swallow turned a somersault, the
first since his previous birthday, and cried out:

"Then I can help them! I can help them!
The land down there"—and he pointed away
to the pale hills and the sea, "is Fairyland!"

Immediately the prince and his friends set
up a great shout. Some laughed also, one
played on a pipe he had, some sang, one stood
on his head and sang, "Merrily, merrily shall
I live now," and another, who was something
like a quaint little monkey, ran up the nearest
tree he could find and chattered.

The swallow, bewildered, looked at the prince for explanation.

"Don't be afraid," said the prince in assurance, "I'll introduce you."

"But," protested the swallow, "I haven't washed. I haven't combed my wings!"

"All of which," answered the prince kindheartedly, "doesn't matter with the best people."

"Of course not," suddenly said a little girl with not very many clothes on, "I shan't mind, for one. That is, I shan't if I can be introduced first," and without more ceremony she introduced herself, "Taffimai Metallumai—is me," she declared.

"Meaning," said the prince, as the swallow gasped, "small-person-without-any-manners-who-ought-to-be-spanked!"

"Which you can always shorten to Taffy if the worst comes to the worst," explained the owner of that name. "Now you know."

The swallow, thanking her, said he would not forget.

But he did forget almost immediately, for during the next ten minutes or so he became so flurried by being introduced to that throng which had gathered on the hill-top that he could scarcely remember their faces, let alone their names.

They were a very mixed crowd up there. Besides the little girl Taffy were three other children who played constantly with a great cat that seemed to belong to a queer old lady with a hat like a tea-cosy and a face like the face of a duchess—and unmistakably so, since she was a duchess and was called "duchess", and awed the swallow much, after the manner of duchesses. But the children, whose names the swallow discovered were Sylvie, Bruno, and Nixie (who would talk about an Uncle Paul), were not the slightest bit afraid. Nor were a sailor named Sinbad, and a lovely woman named Gulnarè, who talked often of the sea, and the strange one, Aladdin, who carried a little lamp he would allow no one to touch.

Oh! no—none were afraid of the duchess, as who, knowing a duchess, would be ? On the contrary, these people would stand together in little groups talking and making friends with each other, and pointing to them the prince would say, "This is the Princess Lirazel and this the youth Alveric," or whomever it might be.

Soon the swallow came to know, besides these, the little fairy-like girl Tourmelise, who said he might sometimes call her Maia instead, and threw him a flower, which he caught in his beak and cherished for many days ; and then those three who were never silent (and never will be silent while there are children like you and men like me), the boy with a pipe who is called the Pied Piper, another fairy thing who spoke in soft bewitching tones, and a sprite who danced to the tune of the pipe and sang till the air quivered; and these two were called respectively Melmillo and Ariel.

Contrasted against that merriment was the quietness of a tall, beautiful girl with short hair, and a little pale-faced Friar, who took the swallow in his hand, and said:

"This is Joan and I am Francis. Don't be afraid."

Thus the swallow knew that all these, even the monkey Nod (who wasn't a monkey really, but a Mulla-mulgar, which is very different), were friends to him. And he was able to perch in peace.

At last the prince said "Hush!" to all the chatter, and asked of the company:

"Where is it we all desire to go?"

And every one answered with a shout:

"Down to the land where the swallow has been!"

"Agreed?" queried the prince.

"Agreed!" said every one as solemnly as town councillors.

"But," the prince warned them, "you forget we know nothing of this land."

To which every one chorused like children in school:

"But the swallow can tell us."

But the little bird blushed, and would have

flown away had not Francis called it back
again.

" Tell us?" he asked quietly.

And, unable to resist this little man, who
treated him as he had never been treated
before, even more sweetly than the Prince
had done, he told the company what he had
seen in the new land.

"You can go day after day and night after
night, and your legs and wings will not be
tired," he said at the end.

At this every one applauded, most of them
like you and me, with hands, but one or two,
like Ariel, by standing on their heads or
dancing.

"Ah! but," said the mulla-mulgar Nod,
"are there nuts?"

"There are forests," replied the swallow.

"And are there flowers?" asked Maia.

"There is a garden by the sea," replied the
bird, "whose scents will make you drowsier
than a forest of white poppies."

"And are there ships?" asked Sinbad.

"There is a harbour whose ships are like
sunset-clouds that have been caught and
moored there, sodden with colours."

"Wonderful!" said all.

"But, remember," warned the swallow
seriously, being now a creature of importance,
because he was also a creature of experience,
"there are also witches and dragons and

wolves and bogles and ghosts and monsters and giants and tempests and ogres and nightmares and sirens and——" here he must pause for a puff or two of breath, "and—fire!"

There was a solemn silence.

"Valleys of Fire," emphasised the swallow.

The silence became awful. Then the maid Joan said quietly:

"I am no longer afraid of fire."

"Nor I," said Francis. "He is our friend."

So every one brightened. At that point Ariel asked:

"Did you ever in your travels see a fellow named Puck?"

"I did," replied the swallow. "When the scent of flowers overcame me he restored me by the kiss of youth."

"Excellent!" cried Ariel. "We began life together. Now if I could find him we might persuade him to make clear the way into this wonderful land, for otherwise it is surely going to be extremely difficult to gain entrance."

"Horribly difficult," broke in the Duchess. "And the moral of that is . . ."

"Almost impossible," interrupted Sinbad.

"Oh! but nothing is impossible," declared Aladdin, holding up his strange lamp. "Nothing is impossible."

"That is so," agreed the prince. "Therefore let us send Ariel to find this Puck with whom he began life."

"Ariel! Ariel!" called every one at once. "Let us send Ariel!"

But he had vanished, and only his friend Melmillo knew that he had already begun that journey, for only to her had he confided his secret before departing.

V

THE SECRET JOURNEY of Ariel came to an end quickly, and within five minutes those on the hill-crest were watching him return, dropping like a bright leaf through the sky. They watched him anxiously, as bearers of uncertain tidings are always watched, and questioned him when he alighted among them with a smile. And they had nothing to ask but:

"Where is Puck? where is Puck?"

Ariel was playfully scornful in his sudden shout:

"You weren't so foolish as to expect Puck would ever come out of Fairyland again, were you?"

They shook shameful heads at him.

"Oh! no, that's altogether impossible," went on Ariel. He lowered his voice. "But he is over there, sitting on the edge of a cloud till I return"—he flung out a toe in the direction from which he had just come,— "just within the borders of his own land."

Everyone looked.

"But you will not see him," Ariel assured them. "It's many leagues away yet."

"Then what can we do?" asked the prince.

"Write him a letter," suggested Taffy.

"Nonsense," said the duchess, after the manner of duchesses. "You can't do that sort of thing here. You can't write letters to Puck. It's not done."

"Nonsense in one way," agreed Ariel. "But good sense in another, for unless we can convince him of both our earnestness and character he will refuse us the Kiss of Youth."

"In earnest!" suddenly exclaimed Sylvie and Bruno together. "You don't think he can doubt that?"

"Naturally," pointed out Francis. "Everyone will doubt before you make him believe."

"All of which means," said Sinbad, with the air of wisdom which comes to a man who has seen much and says little, "that we must prove to him his land has places where each of us can live happily and without disturbing its peace."

This wisdom the company accepted as final. Francis was the first to speak as a result of it.

"I should be happy," he said simply, "where there are birds and animals."

"And I where it is very, very quiet, and there are no quarrels," said Joan.

"And I," whispered Nixie, "in the heart of Uncle Paul."

"And I where there are flowers," said Maia.

As if in answer to this a voice from the clouds declared suddenly:

"Then steer west of the moon for the Pool of Hippocrine. Fly together. You have the Kiss of Youth on you."

"Fly?" whispered everyone. "But it's not possible!"

"Fly!" repeated the voice, which no one doubted was the voice of Puck.

Thus, almost before any were aware of it Francis and Joan and Maia and Nixie were flying true west of the moon, which means west of the Sea of Dreams and the Never Never Land, over the Valley of Avalon and the Castle of Joyous Gard until you come to the Pool of Hippocrine and the Garden of Proserpine.

When they had disappeared Lirazel said:

"I should be happiest in Elfland because my father is king of it."

"And I with her," declared Alveric.

"Then," said the voice without hesitation, "steer south of the Sirius for Elfin City. Fly together! You have the Kiss of Youth on you."

Thus, almost before any were aware of it, Lirazel and Alveric were flying true south of the Sirius, which means south of the Ferlie Firth and the Palace of Oberon, over the Golden Strand and Kelpie Bay until you come to the Elfin City.

So it went until nearly all the company had been admitted to the land they had so long desired; until Sylvie and Bruno had gone to live by the Well of Youth on the shores of Green Harbour, and Aladdin with Gulnare and Sinbad to dwell near the Gold Caverns which are shining—washed by the Enchanted Sea; and the Mulla-mulgar Nod to dwell in the forests he loved.

To the shadow of the Great Wall went the Duchess and the Cheshire cat, to be neighbours to those queer gentry the Marquis of Carabas and the King of Thule.

All these went openly, all happily and with the Kiss of Youth on them. Only when it came to Ariel and his friends Melmillo and the Pied Piper was there a sign of secrecy; and of these no one can really say when they went or where, or where they are now, for these three were for ever restless and mysterious, like the wind which first bore them from the hill-top.

When they had gone, the Happy Prince, the swallow and Taffy—for only these now remained—looked at each other in silence. Then Taffy, being of course a young-person-without-any-manners, set up a great cry as to why her place had not yet been told her, and when the prince could not answer her satisfactorily, demanded of the silent clouds from where she imagined Puck to be watching her:

"Are you going to keep me waiting for ever?"

She shouted petulantly at the swallow, too. She stamped her feet. She beat her fine brown hands on her naked breast. But there was complete silence.

She wept.

At this the prince, with that kindness which had long ago endeared him to the swallow, said in a consoling whisper:

"Remember that the swallow and I were first, and that so far Puck hasn't taken the slightest notice of us."

"But where am I to go?" she pleaded. "Am I to go anywhere?"

"Yes," answered the voice of Puck from the southward, "you are to come with me. Come now—now!"

Taffy turned her wet face to the great still clouds and obeyed. And it is said—though no one will contradict you if you don't believe it—that she went with Puck to the Queen Titania to teach her all those wonderful signs she taught her Daddy, Tegumai Bopsulai, and all the Neolithic ladies and gentlemen who lived on the banks of the Wagai long, long ago.

The prince and the swallow, left alone, wondered how soon their fate would come, and calling into the air, asked:

"And we, what are we to do?"

Without hesitation the voice came:

"You, too, are wanderers. Go where you wish. You have the Kiss of Youth—and if any question as to why you are here, say you have the secret of happiness also."

So the prince and the swallow were left alone again.

As they flew off, striking out to where they believed the sea to be, great blue armies of cloud came out of the west, and twilight fell. At the same time, the swallow, turning to take one last glance at that hill where he had helped so much to happen, saw a figure standing there. By its stillness and silence it seemed to call to him, so that in a moment he went back to the hill.

There he saw a woman who watched him fly down through the half-darkness, and who, when he asked her name, timidly replied, as if afraid even of him:

"I am Mary Rose."

The swallow looked into her face. "You are lonely," he said.

"Yes."

"What are you searching for?" the swallow asked. "For you are searching for something?"

"I can't tell you," she replied. "I can't tell anyone."

"Come with me. We will find what you seek."

Mary Rose smiled. "I cannot fly," she said.

And the swallow saw that this was true, and also that by lingering on the hill he could not only do nothing to help the woman but might also lose the prince. So he touched her face with his wings as he parted them and whispered again:

"Tell me what you are searching for?"

But the woman answered: "I can never tell you. I can never tell you."

"Is it the Kiss of Youth?" he asked. "Is it the Kiss of Youth?"

"Perhaps," she answered sadly, as he flew up. "Perhaps, perhaps."